"A Yaqui Chief Is No Man's Slave..."

The Yaquis are proud, peaceful Indians who live in the high mountains and plateaus of Mejico, primarily in the Sinaloa area. Their forebears were the Aztecs, who perfected a calendar which set dates without error for a quarter-million years, when the Greeks, from whom our Western civilization sprang, considered any number above ten thousand to be infinite.

In *Yaqui,* the incomparable Zane Grey tells the story of a tribal chief who leads his people through the barren wilderness, as Moses had done centuries before—but in this case, to no promised land. They cannot overcome the hated Mexicans, the *Conquistadores* descendants, who enslave them and force them from the pure, clean air of Sonora into the stinking, killing swamps of Yucatan, where they were to be slaves.

And there was no worse master than the young, arrogant Mexican officer, Perez.

He wanted two things: To break the Indian Zane Grey has chosen only to call *Yaqui,* and the lands of the hugest *finca* in the state, which meant he had to marry the landlord's beautiful daughter.

He managed to become wed to his high-spirited bride, but never broke the one called Yaqui.

Their wedding day has become legend.

One which causes old, black-clad women to cross themselves and mutter prayers....

As only Zane Grey could have told it.

Our free catalogue is available upon request. Any titles not in your local bookstore can be purchased through the mail. Simply send 25¢ plus the retail price of the book and write Belmont Tower Books, 185 Madison Avenue, New York, New York 10016.

Any titles currently in print are available in quantity for industrial and sales-promotion use at reduced rates. Address inquiries to our Promotion Dept.

ZANE GREY'S

YAQUI

and Other Great Indian Stories

**Edited by
Loren Grey**

BELMONT TOWER BOOKS • NEW YORK CITY

A BELMONT TOWER BOOK—

Published by

Belmont Tower Books
185 Madison Avenue
New York, N.Y. 10016

Copyright © 1976 by Loren Grey

YAQUI
    Copyright © 1920 by Curtis Publishing Co.
    Copyright © 1948 by Lina Elise Grey
ESCAPE
    Copyright © 1920 by Harper and Brothers
    Copyright © 1941 by Lina Elise Grey
THE BREAKER OF WILD MUSTANGS
    Copyright © 1920 by Harper and Brothers
    Copyright © 1937 by Zane Grey
THE LAND OF THE WILD MUSK-OX
    Copyright © 1975 by Loren Grey
THE HOGAN OF NAS TA BEGA
    Copyright © 1915 by Argosy Magazine
    Copyright © 1943 by Lina Elise Grey

All rights reserved

Printed in the United States of America

TABLE OF CONTENTS

I	YAQUI	7
II	ESCAPE	45
III	THE BREAKER OF WILD MUSTANGS	97
IV	THE LAND OF THE WILD MUSK-OX	103
V	THE HOGAN OF NAS TA BEGA	141

YAQUI

This story depicts the savage strife and hatred between the Mexicans and the Yaqui Indians during the middle and latter part of the 19th century. The Yaquis, who were mountain Aztecs, when captured by the Mexicans were sent as slaves to the Henequen fields in northern Yucatan and were treated with a cruelty that even far exceeded that by Americans in their abuse of Indians in the United States. In this case the Yaqui chieftain wreaks his own kind of bloody vengeance on the hated lieutenant of the army which had enslaved him.

I

Sunset... it was the hour of Yaqui's watch. Chief of a driven remnant of the once mighty tribe, he trusted no sentinel so well as himself at the end of the day's march. While his braves unpacked the tired horses, and his women prepared the evening meal, and his bronze-skinned children played in the sand, Yaqui watched the bold desert horizon.

Long years of hatred had existed between the Yaquis of upland Sonora and the Mexicans from the east. Like eagles, the Indian tribe had lived for centuries in the mountain fastnesses of the Sierra Madre, free, happy, self-sufficient. But wandering prospectors had found gold in their country and that had been the end of their peace. At first the Yaquis, wanting only the wildness and loneliness of their homes, moved farther and farther back from the ever-encroaching advance of the gold diggers. At last, driven from the mountains into the desert, they realized that gold was the doom of their tribe and they began to fight for their land. Bitter and bloody were the battles; and from father to son this wild, free, proud race bequeathed a terrible hatred.

Yaqui was one of the last chiefs of his once great tribe. All his life he remembered the words of his father and grandfather—that the Yaquis must find an unknown and impenetrable hiding place or perish from the earth. When Mexican soldiers at the decree of their government made war upon this tribe, killing those who resisted and making slaves of the captured, Yaqui with his family and followers set out upon a last journey across the Sonora wilderness. Hateful and fearful of the east, whence this blight of gold diggers and land robbers appeared to come, he had fled toward the setting sun into a waste of desert land unknown to his people—a desert of scorching heat and burning sand and tearing cactus and treacherous lava, where water and wood and grass seemed days apart. Some of the youngest children died on the way and all except the strong braves were wearing out.

Alone, on a ridge of rising ground, Yaqui faced the back trail and watched with hawk eyes. Miles distant though that horizon was, those desert eyes could have made out horses against the clear sky. He did not gaze steadily, for the Indian way was to flash a look across the spaces, from near to far, and to fix the eye momentarily, to strain the vision and magnify all objects, then to avert the gaze from that direction and presently flash it back again.

Lonely, wild, and grand, the scene seemed one of lifelessness. Only the sun lived, still hot, as it burned red-gold, distant on the rugged rim of this desert world. Nothing breathed in that vastness. To Yaqui's ear the silence was music. The red sun slipped down and the desert changed. The golden floor of sand and rock shaded cold to the horizon and above that the sky lost its rose, turning to intense luminous blue. In the distance the peaks dimmed and vanished in purple. The fire of the western heavens paled and died, and over all the rock-ribbed, sand-encumbered plateau stole a wondrous gray shade. Yaqui watched until that gray changed to black and the horizon line was lost in night. Safe now from pursuers were he and his people until the dawn.

Then, guided by a campfire, he returned to his silent men and moaning women and a scant meal that he divided. Hunger was naught to Yaqui, nor thirst. Four days could he travel the desert without drink, an endurance most of his hardy tribe were trained to. And as for toil, the strength of his giant frame had never reached its limit. But chief that he was, when he listened to the moaning women and gazed at the silent faces of the children under the starlight he sagged to the sands and, bowing his head, prayed to his gods. He prayed for little—only life, freedom, loneliness and a hidden niche where his people would hear no steps and fear no specters on their trail. Then with unquenchable faith he stretched his great length on the sands; and the night was as a moment.

In the gray of a dawn cold, pure, and silent, with the radiant morning star shining like a silver moon, the long file of Yaquis rode and tramped westward, down the rugged bare slopes of this unknown desert.

And out of the relentless east, land of enemies, rose the glaring sun. The frost melted off the rocks and the cool freshness of morning changed to a fiery breath. The sun climbed, and the leagues were as long as the hours. Down into a broad region of lava toiled the fugitives. Travel over the jagged crusts and through the poison-spiked cholla lamed the horses and made walking imperative. Yaqui drove his people before him, and some of the weakest fell by the way.

Out of the hot lava and stinging cactus the Indians toiled and entered a region of bare stone, cut by the wind and water into labyrinthine passages where, even if they had left tracks on the hard rocks, few pursuers could have followed. Yaqui told this to his people, told them he saw sheep on the peaks above and smelled water, and thus urged them on and on league after league toward this distant purple heights. Vast and hard as had been the desert behind them, this strange upflung desert before them seemed vaster and grimmer. The trackless way led ever upward by winding passages and gorges—a gloomy and weird region of colored stone. And over all reigned the terrible merciless sun.

Yaqui sacrificed horses to the thirst and hunger of his people and abandoned the horror of toil under the sun to a slower progress by night. Blanched and magnified under the great stars, the iron-bound desert of riven rock, so unreal and weird, brought forth a chant from the lips of Yaqui's women. His braves, stoic like himself, endured and plodded on, lightening burdens of the weaker and eventually carrying the children. That night passed and a day of stupor in the shade of sun-heated rock; another night led the fugitives onward and upward through a maze of shattered cliffs, black and wild. Day dawned once more, showing Yaqui by the pitiless light that only his men could endure much more of this dragging on.

He made camp there and encouraged his people by a faith that had come to him during the night—a whisper from the spirit of his forefathers—to endure, to live, to go to a beautiful end his vision could not see. Then Yaqui stalked alone off into the fastnesses of the rocks and prayed to his gods for guidance. All about him were silence, desolation, a gray world of rock; a black barren world of lava. Far as his eye could see to the north and east and south stretched the illimitable glaring desert; rough, peaked, spiked, riven, ghastly with yellow slopes, bleak with its bare belts, terrible with its fluted and upflung plateaus, stone faced by endless ramparts and fast bound to the fading distance. From the west, up over the dark and forlorn heights, Yaqui heard the whispers of his dead forefathers.

Another dawn found Yaqui with his young son on the great heights with the sunrise at his back and with another and more promising world at his feet.

"Land of our forefathers!" he cried out sonorously to his people, gazing mutely down into the promised land. A vast gray-green valley yawned at their feet. Leagues of grassy, rock-ribbed, and tree-dotted slopes led down to a gleaming white stream, winding like a silver ribbon down the valley, to lose itself far in the lower country, where the colored desert merged into an immense and boundless void of hazy blue—the sea.

"Great Water, where the sun sleeps," said Yaqui with long arm outstretched. "Yaqui's father's father saw it."

Yaqui carried his son and led the way down from the heights. Mountain sheep and wild horses and deer and quail that had never before seen man showed no fear of this invasion of their home. And Yaqui's people, footsore and starved, gazed round them and, in the seeming safety of this desert-locked valley with its grass and water and wood and abundant game, they took hope again and saw their prayers answered and happiness once more possible. New life flushed their veins. The long slopes, ever greener as they descended, were welcome to aching eyes so tired of the glaring expanses of the desert.

For an encampment Yaqui chose the head of the valley. Wide and gently sloping, with a rock-walled spring that was the source of the stream, and large ironwood trees and pines and paloverdes, this lonely hidden spot satisfied the longing in Yaqui's heart. Almost his joy was complete. But never could he feel wholly secure again, even had he wings of an eagle. For Yaqui's keen eyes had seen gold in the sands of the stream; and gold spelled the doom of the Indian.

Still Yaqui was grateful and content. Not soon would his people be tracked to this fastness, and perhaps never. He cautioned his braves to save their scant ammunition, sending them with bows and arrows to kill the deer and antelope. The weary squaws no longer chanted the melancholy songs of their woe. The long travel had ended. They unpacked under the pines, made fires to roast the meat that would soon be brought, and attended to the ailments of the few children left to them. Soon the naked little ones, starved and cut and worn as they were, took to the clear cool water like goslings.

Yaqui, carrying his rifle, stalked abroad to learn more of

this wonderful valley. Stretching at length along the stream, he drank deeply, as an Indian who loved mountain water. The glint of gold in the wet sand did not please him as had the sweetness of the cold water. Grasping up a handful of sand and pebbles, he rubbed and washed it in his palm. Tiny grains of gold and little nuggets of gold! Somewhere up at the head of this valley lay the mother lode from which the gold had washed down.

Yaqui knew that here was treasure for which the white men would spill blood and sell their souls. But to the Indians—the Papagos, the Yumas, the man-eating Seris, and especially to the Yaquis—gold was no more than rock or sand, except that they hated it for the curse of white hunters it lured to the desert. Yaqui had found many a rich vein and ledge and placer of gold. He had hated them, and now more than any other he hated this new discovery. It would be a constant peril to his people. In times of flood this mountain stream would carry grains of gold as it flowed down on the desert. Yaqui saw in it a menace. But there was hope in the fact that many treasures of the desert heights would never be seen by white men. His father had told him that. This gray valley was high, cradled in the rocky uplands, and it might be inaccessible from below.

Yaqui set out to see. His stride was that of the strongest and tallest of his tribe, and distance meant little to him. Hunger gnawed at his vitals, but the long march across the wastes and heights had not tired him. Yaqui had never known exhaustion. Before the sun stood straight overhead he had ascertained that this valley of promise was shut off from the west and that the stream failed in impassable desert. From north and east he had traveled, and therefore felt a grim security. But to the south he turned apprehensive eyes. Long he tramped and high he climbed, at last to see that the valley, this land of his forefathers, could be gained from the south. Range and ridge sloped gradually to a barren, desolate land of sun and cacti, far as his desert eyes could see. That must be the land of the Seris, the man-eaters. But it was a waterless hell in summer. No fear from the south till the winter rains fell! Yaqui returned to his camp at sunset. There was joy in the dusky welcoming eyes of his young wife as she placed fresh meat before him.

"Yaqui's only son will live," she said, and pointed to the frail boy as he slept. The chief gazed somberly at the little brown face of his son.

Days passed. With rest and food and water the gloomy spirit of the Yaquis underwent a gradual change. The wild valley was an Indian's happy hunting ground, encompassed by lofty heights known only to sheep and eagles. Like wild animals, Indians, in the peace and loneliness of a secluded region, soon forgot past trials and fears. Still, Yaqui did not forget, but as time passed and nothing disturbed the serenity of this hiding place his vigilance slowly relaxed. The wind and the sun and the solitude and the presence of antelope and wild horses always within sight of camp—these factors of primitive nature had a healing effect upon his sore heart. In the canyons he found graves and bones of his progenitors.

Days passed into weeks. Scarlet blossoms flamed at the long ends of the ocatilla; one morning the paloverdes, which had been bare and shiny green, burst into full bloom; a yellow flowering that absorbed the sunlight. Cacti opened great buds of magenta. From the canyon walls, on inaccessible ledges, hung the exquisite and rare desert flowers, *lluvia d'oro,* shower of gold. This magic of spring did not last. The flowers faded, died, and blew away on the dry wind. The tall grasses slowly yellowed and bleached. Summer came. The glaring sun blazed over the eastern ramparts, burned white down over the still solemn valley, and sank like a huge ball of fire into the distant hazy sea. With the torrid heat of desert Sonora came a sense of absolute security to Yaqui. His new home was locked in the furnace of the sun-blasted wasteland. The clear spring of mountain water sank lower and lower, yet did not fail. The birds and beasts that visited the valley attested to the nature of the surrounding country. So the time came when Yaqui forgot the feeling of distant steps upon his trail.

When autumn came the valley was dry and gray and

withered, except the green line along the stream and the perennial freshness of the cactus and the everlasting green of the paloverdes. With the winter came the rains, and a wave of ever-brightening green flushed the vast valley from its eastern height of slope to the far distant mouth, where it opened into the barren desert.

The god of the Yaquis had not forgotten them. As the months passed child after child was born to the women of the tribe. Yaqui's dusky-eyed wife bore him a healthy girl baby. As the chief balanced the tiny brown form in his great hand he remembered a speech of his father's. "Son, let the Yaquis go back to the mountains of the setting sun— to a land free from white men and gold and firewater, to the desert valley where deer graze with horses. There let the Yaquis multiply into a great people or perish from the earth."

Yaqui watched his girl baby with a gleam of troubled hope lighting in his face. His father had spoken prophecy. There waved the green grass of the broad valley, dotted with wild horses, antelope, and deer grazing among his stock. Here in his hand lay another child—a woman child— and he had believed his son to be the last of his race. It was not too late. The god of the Indian was good. His branch of the Yaquis would mother and father a great people. But even as he fondled his babe the toe of his moccasin stirred grains of gold in the sand.

Love of life lulled Yaqui back into his dreams. To live, to have his people round him, to see his dusky-eyed wife at her work, to watch the naked children playing in the grass, to look out over that rolling, endless green valley, so wild, so lonely, so fertile—such a proof of God in the desert—to feel the hot sun and the sweet wind and the cool night, to linger on the heights watching, listening, feeling, to stalk the keen-eyed mountain sheep, to eat fresh meat and drink pure water, to rest through the solemn still noons and sleep away the silent melancholy nights, to enjoy the games of his forefathers—wild games of riding and running—to steal off alone into the desert and endure heat, thirst, cold, dust, starvation while he sought the Indian gods hidden in the rocks, to be free of the white man—to live like the eagles—to live—Yaqui asked no more.

Yaqui laid the baby back in the cradle of its mother's breast and stalked out as a chief to inspire his people.
In that high altitude the morning air was cold, exhilarating, sweet to breathe and wonderful to send the blood racing. Some winter mornings there was just a touch of frost on the leaves. The sunshine was welcome. The day was short, the night long. Yaqui's people reverted to their old order of happy primitive life before the white man had come with greed for gold and lust to kill.

The day dawned in which Yaqui took his son out and put him upon a horse. As horsemen the Yaquis excelled all other Indian tribes. Boys were taught to ride bareback. Thus as youths they developed exceeding skill and strength.

Some braves had rounded up a band of wild horses and driven them into a rough rock-walled triangle, a natural trap, the opening of which they had closed with a rude fence. On this morning the Yaquis all assembled to see the wild horses broken. Yaqui, as an inspiration to his little son and to the other boys of the tribe, chose the vicious leader of the band as the horse he would first ride and break. High on the rocky wall perched the black-eyed boys, eager and restless, excited and wondering. The women and girls of the tribe occupied another position along the outcropping of gray wall, their colorful garments lending contrast to the scene.

The inclosure was wide and long, containing both level and uneven ground, some of which was grass and, some sand and rock. A few ironwood trees and one huge paloverde, under which Indians were lolling, afforded shade. At the edge of the highest slope began a line of pine trees that reached up to the bare gray heights.

Yaqui had his braves drive the vicious leader of the wild horses out into the open. It was a stallion of ungainly shape and rusty color, no longer young. With ugly head high, nostrils distended, mouth open and ears up, showing the white of vicious, fiery eyes, it pranced in the middle of the circle drawn by its captors.

Yaqui advanced with his long leather *riata,* and, once clear of the ring of horsemen inclosing the stallion, he waved them back. Then as the wild steed plunged, seeking an opening in that circle, Yaqui swung the long noose. He missed twice. The third cast caught its mark, the snarling nose of this savage horse. Yaqui hauled the lasso taut. Then with a snort of fright the stallion lunged and reared, pawing the air. Yaqui, hauling hand over hand, pulled him down and approached him at the same time. Shuddering all over, breathing with hard snorts, the stallion faced his captor one moment, as if ready to fight. But fear predominated. He leaped away. At the end of that leap, so powerful was the strain on him, he went down in the sand. Up he sprang, wilder than ever, and dashed forward, dragging the Indian, gaining yards of the lasso. But the mounted Yaquis blocked his passage. He had to swerve; and as he ran desperately in a circle once more the chief hauled hand over hand on the rope. Suddenly Yaqui bounded in and with a tremendous leap, like the leap of a panther, he gained the back of the stallion and seemed to become fixed there. He dropped the lasso, and with the first startled jump of the stallion the noose loosened and slipped off. Except for Yaqui's great, long brown legs, with their strong bands of muscle set like steel, the stallion was free.

The stallion bolted. Only the rock wall checked his headlong flight. Then he wheeled and ran along the wall, bounding over rocks and ditches, stretching out until, with magnificent stride, he was running at his topmost speed. Along one wall and then the other he dashed, round and round and across, until the moment came when panic succeeded to fury, and then his tremendous energies were directed to the displacement of his rider. Wildly he pitched. With head down, legs stiff, feet together, he plunged over the sand, plowing dust, and bounding straight up. But he could not unseat his inexorable rider. Yaqui's legs banded his belly and were as steel. Then the stallion, now lashed into white lather of sweat and froth, lunged high to paw the air and scream and plunge down to pitch again. His motions soon lost their energy, though not their fury. Then he reached back with eyes of fire and open mouth to bite. Yaqui's huge fist met him, first on the right, then on the left. He plunged to his knees and with rumbling heave of anger he fell on his side, meaning to roll over his rider. But Yaqui's leg on that side flashed high while his hands twisted hard in the long mane. When the foiled horse rose again Yaqui rose with him, again fixed tight on his back. Another dash and burst of running, wild and blind this time and plainly losing speed, showed the weakening of the stallion. And the time arrived when, spent and beaten, he fell in the sand.

"Let Yaqui's son learn to ride like his father," said the chief to his gleeful, worshiping son. "Let Yaqui's son watch and remember to tell his son's son," he said.

He scattered his riders to block the first passages out of the valley and ordered his son and all the women of the tribe and their children again to climb high on the rocks, there to watch. The Indian gods said this day marked the rejuvenation of their tribe. Let his son, who would be chief some day, and his people, see the great runner of the Yaquis.

Naked except for his moccasins, the giant chief broke into a slow trot that was habitual with him when alone on a trail. He crossed the stream and headed out into the grassy valley where deer grazed with the horses. Yaqui selected the one that appeared largest and strongest of the deer herd and to it he called in a loud voice, meant as well for the spirit of his forefathers and for his gods, watching and listening from the heights.

"Yaqui runs to kill!"

The sleek gray deer left off their grazing and stood with long ears erect. Then they bounded off. Yaqui broke from his trot into a long, swinging lope and the length of his stride was such that he seemed to fly over the ground. Up the valley, the deer scattered and Yaqui ran in the trail of the one to which he had called. Half a mile off it halted to look back. Then it grazed, but soon lifted its head to look again. Yaqui ran on at the same easy, distance-devouring stride. Presently the deer dashed away and kept on until it was a mere speck in Yaqui's eyes. It climbed a trail that let over the heights. Then it crossed the wide valley to be turned back by insurmountable cliffs. Yaqui kept it in sight and watched it trot and stop, run and walk and stop again, all the way up the long grassy slope toward the head of the valley.

Here among rocks and trees Yaqui lost sight of his quarry, but he trailed it with scarcely a slackening of his pace. At length, coming out upon a bench, he saw the deer he had chosen to run to death. It was looking back.

Down the grassy middle of the vast valley, clear to the mouth where the stream tumbled off into space, across the wide level from slope to slope, back under the beetling heights, Yaqui pursued the doomed deer.

Leagues and leagues of fleet running had availed the deer nothing. It could not shake off the man. More and more the distance between them lessened. Terror now added to the gradual exhaustion of the four-footed creature, designed by nature to escape its foes. Yaqui, perfect in all the primal attributes of man, was its superior. The race was not to the swift but to the enduring.

Within sight of his people and his little son, Yaqui overtook the staggering deer and broke its neck with his naked hands. Then for an instant he stood erect over his fallen quarry, a tall, gaunt giant, bathed in the weird afterglow of sunset. He lifted a long arm to the heights, as if calling upon his spirits there to gaze down upon the victory of the red man.

II

It was toward evening of another day, all the hours of which had haunted Yaqui with a nameless oppression. Like a deer that scented a faint strange taint on the pure air Yaqui pointed his sensitive nose toward the east, whence came the soft wind.

Suddenly his strong vision quivered to the movement of objects on the southern slope. Halting, he fixed his gaze.

Long line of moving dots!

Neither deer nor sheep nor antelope traveled in that formation. The objects were men. Yaqui caught the glint of sunset red on shining guns. Mexican soldiers!

That nameless haunting fear of the south, long lulled, now had its fulfillment.

Yaqui leaped with gigantic bounds down the slope. Like an antelope he sprang over rocks and dips, and once on the grassy downs he ran the swiftest race of his life. His piercing yells warned his people in time to save them from being surprised by the soldiers. The first shots of combat were fired as he hurdled the several courses of the stream. Yaqui saw the running and crawling forms of men in dusty blue—saw them aim short carbines—saw spurts of flame and puffs of smoke.

Yaqui's last few bounds carried him into the stone-walled encampment, and the whistling bullets that missed him told how the line of soldiers was spreading to surround the place. Yaqui flung himself behind the wall and crawled to where his braves knelt with guns and bows ready. Some were shooting. The women and children were huddled out of sight. Steel-jacketed bullets cracked on the rocks and whined away. Yaqui knew how poor was the marksmanship of the Mexicans. It seemed to him they were shooting high. The position of the Indians was open to fire from several angles.

During a lull in the firing a hoarse yell pealed out. Yaqui knew Spanish.

"Surrender, Yaquis!" was the command.

The Yaquis answered by well-aimed bullets that brought sharp cries from the soldiers. Soon the encampment appeared entirely surrounded. Reports came from all sides and bullets whistled high, spatting into the trees. Then occurred another lull in the firing. Again a voice pealed out: "Surrender, Yaquis, save your lives!"

The Indians recognized their doom. Each man had only a few cartridges for his gun. Many had only bows and arrows. They would be shot like wolves in a trap. But no Yaqui spoke a word.

Nevertheless, when darkness put an end to their shooting there were only a few who had a shell left. The Mexicans grasped the situation and grew bold. They built fires off under the trees. They crept down to the walls and threw stones into the encampment and yelled derisively: "Yaqui dogs!" They kept up a desultory shooting from all sides as if to make known to the Indians that they were surrounded and vigilantly watched.

At dawn the Mexicans began another heavy volleying, firing into the encampment without aim but with deadly intent. Then, yelling their racial hatred of the Yaquis, they charged the camp. It was an unequal battle. Outnumbered and without ammunition the Yaquis fought a desperate but losing fight. One by one they were set upon by several, sometimes by half a dozen, Mexicans, and killed or beaten into insensibility.

Yaqui formed the center of several storms of conflict. With clubbed rifle he was like a giant fighting down a horde of little men.

"Kill the big devil!" cried a soldier.

From the thick of that melee sounded Spanish curses and maledictions and dull thuds and groans as well. The Yaqui was match for all that could surround him. A Mexican fired a pistol. Then an officer came running to knock aside the weapon. He shouted to his men to capture the Yaqui chief. The Mexicans pressed closer, dodging the sweeping rifle, and one of them plunged at the heels of the Indian. Another did likewise and they tripped up the giant, who was then piled upon by a number of cursing soldiers. Like a mad bull Yaqui heaved and tossed, but to no avail. He was overpowered and bound with a lasso, and tied upright to the paloverde under which he had so often rested.

His capture ended the battle. The Mexicans began to run about, searching. Daylight had come. From under a ledge of rock, the Indian women and children were driven. One lithe, quick boy eluded the soldiers. He slipped out of their hands and ran. As he looked back over his shoulder his dark face shone wildly. It was Yaqui's son. Like a deer he ran, not heeding the stern calls to halt. "Shoot!" ordered the officer. Then the soldiers leveled rifles and began to fire. Puffs of dust struck up behind, beside and beyond that flying form. But none hit him. They shot until he appeared to be out of range. And all eyes watched him flee. Then a last bullet struck its mark. The watchers heard a shrill cry of agony and saw the lad fall.

All the Indians were tied hand and foot and herded into a small space and guarded as if they had been wild cattle.

After several hours of resting and feasting and celebrating what manifestly was regarded as a great victory, the officer ordered the capture of horses and the burning of effects not transportable. Soon the beautiful encampment of the Yaquis was a blackened and smoking ruin. Then, driving the Yaquis in a herd before them, the Mexicans, most of them now mounted on Indian horses, faced the ascent of the slope by which they had entered the valley.

Far down that ragged mountain slope the Mexicans halted at the camp they had left when they made their attack on the Yaquis. Mules and burros, packsaddles and camp duffel occupied a dusty bench upon which there grew scant vegetation. All round were black slopes of ragged lava and patches of glistening white cholla.

The Yaquis received little water and food, no blankets, no rest from tight bonds, no bandaging of their fly-tormented wounds. But they bore their ills as if they had none.

Yaqui sat with his back to a stone and when unobserved by the guards he would whisper to those of his people nearest to him. Impassively but with intent faces they listened. His words had some strange, powerful, sustaining effect. And all the time his inscrutable gaze swept down off the lava heights to the hazy blue gulf of the sea.

Dawn disclosed the fact that two of the Yaquis were badly wounded and could not be driven to make a start. Perhaps they meant to force the death that awaited them farther down the trail; perhaps they were absorbed in the morbid gloom of pain and departing strength. At last the officer, weary of his subordinate's failure to stir these men, dragged at them himself, kicked and beat them, cursing the while.

"Yaqui dogs! You go to the henequen fields!"

The older of these wounded Indians, a man of lofty stature and mien, suddenly arose. Swiftly his brown arm flashed. He grasped a billet of wood from a packsaddle and struck the officer down. The blow lacked force. It was evident that the Yaqui, for all his magnificent spirit, could scarcely stand. Excitedly the soldiers yelled, and some brandished weapons. The officer staggered to his feet, livid and furious, snarling like a dog, and ordering his men to hold back, he drew a pistol to kill the Yaqui. The scorn, the contempt, the serenity of the Indian, instead of rousing his respect, incurred a fury which demanded more than death.

"You shall walk the cholla torture!" he shrieked, waving his pistol in the air.

In northwest Mexico, for longer than the oldest inhabitant could remember, there had been a notorious rumor of the cholla torture that the Yaquis meted out to their Mexican captives. This cholla torture consisted of ripping the skin off the soles of Mexicans' feet and driving them to walk upon the cactus beds until they died.

The two wounded Indians, with bleeding raw feet, were dragged to the cholla torture. They walked the white, glistening, needle-spiked beds of cholla, blind to the cruel jeers and mute wonderment and vile maledictions of their hereditary foes. The giant Yaqui who had struck down the officer stalked unaided across the beds of dry cholla. The cones cracked like live bits of steel. They collected on the Yaqui's feet until he was lifting pads of cactus. He walked erect, with a quivering of all the muscles of his naked bronze body, and his dark face was set in a terrible hardness of scorn for his murderers.

Then when the mass of cactus cones adhering to the Yaqui's feet grew so heavy that he became anchored in his tracks the Mexican officer, with a fury that was not all hate, ordered his soldiers to dispatch these two Indians who were beyond the reach of a torture hideous and appalling to all Mexicans. Yaqui, the chief, looked on inscrutably, towering above the bowed heads of his women.

This execution sobered the soldiers. Not only extermination did they mean to mete out to the Yaqui, but an extermination of horrible toil, by which the Mexicans were to profit.

Montes, a Brazilian, lolled in the shady spot on the dock. The hot sun of the Yucatan was more than enough for him.

The still air reeked with a hot pungent odor of henequen. Montes had learned to hate the smell. He was in Yucatan on a mission for the Brazilian government and also as an agent to study the sisal product—an advantageous business for him, to which he had devoted himself with enthusiasm and energy.

But two unforeseen circumstances had disturbed him of late and rendered less happy his devotion to his tasks. His vanity had been piqued, his pride had been hurt, his heart had been stormed by one of Merida's coquettish beauties. And the plight of the poor Yaqui Indians, slaves in the henequen fields, had so roused his compassion that he had neglected his work.

So, as Montes idled there in the shade, with his legs dangling over the dock, a time came in his reflection when he was confronted with a choice between the longing to go home and a strange desire to stay. He gazed out into the gulf. The gunboat Esperanza had come to anchor in the roads off Progreso. She had a cargo of human freight— Yaqui Indian prisoners from the wild plateaus of northern Sonora—more slaves to be broken in the terrible henequen fields. At that moment of Montes's indecision he espied Lieutenant Perez coming down the dock at the head of a file of rurales.

Gazing at Perez intently, the Brazilian experienced a slight cold shock of decision. He would prolong his stay in Yucatan. Strange was the nameless something that haunted him. Jealous curiosity, he called it, bitterly. Perez had the favor of the proud mother of Señorita Dolores Mendoza, the coquettish beauty who had smiled upon Montes. She cared no more for Perez than she cared for him or any of the young bloods of Merida. But she would marry Perez.

Montes rose and stepped out of the shade. His commission in Yucatan put him on common ground with Perez, but he had always felt looked down upon by this little Yucatecan.

"Buenos dias, senor," replied Perez to his greeting. "More Yaquis."

A barge was made fast to the end of the dock and the

Yaquis driven off and held there in a closely guarded group.

Perez halted the loading of henequen long enough to allow the prisoners to march up the dock between the files of *rurales*. They passed under the shadows of the huge warehouses, out into a glaring square where the bare sand radiated veils of heat.

At an order from Perez, soldiers began separating the Yaqui women and children from the men. They were formed in two lines. Then Perez went among them, pointing out one, then another.

Montes suddenly grasped the significance of this scene and it had a strange effect upon him. Yaqui father and son—husband and wife—mother and child did not yet realize that here they were to be parted—that this separation was forever. Then one young woman, tall, with striking dark face, beautiful with the grace of some wild creature, instinctively divined the truth and cried out hoarsely. The silence, the stoicism of these Indians seemed broken. This woman had a baby in her arms. Running across the aisle of sand, she faced a huge Yaqui and cried aloud in poignant broken speed. This giant was her husband and the father of that baby. He spoke, laid a hand on her and stepped out. Perez, who had been at the other end of the aisle, saw the movement and strode toward them.

"Back, Yaqui dogs!" he yelled stridently, and he flashed his bright sword.

With tremendous stride the Yaqui reached Perez and towered over him.

"Capitán, let my wife and child go where Yaqui goes," demanded the Indian in deep voice of sonorous dignity. His Spanish was well spoken. His bearing was that of a chief. He asked what seemed his right, even of a ruthless enemy.

But Perez saw nothing but affront to his authority. At his order the rurales clubbed Yaqui back into line. They would have done the same for the stricken wife, had she not backed away from their threatening advances. She had time for a long agonized look into the terrible face of her husband. Then she was driven away in one group and he was left in the other.

Montes thought he would forever carry in memory the tragic face of that Yaqui's wife. Indians had hearts and souls the same as white people. It was a ridiculous and extraordinary and base thing to be callous to the truth. Montes had spent not a little time in the pampas among the Gauchos and for that bold race he had admiration and respect. Indeed, coming to think about it, the Gauchos resembled these Yaquis. Montes took the trouble to go among English and American acquaintances he had made in Progreso, and learned more about this oppressed tribe.

The vast plateau of northwestern Mexico, a desert and mountainous region rich in minerals, was the home of the Yaquis. For more than one hundred and sixty years there had been war between the Yaquis and the Mexicans. And recently, following a bloody raid credited to the Yaquis, the government in power determined to exterminate them. To that end it was hunting the Indians down, killing those who resisted capture, and sending the rest to the torture of the henequen fields.

But more interesting was the new information that Montes gathered. The Yaquis were an extraordinary, able-bodied, and intelligent people. Most of them spoke Spanish. They had many aboriginal customs and beliefs, but some were Roman Catholics. The braves made better miners and laborers than white men. Moreover, they possessed singular mechanical gifts and quickly learned to operate machines more efficiently than most whites. They possessed wonderful physical development and a marvelous endurance. At sixty years Yaquis had perfectly sound white teeth and hair as black as night. These desert men could travel seventy miles on foot in one day with only a bag of piñole. Water they could do without for days. And it was said that some of the Yaqui runners performed feats of speed, strength, and endurance beyond credence. Montes, remembering the stature of that Yaqui chief and the spread of his shoulders and the wonder of his spare, lithe limbs, thought that he could believe much.

The act of Perez in deliberately parting the chief from his loved ones was cruel and despicable, and it seemed to establish in Montes' mind an excuse for the disgust and hate he had come to feel for the tyrannical little officer. But, being frank with himself, Montes confessed that this act had only fixed a hate he already had acquired.

The Brazilian convinced himself that he had intuitively grasped a portent apparently lost on Perez. One of those silent, intent-faced Yaquis was going to kill this epauleted scion of a rich Yucatan house. Montes had read it in their faces. He had lived among the blood-spilling Gauchos and he knew the menace of silent fierce savages. And he did not make any bones about the admission to himself that he hoped some Yaqui would kill the peacocked Mexican. Montes had Spanish in him, and something of the raw passion of the Gauchos he admired. It suited him to absorb this morbid presentiment. The Yaqui chief fascinated him, impelled him. Montes determined to learn where this giant had been sent and to watch him, win his confidence, if such a thing was possible. *Quien sabe?* Montes felt more reasons than one for his desire to know this big Yaqui.

III

In the interior of Yucatan there were vast, barren areas of land fit only for the production of henequen. Nothing but jungle and henequen would grow there. It was a limestone country. The soil could not absorb water. It soaked through. Here and there, miles apart, were *ceñotes*, underground caverns full of water. Usually these marked the location of a hacienda of one of the rich planters. The climate was hot, humid. For any people used to high altitudes it spelled death.

The plantation of Don Sancho Perez, father of the young lieutenant, consisted of fifty thousand acres. It adjoined the hundred-thousand-acre tract of Doña Isabel Mendoza. The old *don* was ambitious to merge the plantations so that he could dominate the fiber output of that region. To this end he had long sought to win for his son the hand of Doña Isabel's beautiful daughter.

Yaqui was in the squad of prisoners that had been picked out by the young officer to work on his father's plantation.

They were manacled at night and herded like wild beasts into a pen and watched by armed guards. They were routed out at dawn and put to work in the fields. For food they had, a single lump of coarse, soggy bread—one lump once every day. When the weaker among them began to lag, to slow down, to sicken, they were whipped.

Yaqui knew that never again would he see his wife and baby—never hear from them—never know what became of them. He worked like a galley slave, all the harder because of his great strength and endurance.

He would be driven until he broke down.

Yaqui's work consisted of cutting henequen fiber leaves. He had a machete and he walked the endless aisles between the lines of great century plants and from each plant he cut the lower circle of leaves. Each plant gave him a heavy load and he carried it to the nearest hand-car tracks that crossed the plantation. The work of other Indians was to push hand cars along these tracks and gather the loads.

It took Yaqui six days to cut one aisle. As far as he could see stretched a vast, hot, green wilderness with its neverending lines and lanes, its labyrinthine maze of intersecting aisles, its hazy, copper-hued horizons speared and spiked by the great bayonet-like leaves. He had been born and raised on the rugged mountain plateaus far to the north, where the clear, sweet, cold morning air stung and the midday sun was only warm to his back. Where there were grass and water and flowers and trees, where the purple canyons yawned and the black peaks searched the sky. Here he was chained in the thick, hot, moist night. The air was foul, and he was driven out in the long day under a fiery sun, where the henequen reeked and his breath clogged in his throat and his eyes were burning balls and his bare feet were like rotting hoofs.

The time came when Montes saw that the Yaqui looked no more toward that northland which he would never see again. He dreamed no more hopeless dreams. Somehow he knew when his wife and baby were no more a part of him on the earth. For something within him died and there were strange, silent voices at his elbow. He listened to them. And in the depths of his being there boiled a maelstrom of blood. He worked. He waited.

At night in the close-crowded filthy pen, with the dampness of tropical dew stealing in, and all about him the silent prostrate forms of his stricken people, he lay awake and waited enduringly through the long hours till a fitful sleep came to him. By day in the henequen fields, with the furnace blasts of wind swirling down the aisles, with the moans of his beaten comrades full in his ears, he waited with a Yaqui's patience.

He saw his people beaten and scourged and starved. He saw them sicken and fail—wilt under the hot sun—die in the henequen aisles—and be thrown like dogs into ditches with quicklime. One by one they went and when they were nearly all gone others took their places. The Yaqui recognized Indians of other tribes of his race. But they did not know him. He had greatly changed. Only the shell of him was left.

And that seemed unbreakable, deathless. He did not tell these newcomers to the fields what torture lay in store for them. He might have been dumb. He only waited, adding day by day, in the horror of the last throes of his old comrades, something more to that hell in his blood. He watched them die and then the beginning of the end for his new comrades. They were doomed. They were to be driven till they dropped. And others would be brought to fill their places, till at last there were no Yaquis left. The sun was setting for his race.

The Yaqui and his fellow toilers had one day of rest—the Sabbath.

There was no freedom. Always there were guards and soldiers. Sunday was the day of bull fights in the great corral at the hacienda. And on these occasions Yaqui was given extra work. Montes knew the Indian looked forward to this day. The old Don's son, Lieutenant Perez, would come from the city to attend the fight. Then Yaqui fed his dark soul with more cunning, more patience, more promise.

It was Yaqui's work to help drag disemboweled and dying horses from the bull ring and to return with sand to cover the gory spots in the arena. Often Montes saw him look up at the crowded circle of seats and at the box where the gray old Don and his people and friends watched the spectacle. There were handsome women with white lace over their heads and in whose dark and slumberous eyes lurked something Yaqui knew. It was something that was in the race. Lieutenant Perez was there leaning toward the proud señorita. The Indian watched her with strange intensity. She appeared indifferent to the efforts of the picadores and the banderilleros, whose duty it was to infuriate the bull for the artist with the sword—the matador. When he appeared the beautiful senorita wakened to interest. But not until there was blood on the bright blade did she show the fire and passion of her nature. It was sight of blood that quickened her. It was death that she wanted to see.

And last Yaqui let his gaze rivet on the dark, arrogant visage of young Perez. Did not the great chief then become superhuman, or was it only Montes' morbid fancy? When Yaqui turned away, did he not feel a promise of fulfillment in the red haze of the afternoon sun, in the red tinge of the stained sand, in the red and dripping tongue of the tortured bull?

Montes knew the Yaqui only needed to live long enough and there would be something.

And death seemed aloof from this Indian. The ferocity of the desert was in him and its incalculable force of life. In his eyes had burned a seared memory of the violent thrust with which Perez had driven his wife and baby forever from his sight.

Montes' changed attitude evidently found favor in the proud señorita's eyes. She had but trifled with an earnest and humble suitor; to the advances of a man, bold, ardent, strange, with something unfathomable in his wooing, she was not indifferent. The fact did not cool Montes' passion, but it changed him somehow. The Spanish in him was the part that so ardently loved and hated. His mother had been French, and from her he had inherited qualities that kept him eternally in conflict with his instincts.

Montes had his living quarters in Merida, where all the rich henequen planters had town houses. It was not a long horseback ride out to the haciendas. His habit of late, after returning from a visit to the henequen fields, had been to choose the early warm hours of the afternoon to call upon Señorita Mendoza. There had been a time when his calls had been formally received by the Doña Isabel, but of late she had persisted in her siesta, leaving Monts to Dolores. Montes had grasped the significance of this—the future of Dolores had been settled and there no longer was risk in leaving her alone. But Montes had developed a theory that the future of any young woman was an uncertainty.

The Mendoza town house stood in the outskirts of fashionable Merida. The streets were white, the houses were white, the native Mayan women wore white, and always it seemed to Montes as he took the familiar walk that the white sun blazed down on an immaculate city. But there were dark records against the purity of Merida and the Yaqui slave driving was one of them. The Mendoza mansion had been built with money coming from the henequen fields. It stood high on a knoll, a stately white structure looking down upon a formal garden, where white pillars and statues gleamed among green palms and bowers of red roses. At the entrance, on each side of the wide flagstone walk, stood a huge henequen plant.

On this day the family was in town and Montes expected that the señorita would see him coming. He derived pleasure from the assurance that, compared with Perez, he was someone good to look at. Beside him the officer was a swarthy undersized youth. But Montes failed to see the white figure of the girl and suffered chagrin for his vanity.

The day was warm. As he climbed the high, wide stone steps his brow grew moist and an oppression weighed upon him. Only in the very early morning here in Yucatan did he ever have any energy. The climate was enervating. No wonder it was that servants and people slept away the warmer hours. Crossing the broad stone court and the spacious outside hall, Montes entered the dim, dark, musty parlors and passed through to the patio.

Here all was colorful luxuriance of grass and flower and palm, great still ferns and trailing vines. It was not cool, but shady and moist. Only a soft spray of falling water and a humming of bees disturbed the deep silence. The place seemed drowned in sweet fragrance, rich and subtle, thickening the air so that it was difficult to breathe. In a bower roofed by roses lay Señorita Mendoza, asleep in a hammock.

Softly Montes made his way to her side and stood looking down at her. As a picture, as something feminine, beautiful and young and soft and fresh and alluring, asleep and therefore sincere, she seemed all that was desirable. Dolores Mendoza was an unusual type for a Yucatecan of Spanish descent. She was blonde. Her hair was not golden, yet nearly so. She had a broad, low, beautiful brow, with level eyebrows, and the effect of her closed lids was fascinating with their promise. Her nose was small, straight, piquant, with delicate nostrils that showed they could quiver and dilate. Her mouth, the best feature of her beauty, was as red as the roses that drooped over her, and its short curved upper lip seemed full, sweet, sensuous. She had the oval face of her class, but fair, not olive-skinned, and her chin, though it did not detract from her charms, was far from being strong. Perhaps her greatest attraction, seen thus in the slumber of abandon, was her slender form, round-limbed and graceful.

Montes gazed at her until he felt a bitterness of revolt against the deceit of nature. She gladdened all the senses of man.

But somehow she seemed false to the effect she created. If he watched her long in this beautiful guise of sleep he would deaden his intelligence. She was not for him. So he pulled a red rose and pushed it against her lips, playfully tapping them until she awoke. Her eyes opened. They were a surprise. They should have been blue, but they were

"You know, of course, señor," she replied mockingly. "The little Alva girl, for instance. You admired her. Perhaps she—"

"She is adorable," he returned complacently. "I go to her for consolation."

Dolores made a sharp passionate gesture, a contrast to her usual languorous movements. Into the sleepy, tawny eyes shot a dilating fire.

"Have you made love to her?" she demanded.

"Dolores, do you imagine any man could resist that girl?" he rejoined.

"Have you?" she repeated with heaving breast.

Montes discarded his tantalizing lightness. "No, Dolores, I have not. I have lived in a torment lately. My love for you seems turning to hate."

"No!" she cried, extending her hands. She softened. Her lips parted. If there were depths in her, Montes had sounded them.

"Dolores, tell me the truth," he said, taking her hands. "You have never been true."

"I am true to my family. They chose Perez for me to marry—before I ever knew you. It is settled. I shall marry him. But—"

"But! Dolores, you love me?"

She drooped her head. "Yes, señor—lately it has come to that. Ah! Don't—don't! Montes, I beg of you! You forget—I'm engaged to Perez."

Montes released her. In her confession and resistance there was proof of his injustice. She was no nobler than her class. She was a butterfly in her fancies, a little cat in her greedy joy of physical life. But in her agitation he saw a deeper spirit.

"Dolores, if I had come first—before Perez—would you have given yourself to me?" he asked.

"Ah, señor, with all my heart!" she replied softly.

"Dearest—I think I must ask you to forgive me for—for something I can't confess. And now tell me—this reception given tomorrow by your mother—is that to announce your engagement to Perez?"

tawny. Sleepy, dreamy, wonderful cat eyes they were, clear and soft, windows of the truth of her nature. Montes suddenly felt safe again, sure of himself.

"Ah, Señor Montes," she said. "You found me asleep. How long have you been here?"

"A long time, I think," he replied, as he seated himself on a bench near her hammock. "Watching you asleep, I forgot time. But alas! time flies... and you awoke."

Dolores laughed. She had perfect white teeth that looked made to bite and enjoy biting. Her smile added to her charm.

"Sir, one would think you liked me best asleep."

"I do. You are always beautiful, Dolores. But when you are asleep you seem sincere. Now you are—Dolores Mendoza."

"Who is sincere? You are not," she retorted. "I don't know you any more. You seem to try to make me dissatisfied with myself."

"So you ought to be."

"Why? Because I cannot run away with you to Brazil?"

"No. Because you look like an angel but are not one. Because your beauty, your charm, your sweetness deceive men. You seem the incarnation of love and joy."

"Ah!" she cried, stretching and drawing a deep breath that swelled her white neck. "You are jealous! But I am happy. I have what I want. I am young and I enjoy. I love to be admired. I love to be loved. I love jewels, gowns, all I have; pleasure, excitement, music, flowers. I love to eat. I love to be idle, lazy, dreamy. I love to sleep. And you, horrid man, awake me to make me think."

"That is impossible, Dolores," he replied. "You cannot think."

"My mind works well. But I'll admit I'm a little animal—a tawny-eyed cat. So, Montes, you must stroke me the right way or I will scratch."

"Well, I'd rather you scratched," said Montes. "A man likes a woman who loves him tenderly and passionately one moment and tears his hair out the next."

35

"Yes and I will be free then till fall—when—when—"

"When you will be married?"

She bowed assent and hesitatingly slid a white hand toward him.

"Fall! It's a long time. Dolores, I must go back to Brazil."

"Ah, señor, that will kill me! Stay!" she entreated.

"But it would be dangerous. Perez dislikes me. I hate him. Something terrible might come of it."

"That is his risk. I have consented to marry him. I will do my duty before and after. But I see no reason why I may not have a little happiness—of my own—until that day comes. Life for me will not contain all I could wish. I told you; now I am happy. But you are included. Señor, if you love me you will remain."

"Dolores, can you think we will not suffer more?" he asked.

"I know we will afterward. But we shall not now."

"Now is perilous to me. To realize you love me! I did not think you capable of it. Listen! Something—something might prevent your marriage—or happen afterward. All—all is so uncertain."

"Quien sabe?" she whispered; and to the tawny, sleepy languor of her eyes there came a fancy, a dream, a mystic hope.

"Dolores, if Perez were lost to you—one way or another—would you marry me?" he broke out huskily. Not until then had he asked her hand in marriage.

"If such forlorn hope will make you stay—make you happy—yes, Señor Montes," was her answer.

There came a time when Yaqui was needed in the factory where the henequen fiber was extracted from the leaves. He had come to be a valuable machine—an instrument of toil that did not run down or go wrong. One guard said to another: "That big black peon takes a lot of killing!" and then ceased to watch him closely. He might have escaped. He might have crossed the miles and miles of henequen fields to the jungle, and under that dense cover made his way northward to the coast. Yaqui had many a chance. But he never looked to the north.

At first they put him to feeding henequen leaves into the maw of a crushing machine. The juicy, sticky, odorous substance of the big twenty-pound leaf was squeezed into a pulp, out of which came the white glistening threads of fiber. These fibers made sisal rope—rope second in quality only to the manila.

Then they put him in the pressing room to work on the ponderous iron press which was used to make the henequen bales. This machine was a high, strange-looking object, oblong in shape, like a box, opening in the middle from the top down. It had several distinct movements, all operated by levers. Long bundles of henequen were carried in from the racks and laid in the press until it was half full. Then a lever was pulled, the machine closed on the fiber and opened again. This operation was repeated again and again.

Then it was necessary for the operator to step from his platform onto the fiber in the machine and stamp it down and jump upon it and press it closely all round. When this had been done the last time the machine seemed wide open and stuffed so full that it would never close. But when the lever was pulled the ponderous steel jaws shut closer and closer and locked. Then the sides fell away, to disclose a great smooth bale of henequen ready for shipment.

The Yaqui learned to operate this press so skillfully that the work was left to him. When his carriers went out to the racks for more fiber he was left alone in the room.

Some strange relation sprang up between Yaqui and his fiber press.

For him it never failed to operate. He knew to a strand just how much fiber made a perfect bale. And he became so accurate that his bales were never weighed. They came out glistening, white, perfect to the pound. There was a strange affinity between this massive, steel-jawed engine and something that lived in the Yaqui's heart, implacable and immutable, appalling in its strength to wait, in its power to crush.

There seemed no failing of the endurance of this primitive giant, but his great frame had wasted away until it was a mere hulk. Owing to his value now to the hacienda, Yaqui was given rations in lieu of the ball of soggy bread. They were not, however, what the Indian needed. Montes at last won Yaqui's gratitude.

"Señor, if Yaqui wanted to eat it would be meat he needed," said the chief. Then Montes added meat to the wine, bread, and fruit he secretly brought to the Indian.

When Montes began covert kindnesses to the poor Yaqui slaves the chief showed gratitude and pathos: "Señor Montes is good—but the sun of the Yaquis is setting."

Perez in his triumphant arrogance derived pleasure from being magnanimous to the man he instinctively knew was his rival.

One day at the hacienda when Montes rode up to meet Doña Isabel and Dolores he found them accompanied by Perez and his parents. Almost immediately the young officer suggested gaily:

"Señor, pray carry Dolores off somewhere! My father has something to plan with Donna Isabel. It must be a secret from Dolores. Take her a walk—talk to her. Señor—keep her excited—make love to her!"

"I shall be happy to obey. Will you come, señorita?" said Montes.

If they expected Dolores to pout, they were mistaken. Her slow, sleepy glance left the face of her future husband as she turned away silently to accompany Montes. They walked along the palm-shaded road, out toward the huge, open, sunny space that was the henequen domain.

"I hate Perez," she burst out suddenly. "He meant to taunt you. He thinks I am his slave—a creature without mind or heart. Señor, make love to me!"

"You will be his slave—soon," whispered Montes bitterly.

"Never!" she exclaimed passionately.

They reached the end of the shady road. The mill was

—39—

silent. Montes saw the Indian standing motionless close at hand, in the shade of the henequen racks.

"Dolores, did you mean what you just said?" asked Montes eagerly.

"That I will never be Perez's slave?"

"No; the other thing you said."

"Yes, I did," she replied. "Make love to me, señor. It was his wish. I must learn to obey."

With sullen scorn she spoke, not looking at Montes, scarcely realizing the actual purport of her speech. But when Montes took her in his arms she started back with a cry. He held her. And suddenly clasping her tightly he bent his head to kiss the red lips she opened to protest.

"Let me go!" she begged wildly. "Oh—I did not—mean—Montes, *not so!* Do not make me—"

"Kiss me!" whispered Montes hoarsely, "or I'll never let you go. It was his wish. Come, I dare you—I beg you!"

One wild moment she responded to his kiss, and then she thrust him away.

"Ah, by the saints!" she murmured with hands over her face. "Now I will love you more—my heart will break."

"Dolores, I can't let Perez have you," declared Montes miserably.

"Too late, my dear. I am to be his wife."

"But you love me, Dolores?"

"Alas! Too true. I do. Oh, I never knew how well!" she cried.

"Let us run away," he implored eagerly.

Mournfully she shook her head, and looking up suddenly she espied the Yaqui. His great burning cavernous eyes, like black fire, were fixed upon her.

"Oh, that terrible Yaqui," she whispered. "It is he who watches us at the bull fights—Let us go, Montes—Oh, he saw us—he saw me—*Come!*"

Upon their return to the house the old don greeted them effusively. He seemed radiant with happiness. He had almost united two of the first families of Yucatan, which unison would make the greatest henequen plantation. The beautiful señorita had other admirers. But this marriage had unusual advantages. The peculiar location and productiveness of the plantations and the obstacles to greater and quicker output that would be done away with, and the fact that Lieutenant Perez through his military influence could work the fields with peon labor—these facts had carried the balance in favor of the marriage. The old don manifestly regarded the arrangement as a victory for him which he owed to the henequen, and he had decided to make the wedding day one on which the rich product of the plantation should play a most important part.

"But how to *bring in* the henequen!" he asked. "I've racked my brain. Son, I leave it to you."

Young Perez magnificently waved the question aside.

Possessing himself of his fiancee's reluctant hand, he spoke in a whisper audible to Montes. "We planned the wedding presents. That was the secret. But you shall not see—not know—until we are married!"

Montes dropped his eyes and his brow knit thoughtfully. Later, as a peon brought his horse, he called Perez aside.

"I've an idea," he said confidentially. "Have Yaqui select the most perfect henequen fiber to make the most beautiful and perfect bale of henequen ever pressed. Have Yaqui place the wedding presents inside the bale before the final pressing. Then send it to Doña Isabel's house after the wedding and open it there."

Young Perez clapped his hands in delight. What a capital plan! He complimented Montes and thanked him and asked him to keep secret the idea. Indeed, the young lieutenant waxed enthusiastic over the plan. It would be unique; it would be fitting to the occasion. Perez would have Yaqui pick over and select from the racks the most perfect fibers, to be laid aside. Perez would go himself to watch Yaqui at his work. He would have Yaqui practice the operation of pressing, so at the momentous hour there could be no hitch. And on the wedding day Perez would carry the presents himself. No hands but his own would be trusted with those jewels, especially the exquisite pearls that were his own particular gift.

At last the day arrived for the wedding. It was to be a holiday. Yaqui alone was not to lie idle. It was to fall to him to press that bale of henequen and to haul it to the bride's home.

But Perez did not receive all his gifts when he wanted them. Messengers arrived late and some were yet to come. He went to the mill, however, and put Yaqui to work at packing the henequen in the press and building it up. The Indian was bidden to go so far with the bale, leaving a great hole in the middle for the gifts and to have the rest of the fiber all ready to pack and press. Perez would not trust anyone else with his precious secret. He himself would hurry down with the gifts, and secretly, for the manner of presentation was to be a great surprise.

Blue was the sky, white gold the sun, and the breeze waved the palms. But for Montes an invisible shadow hovered over the stately Mendoza mansion where Dolores was to be made a bride. The shadow existed in his mind and took mystic shape—now a vast, copper-hazed, green-spiked plain of henequen, and then the spectral gigantic shape of a toiling man, gaunt, grim, and fire-eyed.

Montes hid his heavy heart behind smiling lips and the speech of a courtier. He steeled himself against a nameless and portending shock, waiting for it even when his mind scorned the delusion. But the shock did not come at sight of Señorita Dolores, magnificently gowned in white, beautiful, serene, imperious, with her proud, tawny eyes and proud, red lips. Nor when those sleepy strange eyes met his. Nor when the priest ended the ceremony that made her a wife.

He noted when Lieutenant Perez laughingly fought his way out of the crowd and disappeared.

Then the unrest of Montes became a haunting suspense.

The guests were directed out to the shaded west terrace,

where in the center of the wide stoned space lay a huge white glistening bale of henequen. Beside it stood the giant Yaqui. Dark, motionless, aloof. The guests clustered round.

When Montes saw the Yaqui like a statue beside the bale of henequen, he sustained the shock for which he had been waiting. He slipped to the front of the circle of guests.

"Ah!" exclaimed the old don, eyeing the bale of henequen with great satisfaction. "This is the surprise our son had in store for us. Here is the jewel case—here are the wedding presents!"

The guests laughed and murmured their compliments.

"Where is Señor Perez?" demanded the don as he looked round.

"The boy is hiding," replied Doña Isabel. "He wants to watch his bride when she sees the gifts."

"No—he would not be hiding," declared the old don in perplexity. Something strange edged into his gladness of the moment. Suddenly he wheeled to the Yaqui. But he never spoke the question on his lips. Slowly he seemed to be blasted by those great black-fired orbs, as piercing as if they had been lightnings from hell.

"Hurry, open the bale," cried the bride, her sweet voice trilling above the gay talk.

Yaqui appeared not to hear. Was he looking into the soul of the father of Lieutenant Perez? All about him betrayed almost a superhuman intensity.

"Open the bale," ordered the bride.

Yaqui cut the wire. He did not look at her. The perfectly folded and pressed strands of fiber shook and swelled and moved apart as if in relief. And like a great white jewel case of glistening silken threads the bale of henequen opened.

It commanded a stilling of the gay murmur—a sudden silence that had a subtle effect upon all. The beautiful bride, leaning closer to look, seemed to lose the light of the tawny proud eyes. Her mother froze into a creature of stone. The old don, in slow strange action, as if his mind had feeble sway over body, bent his gray head away from the gaunt and terrible Yaqui.

Something showed blue down under the center strands

of the glistening fiber. With a swift flash of his huge black hand, with exceeding violence, Yaqui swept the strands aside. Then from his lips pealed an awful cry. Instead of the jewels, there, crushed and ghastly, lay the bridegroom Perez.

ESCAPE

Qualities of endurance, loyalty, stoicism and the ability to survive in a merciless environment were those which Zane Grey believed were best exemplified not only by early Indians in pre-revolutionary days but by those who inhabited the bleak deserts of northern Mexico and the southwestern part of the United States. Here is a tale of a Yaqui who had been rescued by Ranger Richard Gale from being stomped to death by the horses of a band of Mexican bandits. In return, Yaqui had taught Richard the essential attributes and skills for survival in the desert and saved his life as well.

Richard also helped his friend, cavalryman George Thorne, rescue his beautiful Mexican fiancée, Mercedes Estenada, from the bandit Rojas. They had brought Mercedes back to Arizona to the ranch of Jim Belding, Richard's employer, an immigration inspector for the United States. There Thorne and Mercedes were married. It was not long afterwards that Rojas appeared with a band of men, determined to recapture Mercedes at any cost. Rather than risk the lives of everyone at the ranch it was decided that Thorne and Mercedes should try to escape with Yaqui's guidance over the desert to Yuma where they would be safe. They felt that Rojas would never dare to follow them across the trackless searing lava beds, never before traveled by the white man. Unfortunately they had miscalculated Rojas' lust for the beautiful Mercedes, because it was not long before they saw that the bandit was on their trail.

Loren Grey

I

Blanco Sol showed no inclination to bend his head to the alfalfa which swished softly about his legs. Richard Gale felt the horse's sensitive, almost human alertness. Sol knew as well as his master the nature of that flight.

At the far corner of the field the Yaqui halted, and slowly the line of white horses merged into a compact mass. There was a trail leading down to the river. The campfires were so close that the bright blazes could be seen in movement, and dark forms crossed them. Yaqui slipped out of his saddle. He ran his hand over Diablo's nose and spoke low, and repeated this action for each of the other horses. Gale had long ceased to question the strange Indian's behavior. There was no explaining or understanding many of his manoeuvers. But the results of them were always thought-provoking. Gale had never seen horses stand so silently as in this instance; no stamp—no champ of bit—no toss of head—no shake of saddle or pack—no heave or snort! It seemed they had become imbued with the spirit of the Indian, the nameless one called Yaqui.

Yaqui moved away into the shadows as noiselessly as if he were one of them. The darkness swallowed him. He had taken a direction parallel with the trail. Gale wondered if Yaqui meant to try to lead his string of horses by the rebel sentinels. Ladd had his head bent low, his ear toward the trail. Jim Lash's long neck had the arch of a listening deer. Gale listened, too, and as the slow, silent moments went by his faculty of hearing grew more acute from strain. He heard Blanco Sol breathe. He heard the pound of his own heart; the silken rustle of the alfalfa, a faint, far-off sound of voice, like a lost echo. Then his ear seemed to register a movement of air, a disturbance so soft as to be nameless. Then followed long, silent moments.

Yaqui appeared as he had vanished. He might have been part of the shadows. But he was there. He started off down the trail leading Diablo. Again the white line stretched slowly out. Gale fell in behind. A bench of ground, covered with sparse greasewood, sloped gently down to the deep, wide arroyo of Forlorn River. Blanco Sol shied a few feet out of the trail. Peering low with keen eyes, Gale made out three objects—a white sombrero, a blanket, and a Mexican lying face down. The Yaqui had stolen upon this sentinel like a silent wind of death. Just then a desert coyote wailed, and the wild cry fitted the darkness and the Yaqui's deed.

Once under the dark lee of the river bank Yaqui caused another halt, and he disappeared as before. It seemed to Gale that the Indian started to cross the pale level sand bed of the river, where stones stood out gray, and the darker line of opposite shore was visible. But he vanished, and it was impossible to tell whether he went one way or another. Long minutes passed. The horses held their heads up, looked toward the glimmering campfires and listened. Gale thrilled with the meaning of it all—the night—the silence—the flight—and the wonderful Indian stealing with the slow inevitableness of doom upon another sentinel. An hour passed and Gale seemed to have become deadened to all sense of hearing. There were no more sounds in the world. The desert was as silent as it was black. Yet again came that strange change in the tensity of Gale's ear-strain, a check, a break, a vibration—and this time the sound did not go nameless. It might have been moan of wind or wail of far-distant wolf, but Gale imagined it was the strangling death-cry of another guard, or that strange, involuntary utterance of the Yaqui. Blanco Sol trembled in all his great frame, and then Gale was certain the sound was not imagination.

That certainty, once and for all, fixed in Gale's mind the mood of his flight. The Yaqui dominated the horses and the rangers. Thorne and Mercedes were as persons under a spell. The Indian's strange silence, the feeling of mystery and power he seemed to create, all that was incomprehensible about him were emphasized in the light of his slow, sure, and ruthless action. If he dominated the others, surely he did more for Gale—colored his thoughts—presaged the wild and terrible future of that flight. If Rojas embodied all the hatred and passion of the peon—scourged slave for a thousand years—then Yaqui embodied all the darkness, the cruelty, the white, sun-heated blood, the ferocity, the tragedy of the desert.

Suddenly the Indian stalked out of the gloom. He mounted Diablo and headed across the river. Once more the line of moving white shadows stretched out. The soft sand gave forth no sound at all. The glimmering campfires sank behind the western bank. Yaqui led the way into the willows, and there was faint swishing of leaves; then into the mesquite, and there was soft rustling of branches. The glimmering lights appeared again, and grotesque forms of *saguaros* loomed darkly. Gale peered sharply along the trail, and, presently, on the pale sand under a cactus, there lay a blanketed form, prone, outstretched, a carbine clutched in one hand, a cigarette, still burning, in the other.

The cavalcade of white horses passed within five hundred yards of campfires, around which dark forms moved in plain sight. Soft pads in sand, faint metallic tickings of steel on thorns, low, regular breathing of horses—these were all the sounds the fugitives made, and they could not have been heard at one-fifth the distance. The lights disappeared from time to time, grew dimmer, more flickering, and at last they vanished altogether. Belding's fleet and tireless steeds were out in front. The desert opened ahead wide, dark, vast. Rojas and his rebels were behind, eating, drinking, careless. The somber shadow lifted from Gale's heart. He held now an unquenchable faith in Yaqui. Belding would be listening back there along the river. He would hear of the escape. He would tell Nell, and then hide her safely. As Gale had accepted a strange and fatalistic foreshadowing of toil, blood, and agony in this desert journey, so he believed in Mercedes's ultimate freedom and happiness, and his own return to the girl who had grown dearer than life.

A cold, gray dawn was fleeing before a rosy sun when Yaqui halted the march at Papago Well. The horses were taken to water, then led down the arroyo into the grass. Here packs were slipped, saddles removed. Mercedes was cold, lame, tired, but happy. It warmed Gale's blood to look at her. The shadow of fear still lay in her eyes, but it was passing. Hope and courage shone there, and affection for her ranger protectors and the Yaqui, and unutterable love for the cavalryman. Jim Lash remarked how cleverly they had fooled the rebels.

"Shore they'll be comin' along," replied Ladd.

They built a fire, cooked and ate. The Yaqui spoke only one word: "Sleep." Blankets were spread. Mercedes dropped into a deep slumber, her head on Thorne's shoulder. Excitement kept Thorne awake. The two rangers dozed beside the fire. Gale shared the Yaqui's watch. The sun began to climb and the icy edge of dawn to wear away. Rabbits bobbed their cotton tails under the mesquite. Gale climbed a rocky wall above the arroyo bank, and there, with command over the miles of the backtrail, he watched.

It was a sweeping, rolling, wrinkled, and streaked range

of desert that he saw, ruddy in the morning sunlight, with patches of cactus and mesquite rough-etched in shimmering gloom. No Name Mountains split the eastern sky, towering high, gloomy, grand, with purple veils upon their slopes. They were forty miles away and looked five. Gale thought of the girl who was there under their shadow. Nell.

Yaqui kept the horses bunched, and he led them from one little park of galleta grass to another. At the end of three hours he took them to water. Upon his return Gale clambered down from his outlook, the rangers grew active, Mercedes was awakened and soon the party faced westward, their long shadows moving before them. Yaqui led with Blanco Diablo in a long, easy lope. The arroyo washed itself out into flat desert, and the greens began to shade into gray, and then the gray into red. Only sparse cactus and weathered ledges dotted the great low roll of a rising escarpment. Yaqui suited the gait of his horse to the lay of the land, and his followers accepted his pace. There were canter and trot, and swift walk and slow climb, and long swing—miles up and down and forward. The sun soared hot. The heated air lifted, and incoming currents from the west swept low and hard over the barren earth. In the distance, all around the horizon, accumulations of dust seemed like ranging, mushrooming yellow clouds.

Yaqui was the only one of the fugitives who never looked back. Mercedes did often. Gale could not resist it himself, but it was a vain search. For a thousand puffs of white and yellow dust rose from that backward sweep of desert, and any one of them might have been from horses' hoofs. Gale had a conviction that when Yaqui gazed back toward the well and the shining plain beyond, there would be reason for it. But when the sun lost its heat and the wind died down. Yaqui took long and careful surveys westward from the high points on the trail. Sunset was not far off, and there in a bare, spotted valley lay Coyote Tanks, the only waterhole between Papago Well and the Sonoyta Oasis. Gale used his glass, told Yaqui there was no smoke, no sign of life. Still the Indian fixed his falcon eyes on distant spots and looked long. It was as if his vision could not detect what reason or intuition, perhaps an instinct, told him was there. Presently in a sheltered spot, where blown sand had not obliterated the trail, Yaqui found the tracks of horses. The curve of the iron shoes pointed westward. An intersecting trail from the north came in here. Gale thought the tracks either one or two days old. Ladd said they were one day. The Indian shook his head.

No farther advance was undertaken. The Yaqui headed south and traveled slowly, climbing to the brow of a bold height of weathered mesa. There he sat his horse and waited. No one questioned him. The rangers dismounted to stretch their legs, and Mercedes was lifted to a rock, where she rested. Thorne had gradually yielded to the desert's influence for silence. He spoke once or twice to Gale, and occasionally whispered to Mercedes. Gale fancied his friend would soon learn that necessary speech in desert travel meant a few greetings, a few words to make real the fact of human companionship, a few short, terse terms for the business of day or night, and perhaps a stern order or a soft call to a horse.

The sun went down, and the golden, rosy veils turned to blue and shaded darker till twilight was there in the valley. Only the spurs of mountains, spiring the near and far horizon, retained their clear outline. Darkness approached, and the clear peaks faded. The horses stamped to be on the move.

"Malo!" exclaimed the Yaqui.

He did not point with arm, but his piercing eyes gazed at the blurring spot which marked the location of Coyote Tanks.

"Jim, can you see anything?" asked Ladd.

"Nope, but I reckon he can."

Darkness increased momentarily till night shaded the deepest part of the valley. Gale's eyes, keen as they were, were last of the rangers to see tiny needle-points of light just faintly perceptible in the blackness.

"Laddy! Campfires?" he asked, quickly.

"Shore's you're born, my boy."

"How many?"

Ladd did not reply, but Yaqui held up his fingers wide. Five campfires! A strong force of rebels or raiders or some other desert troop was camping at Coyote Tanks.

Yaqui sat his horse for a moment, motionless as stone, his dark face immutable and impassive. Then he stretched wide his right arm in the direction of No Name Mountains, now losing their last faint traces of afterglow, and he shook his head. He made the same impressive gesture toward the Sonoyta Oasis with the same somber negation.

Thereupon he turned Diablo's head to the south and started down the slope. His manner had been decisive, even stern. Lash did not question it, nor did Ladd. Both rangers hesitated, however, and showed a strange, almost a sullen reluctance which Gale had never seen in them before. Raiders were one thing, Rojas was another; Camino del Diablo still another, but that vast and desolate and unwatered waste of cactus and lava, the Sonora Desert, might appall the stoutest heart. Gale felt his own sink—felt himself flinch.

"Oh, where is he going?" cried Mercedes. Her poignant voice seemed to break a spell.

"Shore, lady, Yaqui's goin' home," replied Ladd gently. "An' considerin' our troubles I reckon we ought to thank God he knows the way."

They mounted and rode down the slope toward the darkening south.

Not until night travel was obstructed by a wall of cactus did the Indian halt to make a dry camp. Water and grass for the horses and fire to cook by were not to be had. Mercedes bore up surprisingly well but she fell asleep almost the instant her thirst had been allayed. The men ate and drank. Diablo was the only horse that showed impatience but he was angry, and not in distress. Blanco Sol licked Gale's hand and stood patiently. Many a time had he taken his rest at night without a drink. Yaqui again bade the men sleep. Ladd said he would take the early watch; but from the way the Indian shook his head and settled himself against a stone, it appeared if Ladd remained awake he would have company. Gale lay down weary of limb and eye. He heard

the soft thump of hoofs, the sigh of wind in the cactus—
then no more.

When he awoke there was bustle and stir about him. Day
had not yet dawned, and the air was freezing cold. Yaqui
had found a scant bundle of greasewood which served to
warm them and to cook breakfast. Mercedes was not
aroused till the last moment.

Day dawned with the fugitives in the saddle. A picketed
wall of cactus hedged them in, yet the Yaqui made a
tortuous path, that, zigzag as it might, in the main always
headed south. It was wonderful how he slipped Diablo
through the narrow aisles of thorns, saving the horse and
saving himself. The others were torn and clutched and held
and stung. The way was a flat, sandy pass between low
mountain ranges. There were open spots and aisles and
squares of sand; and hedging rows of prickly pear and the
huge spider-legged *ocatillo* and hummocky masses of
clustered *bisnagi*. The day grew dry and hot. A fragrant
wind blew through the pass. Cactus flowers bloomed red
and yellow and magenta. The sweet, pale Ajo lily gleamed
in shady corners.

Ten miles of travel covered the length of the pass. It
opened wide upon a wonderful scene, an arboreal desert,
dominated by its pure light green, yet lined by many
merging colors. And it rose slowly to a low dim and dark-
red zone of lava, spurred, peaked, domed by volcano cones;
a wild and ragged region, illimitable as the horizon.

The Yaqui was uncertain. His hawk eyes searched and
roved, and became fixed at length at the southwest, and
toward this he turned his horse. The great, fluted *saguaros*,
fifty, sixty feet high, raised columnal forms, and their
branching limbs and curving lines added a grace to the
desert. It was the low-bushed cactus that made the toil and
pain of travel. Yet those thorny forms were beautiful.

In the basins between the ridges, to right and left along
the floor of low plains the mirage glistened, wavered, faded,
vanished—lakes and trees and clouds. Inverted mountains
hung suspended in the lilac air and faint tracery of white-
walled cities.

At noon Yaqui halted the cavalcade. He had selected a field of *bisnagi* cactus for the place of rest. Presently his reason became obvious. With long, heavy knife he cut off the tops of these barrel-shaped plants. He scooped out soft pulp, and with stone and hand then began to pound the deeper pulp into a juicy mass. When he threw this out there was a little water left, sweet, cool water which man and horse shared eagerly. Thus he made even the desert's fiercest growths minister to their needs.

But he did not halt long. Miles of gray-green spiked walls lay between him and that line of ragged, red lava which manifestly he must reach before dark. The travel became faster, straighter. And the glistening thorns clutched and clung to leather and cloth and flesh. The horses reared, snorted, balked, leaped—but they were sent on. Only Blanco Sol, the patient, the plodding, the indomitable, needed no goad or spur. Waves of heat smoked up from the sand. Mercedes reeled in her saddle. Thorne bade her drink, bathed her face, supported her, and then gave way to Ladd, who took the girl with him on Torres's broad back. Yaqui's unflagging purpose and iron arm were bitter and hateful to the proud and haughty spirit of Blanco Diablo. For once Belding's great white devil had met his master. He fought rider, bit, bridle, cactus, sand—and yet he went on and on, zigzagging, turning, winding, crashing through the barbed growths. The middle of the afternoon saw Thorne reeling in his saddle, and then, wherever possible, Gale's powerful arm lent him strength to hold his seat.

The giant cactus came to be only so in name. These *saguaros* were thinning out, growing stunted, and most of them were single columns. Gradually other cactus forms showed a harder struggle for existence, and the spaces of sand between were wider. But now the dreaded, glistening *choya* began to show pale and gray and white upon the rising slope. Roundtopped hills, sunset-colored above, blue-black below, intervened to hide the distant spurs and peaks. Mile and mile long tongues of red lava streamed out between the hills and wound down to stop abruptly upon the slope.

The fugitives were entering a desolate, burned-out world. It rose above them in limitless, gradual ascent and spread wide to east and west. Then the waste of sand began to yield to cinders. The horses sank to their fetlocks as they toiled on. A fine, choking dust blew back from the leaders. Men coughed and horses snorted. The huge, round hills rose smooth, symmetrical, colored as if the setting sun was shining on bare, blue-black surfaces. But the sun was now behind the hills. In between ran the streams of lava. The horsemen skirted the edge between slope of hill and perpendicular ragged wall. This red lava seemed to have flowed and hardened there only yesterday. It was broken, sharp, dull rust color, full of cracks and caves and crevices, and everywhere upon its jagged surface grew the white-thorned *choya*.

Again twilight encompassed the travelers. But there was still light enough for Gale to see the constricted passage open into a wide, deep space where the dull color was relieved by the gray of gnarled and dwarfed mesquite. Blanco Sol, keenest of scent, whistled his welcome herald of water. The other horses answered, quickened their gait. Gale smelled it, too, sweet, cool, damp on the dry air.

Next day the Yaqui's relentless driving demand on the horses was no longer in evidence. He lost no time, but he did not hasten. His course wound between low cinder dunes which limited their view of the surrounding country. These dunes finally sank down to a black floor as hard as flint with tongues of lava to the left, and to the right the slow descent into the cactus plain. Yaqui was now traveling due west. It was Gale's idea that the Indian was skirting the first sharp-toothed slope of a vast volcanic plateau which formed the western half of the Sonora Desert and extended to the Gulf of California. Travel was slow, but not exhausting for rider or beast. A little sand and meager grass gave a grayish tinge to the strip of black ground between lava and plain.

That day, as the manner rather than the purpose of the

Yaqui changed, so there seemed to be subtle differences in the others of the party. Gale himself lost a certain sickening dread, which had not been for himself, but for Mercedes and Nell, and Thorne and the rangers. Jim Lash, good natured again, might have been patrolling the boundary line. Ladd lost his taciturnity and his gloom changed to a cool, careless air. A mood that was almost defiance began to be manifested in Thorne. It was in Mercedes, however, that Gale marked the most significant change. Her collapse the preceding day might never have been. She was lame and sore; she rode side-saddle and often she had to be rested and helped but she found a reserve fund of strength, and her mental condition was not the same that it had been. Her burden of fear had been lifted. Gale saw in her the difference he always felt in himself after a few days in the desert. Already Mercedes and he, and all of them, had begun to respond to the desert spirit. Moreover, Yaqui's strange influence must have been a call to the primitive.

Thirty miles of easy stages brought the fugitives to another waterhole, a little round pocket under the heaved-up edge of lava. There was spare, short, bleached grass for the horses, but no wood for a fire. This night there were question and reply; conjecture, doubt, opinion and conviction expressed by the men of the party. But the Indian, who alone could have told where they were, where they were going, what chance they had to escape, maintained his stoic silence. Gale took the early watch, Ladd the midnight one, and Lash that of the morning.

The day broke rosy, glorious, cold as ice. Action was necessary to make useful benumbed hands and feet. Mercedes was fed while yet wrapped in blankets. Then, while the packs were being put on and horses saddled, she walked up and down, slapping her hands, warming her ears. The rose color of the dawn was in her cheeks, and the wonderful clearness of desert light in her eyes. Thorne's eyes sought her constantly. The rangers watched her. The Yaqui bent his glance upon her only seldom; but when he did look it seemed that his strange, fixed, and inscrutable face was about to break into a smile. Yet that never happened. Gale himself was surprised to find how often his own glance found the slender, dark, beautiful Spaniard. Was this because of her beauty? he wondered. He thought not altogether. Mercedes was a woman. She represented something in life that men of all races for thousands of years had loved to see and own, to reverse and debase, to fight and die for.

It was a significant index to the day's travel that Yaqui should keep a blanket from the pack and tear it into strips to bind the legs of the horses. It meant the dreaded *choya* and the knife-edged lava. That Yaqui did not mount Diablo was still more significant. Mercedes would ride, but the others must walk.

The Indian led off into one of the gray notches between the tumbled streams of lava. These streams were about thirty feet high, a rotting mass, rougher than any other kind of roughness in the world. At the apex of the notch, where two streams met, a narrow gully wound and ascended. Gale caught sight of the dim, pale shadow of a one-time trail. Near at hand it was invisible. He had to look far ahead to catch the faint tracery. Yaqui led Diablo into it, and then began the most laborious and vexatious and painful of all slow travel.

Once up on top of that lava bed, Gale saw stretching away, breaking into millions of crests and ruts, a vast, red-black field sweeping onward and upward, with ragged, low ridges and mounds and spurs leading higher and higher to a great, split escarpment wall, above which dim peaks shone hazily blue in the distance.

He looked no more in that direction. To keep his foothold, to save his horse, cost him all energy and attention. The course was marked out for him in the tracks of the other horses. He had only to follow. But nothing could have been more difficult. The disintegrating surface of a lava bed was at once the roughest, the hardest, the meanest, the cruelest, the most deceitful kind of ground to travel.

It was rotten, yet it had corners as hard and sharp as pikes. It was rough, yet as slippery as ice. If there was a foot of level surface, that space would be one to break through

under a horse's hoofs. It was seamed, lined, cracked, ridged,
knotted iron. This lava bed resembled a tremendously
magnified clinker. It had been a running sea of molten
flint, boiling, bubbling, spouting, and it had burst its
surface into a million sharp facets as it hardened. The color
was dull, dark, angry red, like no other red, inflaming to the
eye. The millions of minute crevices were dominated by
deep fissures and holes, ragged and rough beyond all
comparison.

The fugitives made slow progress. They picked a
cautious, winding way to and fro in little steps here and
there along the many twists of the trail, up and down the
unavoidable depressions, round and round the holes. At
noon, so winding back upon itself had been their course,
they appeared to have come only a short distance up the
lava slope.

It was rough work for them and was terrible for the
horses. Blanco Diablo refused to answer to the power of the
Yaqui. He balked, he plunged, he bit and kicked. He had to
be pulled and beaten over many places. Mercedes's horse
almost threw her, and she was put upon Blanco Sol. The
white charger snorted a protest, then, obedient to Gale's
stern call, patiently lowered his noble head and pawed the
lava for a footing that would hold.

The lava caused Gale toil and worry and pain, but he
hated the *choyas*. As the travel progressed this species of
cactus increased in number of plants and in size. Everywhere the red lava was spotted with little round patches of
glistening frosty white. And under every bunch of *choya*,
along and in the trail, were the discarded joints, like little
frosty pine cones covered with spines. It was utterly
impossible always to be on the lookout for these, and when
Gale stepped on one, often as not the steel-like thorns
pierced leather and flesh. Gale came almost to believe what
he had heard claimed by desert travelers—that the *choya*
was alive and leaped at man or beast. Certain it was when
Gale passed one, if he did not put all attention to avoiding
it, he was hooked through his chaps and held by barbed
thorns. The pain was almost unendurable. It was like no

other. It burned, stung, beat—almost seemed to freeze. It made useless arm or leg. It made him bite his tongue to keep from crying out. It made the sweat roll off him. It made him sick.

Moreover, bad as the *choya* was for man, it was infinitely worse for beast. A jagged stab from this poisoned cactus was the only thing Blanco Sol could not stand. Many times that day, before he carried Mercedes, he had wildly snorted, and then stood trembling while Gale picked broken thorns from the muscular legs. But after Mercedes had been put upon Sol, Gale made sure no *choya* touched him.

The afternoon passed like the morning, in ceaseless winding and twisting and climbing along this abandoned trail. Gale saw many waterholes, mostly dry, some containing water, all of them catch-basins, full only after rainy season. Little ugly bunched bushes, that Gale scarcely recognized as mesquite, grew near these holes; also stunted greasewood and prickly pear. There was no grass, and the *choya* alone flourished in that hard soil.

Darkness overtook the party as they unpacked beside a pool of water deep under an overhanging shelf of lava. It had been a hard day. The horses drank their fill, and then stood patiently with drooping heads. Hunger and thirst were appeased, and a warm fire cheered the weary and foot-sore fugitives. Yaqui said, "Sleep." And so another night passed.

The following morning, ten miles or more up the slow-ascending lava slope, Gale's attention was called from his somber search for the less rough places in the trail.

"Dick, why does Yaqui look back?" asked Mercedes.

Gale was startled.

"Does he?"

"Every little while," replied Mercedes.

Gale was in the rear of all the other horses, so as to take, for Mercedes's sake, the advantage of the broken trail.

Yaqui was leading Diablo, winding around a break. His head was bent as he stepped slowly and unevenly upon the lava. Gale turned to look back, the first time in several days. The mighty hollow of the desert below seemed wide strip of red—wide strip of green—wide strip of gray—streaking to purple peaks. It was all too vast, too mighty to grasp any little details. He thought, of course, of Rojas in certain pursuit, but it seemed absurd to look for him.

Yaqui led on, and Gale often glanced up from his task to watch the Indian. Presently he saw him stop, turn, and look back. Ladd did likewise, and then Jim and Thorne. Gale found the desire irresistible. Thereafter he often rested Blanco Sol, and looked back the while. He had his field glass, but did not choose to use it.

"Rojas will follow," said Mercedes.

Gale regarded her in amazement. The tone of her voice had been indefinable. If there were fear then he failed to detect it. She was gazing back down the colored slope, and something about her, perhaps the steady gaze of her magnificent eyes, reminded him of Yaqui.

Many times during the ensuing hour the Indian faced about, and always his followers did likewise. It was high noon, with the sun beating hot and the lava radiating heat, when Yaqui halted for a rest. The place selected was a ridge of lava, almost a promontory, considering its outlook. The horses bunched here and drooped their heads. The rangers were about to slip the packs and remove saddles when Yaqui restrained them.

He fixed a changeless, gleaming gaze on the slow descent, but did not seem to look afar.

Suddenly he uttered his strange cry—the one Gale considered involuntary, or else significant of some tribal trait or feeling. It was incomprehensible, but no one could have doubted its potency. Yaqui pointed down the lava slope, pointing with finger and arm and neck and head—his whole body was instinct with direction. His whole being seemed to have been animated and then frozen. His posture could not have been misunderstood, yet his expression had not altered. Gale had never seen the Indian's face change its hard, red-bronze calm. It was the color and the flintiness and the character of the lava at his feet.

"Shore he sees somethin'," said Ladd. "But my eyes are no good."

"I reckon I ain't sure of mine," replied Jim. "I'm bothered by a dim movin' streak down there."

Thorne gazed eagerly down as he stood beside Mercedes, who sat motionless facing the slope. Gale looked and looked till he hurt his eyes. Then he took his glass out of its case on Sol's saddle.

There appeared to be nothing upon the lava but the innumerable dots of *choya* shining in the sun. Gale swept his glass slowly forward and back. Then into a nearer field of vision crept a long white-and-black line of horses and men. Without a word he handed the glass to Ladd. The ranger used it, muttering to himself.

"They're on the lava fifteen miles down in an air line," he said, presently. "Jim, shore they're twice that an' more accordin' to the trail."

Jim had his look and replied: "I reckon we're a day an' a night in the lead."

"It is Rojas?" burst out Thorne, with set jaw.

"Yes, Thorne. It's Rojas and a dozen men or more," replied Gale, and he looked up at Mercedes.

She was transformed. She might have been a medieval princess embodying all the Spanish power and passion of that time, breathing revenge, hate, unquenchable spirit of fire. If her beauty had been wonderful in her helpless and appealing moments, now, when she looked back white-faced and flame-eyed, it was transcendant.

Gale drew a long, deep breath. The mood which had presaged pursuit, strife, blood on this somber desert, returned to him tenfold. He saw Thorne's face corded by black veins, and his teeth exposed like those of a snarling wolf. These rangers, who had coolly risked death many times, and had dealt it often, were white as no fear or pain could have made them. Then, on the moment, Yaqui raised

his hand, not clenched or doubled tight, but curled rigid
like an eagle's claw; and he shook it in a strange, slow
gesture which was menacing and terrible.

It was the woman that called to the depths of these men.
And their passion to kill and to save was surpassed only by
the wild hate which was yet love, the unfathomable
emotion of a peon slave. Gale marveled at it, while he felt
his whole being cold and tense as he turned once more to
follow in the tracks of his leaders. The fight predicted by
Belding was at hand. What a fight that must be! Rojas was
traveling light and fast. He was gaining. He had bought his
men with gold, with extravagent promises, perhaps with
offers of the body and blood of an aristocrat hateful to their
kind. Lastly, there was the wild, desolate environment, a
tortured wilderness of jagged lava and poisoned *choya;* a
lonely, fierce, and repellent world, a red stage most
somberly and fittingly colored for a supreme struggle
between men.

Yaqui looked back no more. Mercedes looked back no
more. But the others looked, and the time came when Gale
saw the creeping line of pursuers with naked eyes.

A level line above marked the rim of the plateau. Sand
began to show in the little lava pits. On and upward toiled
the cavalcade, still very slowly advancing. At last Yaqui
reached the rim. He stood with his hand on Blanco Diablo;
and both were silhouetted against the sky. That was the
outlook for a Yaqui. And his great horse, dazzlingly white
in the sunlight, with head wildly and proudly erect, mane
and tail flying in the wind, made a magnificent picture. The
others toiled on and upward, and at last Gale led Blanco Sol
over the rim. Then all looked down the red slope.

But shadows were gathering there and no moving line
could be seen.

Yaqui mounted and wheeled Diablo away. The others
followed. Gale saw that the plateau was no more than a
vast field of low, ragged circles, levels, mounds, cones, and
whirls of lava. The lava was of a darker red than that down
upon the slope, and it was harder than flint. In places fine

sand and cinders covered the uneven floor. Strange varieties of cactus vied with the omnipresent *choya*. Yaqui, however, found ground that his horse covered at a swift walk.

But there was only an hour, perhaps, of this comparatively easy going. Then Yaqui led them into a zone of craters. The top of the earth seemed to have been blown out in holes from a few rods in width to large craters, some shallow, others deep, and all red as fire. Yaqui circled close to abysses which yawned sheer from a level surface, and he appeared always to be turning upon his course to avoid them.

The plateau had now a considerable dip to the west. Gale marked the slow heave and ripple of the ocean of lava to the south, where high, rounded peaks marked the center of this volcanic region. The uneven nature of the slope westward prevented any extended view, until suddenly the fugitives emerged from a rugged break to come upon a sublime and awe-inspiring spectacle.

They were upon a high point of western slope of the plateau. It was a slope, but so many leagues long in its descent that only from a great height could any slant have been perceptible. Yaqui and his white horse stood upon the brink of a crater miles in circumference, a thousand feet deep, with its red walls patched in frost-colored spots by the silvery *choya*. The giant tracery of lava streams waved down the slope to disappear in undulating sand dunes. And these bordered a seemingly endless arm of blue sea. This was the Gulf of California. Beyond the Gulf rose dim, bold mountains, and above them hung the setting sun, dusky red, flooding all that barren empire with a sinister light.

It was strange to Gale then, and perhaps to the others, to see their guide lead Diablo into a smooth and well-worn trail along the rim of the awful crater. Gale looked down into that red chasm. It resembled an inferno. The dark cliffs upon the opposite side were veiled in blue haze that seemed like smoke. Here Yaqui was at home. He moved and looked about him as a man coming at last into his own. Gale saw him stop and gaze out over that red-ribbed void to the Gulf.

Gale divined that somewhere along this crater of hell the Yaqui would make his final stand; and one look into his strange, inscrutable eyes made imagination picture a fitting doom for the pursuing Rojas.

II

The trail led along a gigantic fissure in the side of the crater, and then down and down into a red-walled, blue-hazed labyrinth.

Presently Gale, upon turning a sharp corner, was utterly amazed to see that the split in the lava sloped out and widened into an arroyo. It was so green and soft and beautiful in all the angry, contorted red surrounding that Gale could scarcely credit his sight. Blanco Sol whistled his welcome to the scent of the water. Then Gale saw a great hole, a pit in the shiny lava, a dark, cool, shady well. There was evidence of the fact that at flood seasons the water had an outlet into the arroyo. The soil appeared to be a fine sand, in which a reddish tinge predominated; and it was abundantly covered with a long grass, still partly green. Mesquites and *paloverdes* dotted the arroyo and gradually closed in thckets that obstructed the view.

"Shore it all beats me," exclaimed Ladd. "What a place to hole-up in! We could have hid here for a long time. Boys, I saw mountain sheep, the real old genuine Rocky Mountain bighorn. What do you think of that?"

"I reckon it's a Yaqui hunting-ground," replied Lash. "That trail we hit must be hundreds of years old. It's worn deep and smooth in the iron lava."

"Well, all I got to say is—Beldin' was shore right about the Indian. An' I can see Rojas's finish somewhere up along that awful hell-hole."

Camp was made on a level spot. Yaqui took the horses to water, and then turned them loose in the arroyo. It was a tired and somber group that sat down to eat. The strain of suspense equaled the wearing effects of the long ride. Mercedes was calm, but her great dark eyes burned in her white face. Yaqui watched her. The others looked at her with unspoken pride. Presently Thorne wrapped her in his blankets, and she seemed to fall asleep at once. Twilight deepened. The campfire blazed brighter. A cool wind played with Mercedes's black hair, waving strands across her brow.

Little of Yaqui's purpose or plan could be elicited from him. But the look of him was enough to satisfy even Thorne. He leaned against a pile of wood which he had collected, and his gloomy gaze pierced the campfire, and at long intervals strayed over the motionless form of the Spanish girl.

The rangers and Thorne, however, talked in low tones. It was absolutely impossible for Rojas and his men to reach the waterhole before noon of the next day. And long before that time the fugitives would have decided on a plan of defense. What that defense would be, and where it would be made, were matters which the men considered gravely. Ladd averred the Yaqui would put them into an impregnable position that at the same time would prove a death-trap for their pursuers. They exhausted every possibility, and then, tired as they were, still kept on talking.

"What stuns me is that Rojas stuck to our trail," said Thorne, his lined and haggard face expressive of dark passion. "He has followed us into this fearful desert. He'll lose men, horses, perhaps his life. He's only a bandit, and he stands to win no gold. If he ever gets out of here it'll be by herculean labor and by terrible hardship. All for a poor little helpless woman—just a woman! My God, I can't understand it."

"Shore—*just* a woman," replied Ladd, solemnly nodding his head.

Then there was a long silence during which the men gazed into the fire. Each, perhaps, had some vague conception of the enormity of Rojas's love or hate—some faint and amazing glimpse of the gulf of human passion. Those were cold, hard, grim faces upon which the light flickered.

"Sleep," said the Yaqui.

Thorne rolled in his blanket close beside Mercedes. Then one by one the rangers stretched out, feet to the fire. Gale found that he could not sleep. His eyes were weary; but they would not stay shut; his body ached for rest, yet he could not lie still. The night was somber, gloomy, and the lava-encompassed arroyo full of shadows. The dark velvet sky, fretted with white fire, seemed to be close. There was an absolute silence, as of death. Nothing moved—nothing outside of Gale's body appeared to live. The Yaqui sat like an image carved out of lava. The others lay prone and quiet. Would another night see any of them lie that way, quiet forever? Gale felt a ripple pass over him that was at once a shudder and a contraction of muscles. Used as he was to the desert and its oppression, why should he feel tonight as if the weight of its lava and the burden of its mystery were bearing him down?

He sat up after a while and again watched the fire. Nell's sweet face floated like a wraith in the pale smoke—glowed and flushed and smiled in the embers. Other faces shone there—his sister's—that of his mother. Gale shook off the tender memories. This desolate wilderness with its forbidding silence and its dark promise of hell on the morrow—this was not the place to unnerve oneself with thoughts of love and home. But the torturing paradox of the thing was that this was just the place and just the night for a man to be haunted.

By and by Gale rose and walked down a shadowy aisle between the mesquites. On his way back the Yaqui joined him. Gale was not surprised. He had become used to the Indian's strange guardianship. But now, perhaps because of Gale's poignancy of thought, the contending tides of love and regret, the deep, burning premonition of deadly strife, he was moved to keener scrutiny of the Yaqui. That, of course, was futile. The Indian was impenetrable, silent, strange. But suddenly, inexplicably, Gale felt Yaqui's human quality. It was aloof, as was everything about this Indian; but it was there. This savage walked silently beside him, without glance or touch or word. His thought was as inscrutable as if mind had never awakened in his race. Yet Gale was conscious of greatness, and, somehow, he was reminded of the Indian's story. His home had been desolated, his people carried off to slavery, his wife and children separated from him to die. What had life meant to the Yaqui? What had been in his heart? What was now in his mind? Gale could not answer these questions. But the difference between himself and Yaqui, which he had vaguely felt as that between savages and civilized men, faded out of his mind forever. Yaqui might have considered he owed Gale a debt, and, with a Yaqui's austere and noble fidelity to honor, he meant to pay it. Nevertheless, this was not the thing Gale found in the Indian's silent presence. Accepting the desert with its subtle and inconceivable influence, Gale felt that the savage and the white man had been bound in a tie which was no less brotherly because it could not be comprehended.

Toward dawn Gale manged to get some sleep. Then the morning broke with the sun hidden back of the uplift of the plateau. The horses trooped up the arroyo and snorted for water. After a hurried breakfast the packs were hidden in holes in the lava. The saddles were left where they were, and the horses allowed to graze and wander at will.

Canteens were filled, a small bag of food was packed, and blankets made into a bundle. Then Yaqui faced the steep ascent of the lava slope.

The trail he followed led up on the right side of the fissure, opposite to the one he had come down. It was a steep climb, and encumbered as the men were they made but slow progress. Mercedes had to be lifted up smooth steps and across crevices. They passed places where the rims of the fissure were but a few yards apart. At length the rims widened out and the red, smoky crater yawned beneath. Yaqui left the trail and began clambering down over the rough and twisted convolutions of lava which formed the rim. Sometimes he hung sheer over the precipice. It was with extreme difficulty that the party followed him. Mercedes had to be held on narrow, footwide ledges. The *choya* was there to hinder passage. Finally the Indian halted upon a narrow bench of flat, smooth lava, and his followers worked with exceeding care and effort down to his position.

At the back of this bench, between bunches of *choya*, was a niche, a shallow cave with floor lined apparently with mold. Ladd said the place was a refuge which had been inhabited by mountain sheep for many years. Yaqui spread blankets inside, left the canteen and the sack of food, and with a gesture at once humble, yet that of a chief, he invited Mercedes to enter. A few more gestures and fewer words disclosed his plan. In this inaccessible nook Mercedes was to be hidden. The men were to go around upon the opposite rim, and block the trail leading down to the waterhole.

Gale marked the nature of this eyrie. It was the wildest and most rugged place he had ever stepped upon. Only a sheep could have climbed up the wall above or along the slanting shelf of lava beyond. Below glistened a whole bank of *choya*, frosty in the sunlight, and it overhung an apparently bottomless abyss.

Ladd chose the smallest gun in the party and gave it to Mercedes.

"Shore it's best to go the limit on bein' ready," he said,

simply. "The chances are you'll never need it. But if you do—"

He left off there, and his break was significant. Mercedes answered him with a fearless and indomitable flash of eyes. Thorne was the only one who showed any shaken nerve. His leave-taking of his wife was hurried. Then he and the rangers carefully stepped in the tracks of the Yaqui.

They climbed up to the level of the rim and went along the edge. When they reached the fissure and came upon its narrowest point, Yaqui showed in his actions that he meant to leap it. Ladd restrained the Indian. They then continued along the rim till they reached several bridges of lava which crossed it. The fissure was deep in some parts, choked in others. Evidently the crater had no direct outlet into the arroyo below. Its bottom, however, must have been far beneath the level of the waterhole.

After the fissure was crossed the trail was soon found. Here it ran back from the rim. Yaqui waved his hand to the right, where along the corrugated slope of the crater there were holes and crevices and cover for a hundred men. Yaqui strode on up the trail toward a higher point, where presently his dark figure stood motionless against the sky. The rangers and Thorne selected a deep depression, out of which led several ruts deep enough for cover. According to Ladd it was as good a place as any, perhaps not so hidden as others, but freer from the dreaded *choya*. Here the men laid down rifles and guns, and, removing their heavy cartridge belts, settled down to wait.

Their location was close to the rim wall and probably five hundred yards from the opposite rim, which was now seen to be considerably below them. The glaring red cliff presented a deceitful and baffling appearance. It had a thousand ledges and holes in its surfaces, and one moment it looked perpendicular and the next there seemed to be a long slant. Thorne pointed out where he thought Mercedes was hidden. Ladd selected another place, and Lash still another. Gale searched for the bank of the *choya* he had seen under the bench where Mercedes's retreat lay, and when he found it the others disputed his opinion. Then Gale brought his field glass into requisition, proving that he was right. Once located and fixed in sight, the white patch of *choya,* the bench, and the sheep eyrie stood out from the other features of that rugged wall. But all the men were agreed that Yaqui had hidden Mercedes where only the eyes of a vulture could have found her.

Jim Lash crawled into a little strip of shade and bided the time tranquilly. Ladd was restless and impatient and watchful, every little while rising to look up the far-reaching slope, and then to the right, where Yaqui's dark figure stood out from a high point of the rim. Thorne grew silent, and seemed consumed by a slow, sullen rage. Gale was neither calm nor free of a gnawing suspense nor of a waiting wrath. But as best he could he put the pending action out of mind.

It came over him all of a sudden that he had not grasped the stupendous nature of this desert setting. There was the measureless red slope, its lower ridges finally sinking into white sand dunes toward the blue sea.. The cold, sparkling light, the white sun, the deep azure of sky, the feeling of boundless expanse all around him—these meant high altitude. Southward the barren red simply merged into distance. The field of craters rose in high, dark wheels toward the dominating peaks. When Gale withdrew his gaze from the magnitude of these spaces and heights the crater beneath him seemed dwarfed. Yet while he gazed it spread and deepened and multiplied its ragged lines. No, he could not grasp the meaning of size or distance here. There was too much to stun the sight. But the mood in which nature had created this convulsed world of lava seized hold upon him.

Meanwhile the hours passed. As the sun climbed, the clear, steely lights vanished. The blue hazes deepened, and slowly the glistening surfaces of lava turned redder. Ladd was concerned to discover that Yaqui was missing from his outlook upon the high point. Jim Lash came out of the shady crevice, and stood up to buckle on his cartridge belt. His narrow, gray glance slowly roved from the height of lava down along the slope, paused in doubt, and then swept on to resurvey the whole vast eastern dip of the plateau.

"I reckon my eyes are pore," he said. "Mebbe it's this damn red glare. Anyway, what's them creepin' spots up there?"

"Shore I seen them. Mountain sheep," replied Ladd.

"Guess again, Laddy. Dick, I reckon you'd better flash the glass up the slope."

Gale adjusted the field glass an began to search the lava, beginning close at hand and working away from him. Presently the glass became stationary.

"I see half a dozen small animals, brown in color. They look like sheep. But I couldn't distinguish mountain sheep from antelope."

"Shore they're bighorn," said Ladd.

"I reckon if you'll pull around to the east an' search under that long wall of lava—there—you'll see what I see," added Jim.

The glass climbed and circled, wavered an instant, then fixed steady as a rock. There was a breathless silence.

"Fourteen horses—two packed—some mounted—others without riders, and lame," said Gale, slowly.

Yaqui appeared far up the trail, coming swiftly. Presently he saw the rangers and halted to wave his arms and point. Then he vanished as if the lava had opened beneath him.

"Lemme have that glass," suddenly said Jim Lash. "I'm seein' red, I tell you.... Well, pore as my eyes are they had it right. Rojas an' his outfit have left the trail."

"Jim, you ain't meanin' they've taken to that awful slope?" queried Ladd.

"I sure do. There they are—still comin', but goin' down, too."

"Mebbe Rojas is crazy, but it begins to look like he—"

"Laddy, I'll be danged if the Mexican hasn't vamoosed. Gone out of sight! Right there not a half mile away, the whole caboddle—gone!"

"Shore they're behind a crust or have gone down into a rut," suggested Ladd. "They'll show again in a minute.

Look sharp, boys, for I'm figgerin' Rojas'll spread his men."

Minutes passed, but nothing moved upon the slope. Each man crawled up to a vantage point along the crest of rotting lava. The watchers were careful to peer through little notches or from behind a spur, and the constricted nature of their hiding-place kept them close together. Ladd's muttering grew into a growl, then lapsed into the silence that marked his companions. From time to time the rangers looked inquiringly at Gale. The field glass, however, like the naked sight, could not catch the slightest moving object out there upon the lava. A long hour of slow, mounting suspense wore on.

"Shore it's all goin' to be as queer as the Yaqui," said Ladd.

Indeed, the strange mien, the silent action, the somber character of the Indian had not been without effect upon the minds of the men. Then the weird, desolate, tragic scene added to the vague sense of mystery. And now the disappearance of Rojas's band, the long wait in the silence, the certainty of invisible foes crawling, circling closer and closer, lent to the situation a final touch that made it unreal.

"I'm reckonin' there's a mind behind them Mexicans," replied Jim. "Or mebbe we ain't done Rojas credit.... If somethin' would only come off!"

"Boys, look sharp!" suddenly called Lash. "Low down to the left—mebbe three hundred years. See, along by them seams of lava—behind the *choyas*. First off I thought it was a sheep. But it's the Yaqui!... Crawlin' swift as a lizard! Can't you see him?"

It was a full moment before Jim's companions could locate the Indian. Flat as a snake Yaqui wound himself along with incredible rapidity. His advance was all the more remarkable for the fact that he appeared to pass directly under the dreaded *choyas*. Sometimes he paused to lift his head and look. He was directly in line with a huge whorl of lava that rose higher than any point on the slope.

This spur was a quarter of a mile from the position of the rangers.

"Shore he's headin' for that high place," said Ladd. "He's going slow now. There, he's stopped behind some *choyas*. He's gettin' up—no' he's kneelin'.... Now what the hell!"

"Laddy, take a peek at the side of that lava ridge," sharply called Jim. "I guess mebbe somethin's comin' off. See! There's Rojas an' his outfit climbin'. Don't make out no hosses.... Dick, use your glass an' tell us what's doin'. I'll watch Yaqui an' tell you what his move means."

Clearly and distinctly, almost as if he could have touched them, Gale had Rojas and his followers in sight. They were toiling up the rough lava on foot. They were heavily armed. Spurs, chaps, jackets, scarfs were not in evidence. Gale saw the lean, swarthy faces, the black straggly hair, the ragged, soiled garments which had once been white.

"They're almost up now," Gale was saying. "There! They halt on top. I see Rojas. He looks wild. By—! Fellows, an Indian!... It's a Papago. Belding's old herder!... The Indian points—this way—then down. He's showing Rojas the lay of the trail."

"Boys, Yaqui's in range of that bunch," said Jim, swiftly. "He's raisin' his rifle slow—Lord, how slow he is!... He's covered some one. Which one I can't say. But I think he'll pick Rojas."

"The Yaqui can shoot. He'll pick Rojas," added Gale, grimly.

"Not on your life!" Ladd's voice cut in with scorn. "Gentlemen, you can gamble Yaqui'll kill the Papago. That traitor Indian knows these sheep haunts. He's tellin' Rojas—"

A sharp rifle shot rang out.

"Laddy's right," called Gale. "The Papago's hit—his arm falls—There, he tumbles!"

More shots rang out. Yaqui was seen standing erect firing rapidly at the darting Mexicans. For all Gale could make out no second bullet took effect. Rojas and his men vanished behind the bulge of lava. Then Yaqui deliberately backed away from his position. He made no effort to run or hide. Evidently he watched cautiously for signs of pursuers in the ruts and behind the *choyas*. Presently he turned and came straight toward the position of the rangers, sheered off perhaps a hundred paces below it, and disappeared in a crevice. Plainly his intention was to draw pursuers within rifle shot.

"Shore, Jim, you had your wish. Somethin' come off," said Ladd. "An' I'm sayin' thank God for the Yaqui! That Papago'd have ruined us. Even so, mebbe he's told Rojas more'n enough to make us sweat blood."

"He had a chance to kill Rojas," cried out the drawn-faced, passionate Thorne. "He didn't take it!... He didn't take it!"

Only Ladd appeared to be able to answer the cavalryman's poignant cry.

"Listen, son," he said, and his voice rang. "We all know how you feel. An' if I'd had that one shot never in the world could I have picked the Papago guide. I'd have had to kill Rojas. That's the white man of it. But Yaqui was right. Only an Indian could have done it. You can gamble the Papago alive meant slim chance for us. Because he'd have led straight to where Mercedes is hidden, an' then we'd have left cover to fight it out... when you come to think of the Yaqui's hate for Mexicans, when you just seen him pass up a shot at one—well, I don't know how to say what I mean, but damn me, my sombrero is off to the Indian!"

"I reckon so, an' I reckon the ball's opened," rejoined Lash, and now that former nervous impatience so unnatural to him was as if it had never been. He was smilingly cool, and his voice had almost a caressing note. He tapped the breach of his Winchester with a sinewy brown hand, and he did not appear to be addressing any one in particular. "Yaqui's opened the ball. Look up your pardners there, gents, an' get ready to dance."

Another wait set in then, and judging by the more direct rays of the sun and a receding of the little shadows cast by the *choyas,* Gale was of the opinion that it was a long wait. But it seemed short. The four men were lying under the bank of a half circular hole in the lava. It was notched and cracked, and its rim was fringed by *choyas.* It sloped down and opened to an unobstructed view of the crater. Gale had the upper position, farthest to the right, and therefore was best shielded from possible fire from the higher ridges of the rim, some three hundred yards distant. Jim came next, well hidden in a crack. The positions of Thorne and Ladd were most exposed. They kept sharp lookout over the uneven rampart of their hiding-place.

The sun passed the zenith, began to slope westward, and to grow hotter. The men waited and waited. Gale saw no impatience even in Thorne. The sultry air seemed to be laden with some burden or quality that was at once composed of heat, menace, color, and silence. Even the light glancing up from the lava seemed red and the silence had substance. Sometimes Gale felt that it was unbearable. Yet he made no effort to break it.

Suddenly this dead stillness was rent by a shot, clear and stinging, close at hand. It was from a rifle, not a carbine. With startling quickness a cry followed—a cry that pierced Gale—it was so thin, so high-keyed, so different from all other cries. It was the involuntary human shriek of death.

"Yaqui's called out another pardner," said Jim Lash, laconically.

Carbines began to crack. The reports were quick, light, like sharp spats without any ring. Gale peered from behind the edge of his covert. Above the ragged wave of lava floated faint whitish clouds, all that was visible of the smokeless powder. Then Gale made out round spots, dark against the background of red, and in front of them leaped out small tongues of fire. Ladd's .405 began to "spang" with its beautiful sound of power. Thorne was firing, somewhat wildly Gale thought. Then Jim Lash pushed his Winchester over the rim under a *choya,* and between shots Gale could hear him singing: "Turn the lady, turn—turn the lady, turn!...Alaman left! Swing your pardners!...forward an' back!... turn the lady, turn!" Gale got into the fight himself, not so sure that he hit any of the round, bobbing objects he aimed at, but growing sure of himself as action liberated something forced and congested within his breast.

Then over the position of the rangers came a hail of bullets. Those that struck the lava hissed away into the crater; those that came biting through the *choyas* made a sound which resembled a sharp ripping of silk. Bits of cactus stung Gale's face, and he dreaded the flying thorns more than he did the flying bullets.

"Hold on, boys," called Ladd, as he crouched down to reload his rifle. "Save your shells. The Mexicans are spreadin' on us, some goin' down below Yaqui, others movin' up for that high ridge. When they get up there I'm damned if it won't be hot for us. There ain't room for all of us to hide here."

Ladd raised himself to peep over the rim. Shots were now scattering, and all appeared to come from below. Emboldened by this he rose higher. A shot from in front, a rip of bullet through the *choya*, a spot of something hitting Ladd's face, a missile hissing onward—these inseparably blended sounds were all registered by Gale's sensitive ear.

With a curse Ladd tumbled down into the hole. His face showed a great gray blotch, and starting blood. Gale felt a sickening assurance of desperate injury to the ranger. He ran to him calling: "Laddy! Laddy!"

"Shore I ain't plugged. It's a damn *choya* burr. The bullet knocked it in my face. Pull it out!"

The oval, long-spiked cone was firmly imbedded in Ladd's cheek. Blood streamed down his face and neck. Carefully, yet with no thought of pain to himself, Gale tried to pull the cactus joint away. It was as firm as if it had been nailed there. That was the damnable feature of the barbed thorns; once set, they held on as that strange plant held to its desert life. Ladd began to writhe, and sweat mingled with the blood on his face. He cursed and raved, and his movements made it almost impossible for Gale to do anything.

"Put your knife-blade under an' tear it out!" shouted Ladd, hoarsely.

Thus ordered, Gale slipped a long blade in between the embedded thorns, and with a powerful jerk literally tore the *choya* out of Ladd's quivering flesh. Then, where the ranger's face was not red and raw, it certainly was white.

A volley of shots from a different angle was followed by the quick ring of bullets striking the lava all around Gale. His first idea, as he heard the projectiles sing and hum and whine away into the air, was that they were coming from above him. He looked up to see a number of low, white and dark knobs upon the high point of lava. They had not been there before. Then he saw little, pale, leaping tongues of fire. As he dodged down he distinctly heard a bullet strike Ladd. At the same instant he seemed to hear Thorne cry out and fall, and Lash's boots scrape rapidly away.

Ladd fell backward still holding the .405. Gale dragged him into the shelter of his own position, and dreading to look at him, took up the heavy weapon. It was with a kind of savage strength that he gripped the rifle; and it was with a cold and deadly intent that he aimed and fired. The first Mexican huddled low, let his carbine go clattering down, and then crawled behind the rim. The second and third jerked back. The fourth seemed to flop up over the crest of lava. A dark arm reached for him, clutched his leg, tried to drag him up. It was in vain. Wildly grasping the air the bandit fell, slid down a steep shelf, rolled over the rim, to go hurtling down out of sight.

Fingering the hot rifle with close-pressed hands, Gale watched the skyline along the high point of lava. It remained unbroken. As his passion left him he feared to look back at his companions, and the cold chill returned to his breast.

"Shore—I'm damn glad—they ain't usin' soft-nose bullets," drawled a calm voice.

Swift as lightning Gale whirled.

"Laddy! I thought you were done for," cried Gale, with a break in his voice.

"I ain't a-mindin' the bullet much. But that *choya* joint

took my nerve, an' you can gamble on it. Dick, this hole's pretty high up, ain't it?"

The ranger's blouse was open at the neck, and on his right shoulder under the collar bone was a small hole just beginning to bleed.

"Sure it's high, Laddy," replied Gale, gladly. "Went clear through, clean as a whistle!"

He tore a handkerchief into two parts, made wads, and pressing them close over the wounds he bound them there with Ladd's scarf.

"Shore it's funny how a bullet can floor a man an' then not do any damage," said Ladd. "I felt a zip of wind an' somethin' like a pat on my chest an' down I went. Well, so much for the small caliber with their steel bullets. Supposin' I'd connected with a .405!"

"Laddy, I—I'm afraid Thorne's done for," whispered Gale. "He's lying over there in that crack. I can see part of him. He doesn't move."

"I was wonderin' if I'd have to tell you that. Dick, he went down hard hit, fallin', you know, limp an' soggy. It was a moral cinch one of us would get it in this fight; but God! I'm sorry Thorne had to be the man."

"Laddy, maybe he's not dead," replied Gale. He called aloud to his friend. There was no answer.

Ladd got up, and, after peering keenly at the height of the lava, he strode swiftly across the space. It was only a dozen steps to the crack in the lava where Thorne had fallen in head first. Ladd bent over, went to his knees, so that Gale saw only his head. Then he appeared rising with arms round the cavalryman. He dragged him across the hole to the sheltered corner that alone afforded protection. He had scarcely reached it when a carbine cracked and a bullet struck the flinty lava, striking sparks, then singing away into the air.

Thorne was either dead or unconscious, and Gale, with a contracting throat and numb heart, decided for the former. Not so Ladd, who probed the bloody gash on Thorne's temple, and then felt his breast.

"He's alive an' not bad hurt. That bullet hit him

glancin'. Shore them steel bullets are some lucky for us. Dick, you needn't look so glum. I tell you he ain't bad hurt. I felt his skull with my finger. There's a hole in it. Wash him off an' tie—Wow! Did you get the wind of that one! An' mebbe it didn't sing off the lava! ... Dick, look after Thorne now while I—"

The completion of his speech was the stirring ring of the .405, and then he uttered a laugh that was unpleasant.

"Shore, there's a man's size bullet for you. No slim, sharp-point, steel-jacket nail! I'm takin' it on me to believe you're appreciatin' of the .405, seein' as you don't make no fuss."

It was indeed a joy to Gale to find that Thorne had not received a wound necessarily fatal, though it was serious enough. Gale bathed and bound it, and laid the cavalryman against the slant of the bank, his head high to lessen the bleeding.

As Gale straightened up Ladd muttered low and deep, and swung the heavy rifle around to the left. Far along the slope a figure moved. Ladd began to work the lever of the Winchester and to shoot. At every shot the heavy firearm sprang up, and the recoil made Ladd's shoulder give back. Gale saw the bullets strike the lava behind, beside, before the fleeing Mexican, sending up dull puffs of dust. On the sixth shot he plunged down out of sight, either hit or frightened into seeking cover.

"Dick, mebbe there's one or two left above; but we needn't figger much on it," said Ladd, as, loading the rifle, he jerked his fingers quickly from the hot breech. "Listen! Jim an' Yaqui are hittin' it up lively down below. I'll sneak down there. You stay here an' keep about half an eye peeled up younder, an' keep the rest my way."

Ladd crossed the hole, climbed down into the deep crack where Thorne had fallen, and then went stooping along with only his head above the level. Presently he disappeared. Gale, having little to fear from the high ridge, directed most of his attention toward the point beyond which Ladd had gone. The firing had become desultory, and the light carbine shots outnumbered the sharp rifle shots five to one. Gale made a note of the fact that for some little time he had not heard the unmistakable report of Jim Lash's automatic. Then ensued a long interval in which the desert silence seemed to recover its grip. The .405 ripped it asunder—*sprang—sprang—sprang*. Gale fancied he heard yells. There were a few shots still farther down the trail. Gale had an uneasy conviction that Rojas and some of his band might go straight to the waterhole. It would be hard to dislodge even a few men from that retreat.

There seemed a lull in the battle. Gale ventured to stand high, and, screened behind *choyas,* he swept the three-quarter circle of lava with his glass. In the distance he saw horses, but no riders. Below him, down the slope along the crater rim and the trail, the lava was bare of all except tufts of *choya*. Gale gathered assurance. It looked as if the day was favoring his side. Then Thorne, coming partly to consciousness, engaged Gale's care. The cavalryman stirred and moaned, called for water, and then for Mercedes. Gale held him back with a strong hand, and presently he was once more quiet.

For the first time in hours, as it seemed, Gale took note of the physical aspect of his surroundings. He began to look upon them without keen gaze strained for crouching form, or bobbing head, or spouting carbine. Either Gale's sense of color and proportion had become deranged during the fight, or the encompassing air and the desert had changed. Even the sun had changed. It seemed lowering, oval in shape, magenta in hue, and it had a surface that gleamed like oil on water. Its red rays shone through red haze. Distances that had formerly been clearly outlined were now dim, obscured. The yawning chasm was not the same. It circled wider, redder, deeper. It was a weird, ghastly mouth of hell. Gale stood fascinated, unable to tell how much he saw was real, how much the exaggeration of overwrought emotions. There was no beauty here, but an unparalleled grandeur, a sublime scene of devastation and desolation which might have had its counterpart upon the burned-out moon. The mood that gripped Gale now added to its somber portent an unshakable forboding of calamity.

He wrestled with the spell as if it were a physical foe. Reason and intelligence had their voices in his mind, but the moment was not one wherein these things could wholly control. He felt life strong within his breast, yet there, a step away, was death; yawning, glaring, smoky, red. It was a moment—an hour for a savage, born, bred, developed in this scarred and blasted place of jagged depths and red distances and silences never meant to be broken. Since Gale was not a savage he fought that call of the red gods which sent him back down the long ages toward his primitive day. His mind combated his sense of sight and the hearing that seemed useless; and his mind did not win all the victory. Something fatal was here, hanging in the balance, as the red haze hung along the vast walls of that crater of hell.

Suddenly harsh, prolonged yells brought him to his feet, and the unrealities vanished. Far down the trails where the crater rims closed in the deep fissure he saw moving forms. They were three in number. Two of them ran nimbly across the lava bridge. The third staggered far behind. It was Ladd. He appeared hard hit. He dragged at the heavy rifle which he seemed unable to raise. The yells came from him. He was calling the Yaqui.

Gale's heart stood still momentarily. Here, then, was the catastrophe! He hardly dared sweep that fissure with his glass. The two fleeing figures halted—turned to fire at Ladd. Gale recognized the foremost one—small, compact, gaudy—Rojas! The bandit's arm was outstretched. Puffs of white smoke rose, and shots rapped out. When Ladd went down Rojas threw his gun aside and with a wild yell bounded over the lava. His companion followed.

A tide of passion, first hot as fire, then cold as ice, rushed over Gale when he saw Rojas take the trail toward Mercedes's hiding-place. The little bandit appeared to have the sure-footedness of a mountain sheep. The Mexican following was not so sure or fast. He turned back. Gale heard the trenchant bark of the .405. Ladd was kneeling. He shot again—again. The retreating bandit seemed to run full into an invisible obstacle, then fell lax, inert, lifeless.

Rojas sped on unmindful of the spurts of dust about him. Yaqui, high above Ladd, was also firing at the bandit. Then both rifles were emptied. Rojas turned at a high break in the trail. He shook a defiant hand, and his exulting yell pealed faintly to Gale's ears. About him there was something desperate, magnificent. Then he clambered down the trail.

Ladd dropped the .405, and rising, gun in hand, he staggered toward the bridge of lava. Before he had crossed it Yaqui came bounding down the slope, and in one splendid leap he cleared the fissure. He ran beyond the trail and disappeared on the lava above. Rojas had not seen this sudden darting move of the Indian.

Gale felt himself bitterly powerless to aid in that pursuit. He could only watch. He wondered, fearfully, what had become of Lash. Presently, when Rojas came out of the cracks and ruts of lava there might be a chance of disabling him by a long shot. His progress was now slow. But he was making straight for Mercedes' hiding place. What was it leading him there—an eagle eye, or hate, or instinct? Why did he go on when there could be no turning back for him on that trail? Ladd was slow, heavy, staggering on the trail; but he was relentless. Only death could stop the ranger now. Surely Rojas must have known that when he chose the trail. From time to time Gale caught glimpses of Yaqui's dark figure stealing along the higher rim of the crater. He was making for a point above the bandit.

Endless moments dragged by. The lowering sun colored only the upper half of the crater walls. Far down the depths were murky blue. Again Gale felt the insupportable silence. The red haze became a transparent veil before his eyes. Sinister, evil, brooding, waiting, seemed that yawning abyss. Ladd staggered along the trail. At times he crawled. The Yaqui gained; he might have had wings as he leaped from jagged crust to jagged crust; his sure-footedness was a wonderful thing.

But for Gale the marvel of that endless period of watching was the purpose of the bandit Rojas. He had now no weapon. Gale's glass made this fact plain. There was death behind him, death below him, death before him, and though he could not have known it, death above him. He never faltered—never made a misstep upon the narrow, flinty trail. When he reached the lower end of the level ledge Gale's poignant doubt became a certainty. Rojas had seen Mercedes. It was incredible, yet Gale believed it. Then, his heart clamped as in an icy vise, Gale threw forward the Remington, and sinking on one knee, began to shoot. He emptied the magazine. Puffs of dust near Rojas did not even make him turn.

As Gale began to reload he was horror-stricken by a low cry from Thorne. The cavalryman had recovered consciousness. He was half raised, pointing with shaking hand at the opposite ledge. His distended eyes were riveted upon Rojas. He was trying to utter speech that would not come.

Gale wheeled, rigid now, steeling himself to one last forlorn hope—that Mercedes could defend herself. She had a gun. He doubted not at all that she would use it. But, remembering her terror of this savage, he feared for her.

Rojas reached the level of the ledge. He halted. He crouched. It was the act of a panther. Manifestly he saw Mercedes within the cave. Then faint shots patted the air, broke in quick echo. Rojas went down as if struck a heavy blow. He was hit. But even as Gale yelled in sheer madness the bandit leaped erect. He seemed too quick, too supple to be badly wounded. A slight, dark figure flashed out of the cave. Mercedes! She backed against the wall. Gale saw a puff of white—heard a report. But the bandit lunged at her. Mercedes ran, not to try to pass him, but straight for the precipice. Her intention was plain. But Rojas outstripped her, even as she reached the verge. Then a piercing scream pealed across the crater—a scream of despair.

Gale closed his eyes. He could not bear to see more.

Thorne echoed Mercedes's scream. Gale looked round just in time to leap and catch the cavalryman as he staggered, apparently for the steep slope. And then, as Gale dragged him back, both fell. Gale saved his friend, but he plunged into a *choya*. He drew his hands away full of the great, glistening cones of thorns.

"For God's sake, Gale, shoot! *Kill him! Kill him!*... Can't—you—see—Rojas—"

Thorne fainted.

Gale, stunned for the instant, stood with uplifted hands, and gazed from Thorne across the crater. Rojas had not killed Mercedes. He was overpowering her. His actions seemed slow, wearing, purposeful. Her's were violent. Like a trapped she-wolf, Mercedes was fighting. She tore, struggled, flung herself.

Rojas's intention was terribly plain.

In agony now, both mental and physical, cold and sick and weak, Gale gripped his rifle and aimed at the writhing forms on the ledge. He pulled the trigger. The bullet struck up a cloud of red dust close to the struggling couple. Again Gale fired, hoping to hit Rojas. The bullet struck high. A third—fourth—fifth time the Remington spoke in vain! The rifle fell from Gale's pain-racked hands.

How horribly plain that fiend's intention! Gale tried to close his eyes, but could not. He prayed wildly for a sudden blindness—to faint as Thorne had fainted. But he was transfixed to the spot with eyes that pierced the red light.

Mercedes was growing weaker, seemed about to collapse.

"Oh, Jim Lash, are you dead?" cried Gale. "Oh, Laddy!"... Oh, Yaqui!"

Suddenly a dark form leaped down the wall behind the ledge where Rojas fought the girl. It sank in a heap, then bounded erect.

"Yaqui!" screamed Gale, and he waved his bleeding hands till the blood bespattered his face. Then he choked. Utterance became impossible.

The Indian bent over Rojas and flung him against the wall. Mercedes, sinking back, lay still. When Rojas got up the Indian stood between him and escape from the ledge. Rojas backed the other way along the narrowing shelf of lava. His manner was abject, stupefied. Slowly he stepped backward.

It was then that Gale caught the white gleam of a knife in Yaqui's hand. Rojas turned and ran. He rounded a corner of wall where the footing was precarious. Yaqui followed slowly. His figure was dark and menacing. But he was not in a hurry. When he passed off the ledge Rojas was edging farther and farther along the wall. He was clinging now to the lava, creeping inch by inch. Perhaps he had thought to work around the buttress or climb over it. Evidently he went as far as possible, and there he clung, an unscalable wall above, the abyss beneath.

The approach of the Yaqui was like a slow dark shadow of doom. If it seemed so to the stricken Gale what must it have been to Rojas? He appeared to sink against the wall. The Yaqui stole closer and closer. He was the savage now, and for him the moment must have been glorified. Gale saw him gaze up at the great circling walls of the crater, then down into the depths. Perhaps the red haze hanging above him, or the purple haze below, or the deep caverns in the lava, held for Yaqui spirits of the desert, his gods to whom he called. Perhaps he invoked shadows of his loved ones and his race, calling them in this moment of vengeance.

Gale heard—or imagined he heard—that wild, strange Yaqui cry.

Then the Indian stepped close to Rojas, and bent low, keeping out of reach. How slow were his motions! Would Yaqui never end it? A wail drifted across the crater to Gale's ears.

Rojas fell backward and plunged downward. The bank of white *choyas* caught him, held him upon their steel spikes. How long did the dazed Gale sit there watching Rojas wrestling and writhing in convulsive frenzy? The bandit now seemed mad to win the delayed death.

When he broke free he was a white patched object no longer human, a ball of *choya* burrs, and he slipped off the bank to shoot down and down into the purple depths of the crater.

The second day after Ladd had been given such thin nourishment as he could swallow he recovered the use of his tongue.

"Shore—this's—hell," he whispered.

That was a characteristic speech for the ranger, Gale thought, and indeed it made all who heard it smile while their eyes were wet.

From that time forward Ladd gained, but he gained so immeasurably slowly that only the eyes of hope could have seen any improvement. Jim Lash threw away his crutch, and Thorne was well, if still somewhat weak, before Ladd could lift his arm or turn his head. A kind of long, immovable gloom passed, like a shadow, from his face. His whispers grew stronger. And the day arrived when Gale, who was perhaps the least optimistic, threw doubt to the winds and knew the ranger would get well. For Gale that joyous moment of realization was one in which he seemed to return to a former self long absent. He experienced an elevation of soul. He was suddenly overwhelmed with gratefulness, humility, awe. A gloomy black terror had passed by. He wanted to thank the faithful Mercedes, and Thorne for getting well, and the cheerful Lash, and Ladd himself, and that strange and wonderful Yaqui, now such a splendid figure. He thought of home and Nell. The terrible encompassing red slopes lost something of their fearsomeness, and there was a good spirit hovering near.

"Boys, come round," said Ladd, in his low voice. "An' you, Mercedes. An' call the Yaqui."

Ladd lay in the shade of the brush shelter that had been erected. His head was raised slightly on a pillow. There seemed little of him but long lean lines, and if it had not been for his keen, thoughtful, kindly eyes, his face would have resembled a death mask of a man starved.

"Shore I want to know what day is it an' what month?" asked Ladd.

Nobody could answer him. The question seemed a surprise to Gale, and evidently was so to the others.

"Look at that cactus," went on Ladd.

Near the wall of lava a stunted *saguaro* lifted its head.

A few shriveled blossoms that had once been white hung along the fluted column.

"I reckon according to that giant cactus it's somewheres along the end of March," said Jim Lash, soberly.

"Shore it's April. Look where the sun is. An' can't you feel it's gettin' hot?"

"Supposin' it is April?" queried Lash, slowly.

"Well, what I'm drivin' at is it's about time you all was hittin' the trail back to Forlorn River, before the waterholes dry out."

"Laddy, I reckon we'll start soon as you're able to be put on a hoss."

"Shore that'll be too late."

A silence ensued, in which those who heard Ladd gazed fixedly at him and then at one another. Lash uneasily shifted the position of his lame leg, and Gale saw him moisten his lips with his tongue.

"Charlie Ladd, I ain't reckonin' you mean we're to ride off an' leave you here?"

"What else is there to do? The hot weather's close. Pretty soon most of the waterholes will be dry. You can't travel then.... I'm on my back here, an' God only knows when I could be packed out. Not for weeks, mebbe. I'll never be any good again, even if I was to get out alive.... You see, shore this sort of case comes round sometimes in the desert. It's common enough. I've heard of several cases where men had to go an' leave a feller behind. It's reasonable. If you're fightin' the desert you can't afford to be sentimental .... Now, as I said, I'm all in. So what's the sense of you waitin' here, when it means the old desert story? By goin' now mebbe you'll get home. If you wait on a chance of takin' me, you'll be too late. Pretty soon this lava'll be one roastin' hell. Shore now, boys, you'll see this the right way? Jim, old pard?"

"No, Laddy, an' I can't figger how you could ever ask me."

"Shore then leave me here with Yaqui an' a couple of the hosses. We can eat sheep meat. An' if the water holes out—"

"No!" interrupted Lash, violently.

Ladd's eyes sought Gale's face.

"Son, you ain't bull-headed like Jim. You'll see the sense of it. There's Nell a-waitin back at Forlorn River. Think what it means to her! She's a damn fine girl, Dick, an' what right have you to break her heart for an old worn-out cowpuncher? Think how she's watchin' for you with that sweet face all sad an' troubled, an' her eyes turnin' black. You'll go, son, won't you?"

Dick shook his head.

The ranger turned his gaze upon Thorne, and now the keen, glistening light in his gray eyes had blurred.

"Thorne, it's different with you. Jim's a fool, an' young Gale has been punctured by *choya* thorns. He's got the desert poison in his blood. But you now—you've no call to stick—you can find that trail out. It's easy to follow, made by so many shod horses. Take your wife an' go.... Shore you'll go, Thorne?"

Deliberately and without an instant's hesitation the cavalryman replied "No."

Ladd then directed his appeal to Mercedes. His face was now convulsed, and his voice, though it had sunk to a whisper, was clear, and beautiful with some rich quality that Gale had never heard in it.

"Mercedes, you're a woman. You're the woman we fought for. An' some of us are shore goin' to die for you. Don't make it all for nothin'. Let us feel we saved the woman. Shore you can make Thorne go. He'll have to go if you say. They'll all have to go. Think of the years of love an' happiness in store for you. A week or so an' it'll be too late. Let me tell you, Mercedes, when the summer heat hits the lava we'll all wither an' curl up like shavin's near a fire. A wind of hell will blow up this slope. Look at them mesquites. See the twist in them. That's the torture of heat an' thirst. Do you want me or all us men seein' you like that? Mercedes, don't make it all for nothin'. Say you'll persuade Thorne, if not the others."

For all the effect his appeal had to move her Mercedes might have possessed a heart as hard and fixed as the surrounding lava.

"Never!"

White-faced, with great black eyes flashing, the Spanish

girl spoke the word that bound her and her companions to the desert.

The subject was never mentioned again. Gale thought that he read a sinister purpose in Ladd's mind. To his astonishment, Lash came to him with the same fancy. After that they made certain there never was a gun within reach of Ladd's clutching, clawlike hands.

Gradually the somber spell lifted from the ranger's mind. When he was entirely free of it he began to gather strength daily. Then it was as if he had never known patience—he who had shown so well how to wait. He was in a frenzy to get well. His appetite could not be satisfied.

The sun climbed higher, whiter, hotter. At midday a wind from gulfward roared up the arroyo, and now only the *paloverdes* and the few *saguaros* were green. Every day the water in the lava hole sank an inch.

The Yaqui alone spent the waiting time in activity. He made trips up on the lava slope, and each time he returned with guns or boots or sombreros, or something belonging to the bandits that had fallen. He never fetched in a saddle or bridle, and from that the rangers concluded Rojas's horses had long before taken their back trail. What speculation, what consternation those saddled horses would cause if they returned to Forlorn River!

As Ladd improved there was one story he had to hear every day. It was the one relating to what he had missed— the sight of Rojas pursued and plunged to his doom. The thing had a morbid fascination for the sick ranger. He reveled in it. He tortured Mercedes. His gentleness and consideration, heretofore so marked, were in abeyance to some sinister, ghastly joy. But to humor him Mercedes racked her soul with the sensations she had suffered when Rojas hounded her out on the ledge, when she shot him, when she sprang to throw herself over the precipice, when she fought him, when with half-blinded eyes she looked up to see the merciless Yaqui reaching for the bandit.

Ladd fed his cruel longing with Thorne's poignant recollections, with the keen, clear, never-to-be-forgotten shocks to Gale's eye and ear. Jim Lash, for one at least, never tired of telling how he had seen and heard the tragedy, and every time in the telling it gathered some more tragic and gruesome detail. Jim believed in satiating the ranger. Then in the twilight, when the campfire burned, Ladd would try to get the Yaqui to tell his side of the story. But this the Indian would never do. There was only the expression of his fathomless eyes and the set passion of his massive face.

Those waiting days grew into weeks. Ladd gained very slowly. Nevertheless, at last he could walk about, and soon he averred that, strapped to a horse, he could last out the trip to Forlorn River.

There was rejoicing in camp, and plans were eagerly suggested. The Yaqui happened to be absent. When he returned the rangers told him they were now ready to undertake the journey back across lava and cactus.

Yaqui shook his head. They declared again their intention.

"No!" replied the Indian, and his deep, sonorous voice rolled out upon the quiet of the arroyo. He spoke briefly then. They had waited too long. The smaller waterholes back in the trail were dry. The hot summer was upon them. There could be only death waiting down in the burning valley. Here was water and grass and wood and shade from the sun's rays, and sheep to be killed on the peaks. The water would hold unless the season was that dreaded *ano seco* of the Mexicans.

"Wait for rain," concluded Yaqui, and now as never before he spoke as one with authority. "If no rain—" Silently he lifted a hand.

What Gale might have thought an appalling situation, if considered from a safe and comfortable home away from the desert, became, now that he was shut in by the red-ribbed lava walls and great dry wastes, a matter calmly accepted as inevitable. So he imagined it was accepted by the others. Not even Mercedes uttered a regret. No word was spoken of home. If there was thought of loved ones, it was locked deep in their minds. In Mercedes there was no change in womanly quality, perhaps because all she had to love was there in the desert with her.

Gale had often pondered over this singular change in character. He had trained himself, in order to fight a paralyzing something in the desert's influence, to oppose with memory and thought an insidious primitive retrogression to what was scarcely consciousness at all, merely a savage's instinct of sight and sound. He felt the need now of redoubled effort. For there was a sheer happiness in drifting. Not only was it easy to forget, it was hard to remember. His idea was that a man laboring under a great wrong, a great crime, a great passion might find the lonely desert a fitting place for either remembrance or oblivion, according to the nature of his soul. But an ordinary, healthy, reasonably happy mortal who loved the open with its blaze of sun and sweep of wind would have a task to keep from going backward to the natural man as he was before civilization.

By tacit agreement Ladd again became the leader of the party. Ladd was a man who would have taken all the responsibility whether or not it was given him. In moments of hazard, of uncertainty, Lash and Gale, even Belding, had unconsciously looked to the ranger. He had that kind of power. The first thing Ladd asked was to have the store of food that remained spread out upon a tarpaulin. Assuredly, it was a slender enough supply. The ranger stood for long moments gazing down at it. He was groping among past experiences, calling back from his years of life on range and desert that which might be valuable for the present issue. It was impossible to read the gravity of Ladd's face, for he still looked like a dead man, but the slow shake of his head told Gale much. There was a grain of hope, however, in the significance with which he touched the bags of salt and said, "Shore it was sense packin' all that salt!"

Then he turned to face his comrades.

"That's little grub for six starvin' people corralled in the desert. But the grub end ain't worryin' me. Yaqui can get sheep up the slopes. Water! That's the beginnin' an' middle an' end of our case."

"Laddy, I reckon the waterhole here never goes dry," replied Jim.

"Ask the Indian."

Upon being questioned, Yaqui repeated what he had said about the dreaded *año seco* of the Mexicans. In a dry year this waterhole failed.

"Dick, take a rope an' see how much water's in the hole."

Gale could not find bottom with a thirty foot lasso. The water was as cool, clear, sweet as if it had been kept in a shaded iron receptacle.

Ladd welcomed this information with surprise and gladness.

"Let's see. Last year was shore pretty dry. Mebbe this summer won't be. Mebbe our wonderful good luck'll hold. Ask Yaqui if he thinks it'll rain."

Mercedes questioned the Indian.

"He says no man can tell surely. But he thinks the rain will come," she replied.

"Shore it'll rain, you can gamble on that now," continued Ladd. "If there's only grass for the hosses! We can't get out of here without hosses. Dick, take the Indian an' scout down the arroyo. Today I seen the hosses were gettin' fat. Gettin' fat in this desert! But mebbe they've about grazed up all the grass. Go an' see, Dick. An' may you come back with more good news!"

Gale, upon the few occasions when he had wandered down the arroyo, had never gone far. The Yaqui said there was grass for the horses, and until now no one had given the question more consideration. Gale found that the arroyo widened as it opened. Near the head, where it was narrow, the grass lined the course of the dry stream bed. But farther down this stream bed spread out. There was every indication that at flood seasons the water covered the floor of the arroyo. The farther Gale went the thicker and larger grew the gnarled mesquites and *paloverdes,* the more cactus and greasewood there were, and other desert growths. Patches of gray grass grew everywhere. Gale began to wonder where the horses were. Finally the trees and brush thinned out, and a mile-wide gray plain stretched down to reddish sand dunes. Over to one side were the white horses, and even as Gale saw them both Blanco Diablo and Sol lifted their heads and, with white manes tossing in the wind, whistled clarion calls. Here was grass enough for many horses; the arroyo was indeed an oasis.

Ladd and the others were awaiting Gale's report, and they received it with calmness, yet with a joy no less evident because it was restrained. Gale, in his keen observation at the moment, found that he and his comrades turned with glad eyes to the woman of the party.

"Senor Laddy, you think—you—believe—we shall—" she faltered, and her voice failed. It was the woman in her, weakening in the light of real hope, of the happiness now possible beyond that desert barrier.

"Mercedes, no white man can tell what'll come to pass out here," said Ladd, earnestly. "Shore I have hopes now I never dreamed of. I was pretty near a dead man. The Indian saved me. Queer notions have come into my head about Yaqui. I don't understand them. He seems when you look at him only a squalid, sullen, vengeful savage. But Lord! that's far from truth. Mebbe Yaqui's different from most Indians. He *looks* the same, though. Mebbe the trouble is we white folks never knew the Indian. Anyway, Beldin' had it right. Yaqui's our godsend. Now as to the future, I'd like to know mebbe as well as you if we're ever to get home. Only bein' what I am, I say *quien sabe?* But somethin' tells me Yaqui knows. Ask him, Mercedes. Make him tell. We'll all be the better for knowin'. We'd be stronger for havin' more'n our faith in him. He's a silent Indian, but make him tell."

Mercedes called to Yaqui. At her bidding there was always a suggestion of hurry, which otherwise was never manifest in his actions. She put a hand on his bared muscular arm and began to speak in Spanish. Her voice was low, swift, full of deep emotion, sweet as the sound of a bell. It thrilled Gale, though he understood scarcely a word she said. He did not need translation to know that here spoke the longing of a woman for life, love, home, the heritage of a woman's heart.

Gale doubted his own divining impression. It was that the Yaqui understood this woman's longing. In Gale's sight the Indian's stoicism, his inscrutability, the lavalike hardness of his face, although they did not change, seemed to give forth light, gentleness, loyalty. For an instant Gale seemed to have a vision; but it did not last, and he failed to hold some beautiful illusive thing.

"Si!" rolled out the Indian's reply, full of power and depth.

Mercedes drew a long breath, and her hand sought Thorne's.

"He says yes," she whispered. "He answers he'll save us. He'll take us all back—he knows!"

THE BREAKER OF WILD MUSTANGS

One of the traditional skills assigned to cowboys by most Western writers was that of roping and breaking wild mustangs for saddle horses. However, Indians were also often called upon to do this. This story tells of one who demonstrated a skill and perseverance that few white broncobusters could imitate.

I

Silvermane snorted defiance from the cedar corral when the Naabs, and Indians, and Hare appeared. A half-naked sinewy Navajo with a face as changeless as a bronze mask sat astride August's blindfolded roan, Charger. He rode bareback except for a blanket strapped upon the horse. He carried only a long, thick halter, with a loop and a knot. When August opened the improvised gate, with its sharp bayonet-like branches of cedar, the Indian rode into the corral. The watchers climbed to the knoll. Silvermane snorted a blast of fear and anger. August's huge roan showed uneasiness. He stamped, and shook his head, as if to rid himself of the blinders.

Into the farthest corner of densely packed cedar boughs Silvermane pressed himself and watched. The Indian rode around the corral, circling closer and closer, yet appearing not to see the stallion. Many rounds he made and closer he got, always with the same steady gait. Silvermane left his corner and tried another. The old unwearying round brought Charger and the Navajo close by him. Silvermane pranced out of his thicket of boughs; he whistled, he wheeled with his shiny hoofs lifting. In an hour the Indian was edging the outer circle of the corral, with the stallion pivoting in the centre, ears laid back, eyes shooting sparks, fight in every line of him.

And the circle narrowed inward.

Suddenly the Navajo sent the roan at Silvermane and threw his halter. It spread out like a lasso, and the loop went over the head of the stallion, slipped to the knot and held fast, while the rope tightened. Silvermane leaped up, forehoofs pawing the air, and his long shrill cry was neither whistle, snort, nor screech, but all combined. He came down, missing Charger with his hoofs, sliding off his haunches. The Indian, his bronze muscles rippling, close-hauled the rope, making half hitches round his bony wrist.

In a whirl of dust the roan drew closer to the gray, and Silvermane began a mad race around the corral. The roan ran with him nose to nose. When Silvermane saw he could not shake him, he opened his jaws, rolled back his lip in an ugly snarl, his white teeth glistening, and tried to bite. But the Indian's moccasined foot shot up under the stallion's ear and pressed him back. Then the roan hugged Silvermane so close that half the time the Navajo almost rode two horses. But for the rigidity of his arms, and the play and sudden tension of his leg muscles, the Indian's work would have appeared commonplace, so dexterous was he, so perfectly at home in his dangerous seat. Suddenly he whooped and August Naab hauled back the gate, and the two horses, neck and neck, thundered out upon the level stretch.

"Good!" cried August. "Let him rip now, Navvy. All over but the work, Jack. I feared Silvermane would spear himself on some of those dead cedar spikes in the corral. He's safe now."

Jack watched the horses plunge at breakneck speed

down the stretch, circle at the forest edge, and come tearing back. Silvermane was pulling the roan faster than he had ever gone in his life, but the dark Indian kept his seat. The speed slackened on the second turn, and decreased as, mile after mile, the imperturbable Indian held roan and gray side to side and let them run.

Time passed, but Hare's interest in the breaking of the stallion never flagged. He began to understand the Indian, and to feel what the restraint and drag must be to the horse. Never for a moment could Silvermane elude the huge roan, the tight halter, the relentless Navajo. Gallop fell to trot, and trot to jog, and jog to walk; and hour by hour, without whip or spur or word, the breaker of desert mustangs drove the wild stallion. If there were cruelty it was in his implacable slow patience, his farsighted purpose. Silvermane would have killed himself in an hour; he would have cut himself to pieces in one headlong dash, but that steel arm suffered him only to wear himself out. Late that afternoon the Navajo led a dripping, drooping, foam-lashed stallion into the corral, tied him with the halter, and left him.

Later Silvermane drank of the water poured into the corral trough, and had not the strength or spirit to resent the Navajo's caressing hand on his mane.

Next morning the Indian rode again into the corral on blindfolded Charger. Again he dragged Silvermane out on the level and drove him up and down with remorseless, machine-like persistence. At noon he took him back, tied him up, and roped him fast. Silvermane tried to rear and kick, but the saddle went on, strapped with a flash of the dark-skinned hands. Then again Silvermane ran the level stretch beside the giant roan, only he carried a saddle now. At the first, he broke out with free wild stride as if to run forever from under the hateful thing. But as the afternoon waned he crept wearily back to the corral.

On the morning of the third day the Navajo went into the corral without Charger, and roped the gray, tied him fast, and saddled him. Then he loosed the lassoes except the one around Silvermane's neck, which he whipped under his foreleg to draw him down. Silvermane heaved a groan which plainly said he never wanted to rise again. Swiftly the Indian knelt on the stallion's head; his hands flashed; there was a scream, a click of steel on bone; and proud Silvermane jumped to his feet with a bit between his teeth.

The Navajo, firmly in the saddle, rose with him, and Silvermane leaped through the corral gate, and out upon the stretch, lengthening out with every stride, and settling into a wild, despairing burst of speed. The white mane waved in the wind; the half-naked Navajo swayed to the motion. Horse and rider disappeared in the cedars.

They were gone all day. Toward night they appeared on the stretch. The Indian rode into camp and, dismounting, handed the bridle-rein to Naab. He spoke no word; his dark impassiveness invited no comment. Silvermane was dust-covered and sweat-stained. His silver crest had the same proud beauty, his neck still the splendid arch, his head the noble outline, but his was a broken spirit.

"Here, my lad," said August Naab, throwing the bridle-rein over Hare's arm. "What did I say once about seeing you on a great gray horse? Ah! Well, take him and know this: you've the swiftest horse in this desert country."

THE LAND OF THE WILD MUSK-OX

The adventuring spirit of the English pioneers brought them to many strange and dangerous lands. None was stranger than the vast snowy landscapes of the Frozen North, and no pioneers bolder than those who went forth across the frozen plains and into the great green cathedral aisles of the forest in search of the treasure of fur and game that was the wealth of the Arctic lands. Some traded for caribou, many for beaver, marten, mink and fox.

This is the tale of an American plainsman resolved to capture and tame the mighty musk-ox, and the tale of his struggle against an unforgiving Nature and against the religious taboos of the Indians.

I

It was a waiting day at Fort Chippewayan. The lonesome, far-northern Hudson's Bay Trading Post seldom saw such life. Tepees dotted the banks of the Slave River and lines of blanketed Indians paraded its shores. Near the boat landing a group of chiefs, grotesque in semibarbaric, semi-civilized splendor, but black-browed, austere-eyed, stood in savage dignity with folded arms and high-held heads. Lounging on the grassy bank were white men, traders, trappers and officials of the post.

All eyes were on the distant curve of the river where, as it lost itself in a fine-fringed bend of dark green, white-glinting waves danced and fluttered. A June sky lay blue in the majestic stream; ragged, spear-topped, dense green trees massed down to the water; beyond rose bold, balk-knobbed hills, in remote purple relief.

A long Indian arm stretched south. The waiting eyes discerned a black speck on the green, and watched it grow. A flatboat, with a man standing to the oars, bore down swiftly.

Not a red hand, nor a white one, offered to help the voyager in the difficult landing. The oblong, clumsy, heavily laden boat surged with the current and passed the dock despite the boatman's efforts. He swung his craft in below upon a bar and roped it fast to a tree. The Indians crowded above him on the bank. The boatman raised his powerful form erect, lifted a bronzed face which seemed set in craggy hardness, and cast from narrow eyes a keen, cool glance on those above. The silvery gleam in his fair hair told of years.

Silence, impressive as it was ominous, broke only to the rattle of camping paraphernalia, which the voyager threw to a level, grassy bench on the bank. Evidently this unwelcome visitor had journeyed from afar, and his boat, sunk deep into the water with its load of barrels, boxes and bags, indicated that the journey had only begun. Significant, too, were a couple of long Winchester rifles shining on a tarpaulin.

The cold-faced crowd stirred and parted to permit the passage of a tall, thin, gray personage of official bearing, in a faded military coat.

"Are you the musk-ox hunter?" he asked, in tones that contained no welcome.

The boatman greeted this peremptory interlocutor with a cool laugh—a strange laugh, in which the muscles of his face appeared not to play.

"Yes, I am the man," he said.

"The chiefs of the Chippewayan and Great Slave tribes have been apprised of your coming. They have held council and are here to speak with you."

At a motion from the commandant, the line of chieftains

piled down to the level bench and formed a half-circle before the voyager. To a man who had stood before grim Sitting Bull and noble Black Thunder of the Sioux, and faced the falcon-eyed Geronimo, and glanced over the sights of a rifle at gorgeous-feathered, wild, free Comanches, this semicircle of savages—lords of the north— was a sorry comparison. Bedaubed and betrinketed, slouchy and slovenly, these low-statured chiefs belied in appearance their scorn-bright eyes and lofty mien. They made a sad group.

One who spoke in unintelligible language, rolled out a haughty, sonorous voice over the listening multitude. When he had finished, a half-breed interpreter, in the dress of a white man, spoke at a signal from the commandant.

"He says listen to the great orator of the Chippewayan. He has summoned all the chiefs of the tribes south of Great Slave Lake. He has held council. The cunning of the paleface hunter who comes to take the musk-oxen, is well known. Let the pale-face hunter return to his own hunting grounds; let him turn his face from the north. Never will the chiefs permit the white man to take musk-oxen alive from their country. The Ageter, the Musk-ox, is their god. He gives them food and fur. He will never come back if he is taken away, and the reindeer will follow him. The chiefs and their people would starve. They command the pale-face hunter to go back. They cry Naza! Naza! Naza!"

"Say, for a thousand miles, I've heard that word Naza!" returned the hunter, with mingled curiosity and disgust. "At Edmonton Indian runners started ahead of me, and every village I struck the redskins would crowd around me and an old chief would harangue at me, and motion me back, and point north with Naza! Naza! Naza! What does it mean?"

"No white man knows, no Indian will tell," answered the interpreter. "The traders think it means the Great Slave, the North Star, the North Spirit, the North Wind, the North Lights and Ageter, the musk-ox god."

"Well, say to the chiefs to tell Ageter I have been four moons on the way after some of his little Ageters, and I'm going to keep on after them."

"Hunter, you are most unwise," broke in the commandant, in his officious voice. "The Indians will never permit you to take a musk-ox alive from the north. They worship him, pray to him. It is a wonder you have not been stopped."

"Who'll stop me?"

"The Indians. They will kill you if you do not turn back."

"Faugh! to tell an American plainsman that!" The hunter paused a steady moment, with his eyelids narrowing over slits of blue fire. "There is no law to keep me out, nothing but Indian superstition and the greed of Hudson's Bay people. And I am an old fox, not to be fooled by pretty baits. For years the officers of this fur-trading company have tried to keep out explorers. Even Sir John Franklin, an Englishman, could not buy food of them. The policy of the company is to side with the Indians, to keep out traders and trappers. Why? So they can keep on cheating the poor savages out of clothing and food by trading a few trinkets and blankets, a little tobacco and rum for millions of dollars worth of furs. Have I failed to hire man after man, Indian after Indian, not to know why I cannot get a helper? Have I, a plainsman, come a thousand miles alone to be scared by you, or a lot of craven Indians? Have I been dreaming of musk-oxen for forty years, to slink south now, when I begin to feel the north? Not I."

Deliberately every chief, with the sound of a hissing snake, spat in the hunter's face. He stood immovable while they perpetrated the outrage, then calmly wiped his cheeks, and in his strange, cool voice, addressed the interpreter.

"Tell them thus they show their true qualities, to insult in council. Tell them they are not chiefs, but dogs. Tell them they are not even squaws, only poor, miserable starved dogs. Tell them I turn my back on them. Tell them the paleface has fought real chiefs, fierce, bold, like eagles, and he turns his back on dogs. Tell them he is the one who could teach them to raise the musk-oxen and the reindeer, and to keep out the cold and the wolf. But they are blinded. Tell them the hunter goes north."

Through the council the chiefs ran a low mutter, as of gathering thunder.

True to his word, the hunter turned his back on them. As he brushed by, his eye caught a gaunt savage slipping from the boat. At the hunter's stern call, the Indian leaped ashore, and started to run. He had stolen a parcel, and would have succeeded in eluding its owner but for an unforeseen obstacle, as striking as it was unexpected.

A white man of colossal stature had stepped in the thief's passage, and laid two great hands on him. Instantly the parcel flew from the Indian, and he spun in the air to fall into the river with a sounding splash. Yells signaled the surprise and alarm caused by this unexpected incident. The Indian frantically swam to the shore. Whereupon the champion of the stranger in a strange land lifted a bag, which gave forth a musical clink of steel, and throwing it with the camp articles on the grassy bench, he extended a huge, friendly hand.

"My name is Rea," he said, in deep, cavernous tones.

"Mine is Jones," replied the hunter, and right quickly did he grip the proffered hand. He saw in Rea a giant, of whom he was but a stunted shadow. Six and one-half feet Rea stood, with yard-wide shoulders, a hulk of bone and brawn. His ponderous, shaggy head rested on a bull neck. His broad face, with its low forehead, its close-shut mastiff under jaw, its big, opaque eyes, pale and cruel as those of a jaguar, marked him a man of terrible brute force.

"Free-trader!" called the commandant. "Better think twice before you join fortunes with the musk-ox hunter."

"To hell with you an' your rantin', dog-eared redskins!" cried Rea. "I've run agin a man of my own kind, a man of my own country, an' I'm goin' with him."

With this he thrust aside some encroaching, gaping Indians so unconcernedly and urgently that they sprawled upon the grass.

Slowly the crowd mounted and once more lined the bank.

Jones realized that by some late-turning stroke of fortune, he had fallen in with one of the few free-traders of the province. These freetraders, from the very nature of their calling—which was to defy the fur company, and to trap and trade on their own acount—were a hardy and intrepid class of men. Rea's worth to Jones exceeded that of a dozen ordinary men. He knew the ways of the north, the language of the tribes, the habits of the animals, the handling of dogs, the uses of food and fuel. Moreover, it soon appeared that he was a carpenter and blacksmith.

"There's my kit," he said, dumping the contents of his bag. It consisted of a bunch of steel traps, some tools, a broken ax, a box of miscellaneous things such as trappers used, and a few articles of flannel. "Thievin' redskins," he added, in explanation of his poverty. "Not much of an outfit, but I'm the man for you. Besides, I had a pal once who knew you on the plains, called you 'Buff' Jones. Old Jim Bent he was."

"I recollect Jim," said Jones. "He went down in Custer's last charge. So you were Jim's pal. That'd be a recommendation if you needed one. But the way you chucked the Indian overboard got me."

Rea soon manifested himself as a man of few words and much action. With the planks Jones had on board he heightened the stern and bow of the boat to keep out the beating waves in the rapids; he fashioned a steering-gear and a less awkward set of oars, and shifted the cargo so as to make more room in the craft.

"Buff, we're in for a storm. Set up a tarpaulin an' make a fire. We'll pretend to camp to-night. These Indians won't dream we'd try to run the river after dark, and we'll slip by undercover."

The sun clouded over; clouds moved from the north; a cold wind swept the tips of the spruces, and rain commenced to drive in gusts. By the time it was dark not an Indian showed himself. They were housed from the storm. Lights twinkled in the tepees and the big log cabins of the trading company. Jones scouted round till pitchy black night, when a freezing, pouring blast sent him back to the protection of the tarpaulin. When he got there he found that Rea had taken it down and awaited him. "Off!" said the free-trader; and with no more noise than a drifting feather the boat swung into the current and glided down till the tinkling fires no longer accentuated the darkness.

By night the river, in common with all swift rivers, had a sullen voice, and murmured its hurry, its restraint, its menace, its meaning. The two boatmen, one at the steering gear, one at the oars, faced the pelting rain and watched the dim, dark line of trees. The craft slid noiselessly onward into the gloom.

And into Jones's ears, above the storm, poured another sound, a steady, muffled rumble, like the roll of giant chariot wheels. It had come to be a familiar roar to him, and the only thing which, in his long life of hazard, had ever sent the cold, prickling, tight shudder over his warm skin. Many times on the Athabasca that rumble had presaged the dangerous and dreaded rapids.

"Hell Bend Rapids!" shouted Rea. "Bad water, but no rocks."

The rumble expanded to a roar, the roar to a boom that charged the air with heaviness, with a dreamy burr. The whole indistinct world appeared to be moving to the lash of wind, to the sound of rain, to the roar of the river. The boat shot down and sailed aloft, met shock on shock, breasted leaping dim white waves, and in a hollow, unearthly blend of watery sounds, rode on and on, buffetted, tossed, pitched into a black chaos that yet gleamed with obscure shrouds of light. Then the convulsive stream shrieked out a last defiance, changed its course abruptly to slow down and

111

drown the sound of rapids in muffling distance. Once more the craft swept on smoothly, to the drive of the wind and the rush of the rain.

By midnight the storm cleared. Murky clouds split to show shining, blue-white stars and a fitful moon, that silvered the crests of the spruces and sometimes hid like a gleaming, black-threaded pearl behind the dark branches.

Jones, a plainsman all his days, wonderingly watched the moon-blanched water. He saw it shade and darken under shadowy walls of granite, where it swelled with hollow song and gurgle. He heard again the far-off rumble, faint on the night wind. High cliff banks appeared, walled out the mellow light, and the river suddenly narrowed. Yawning holes, whirling pools of a second, opened with a gurgling suck and raced with the boat.

On the craft flew. Far ahead, a long, declining plane of jumping frosted waves played dark and white with the moonbeams. The Slave plunged to his freedom, down his rivers, stone-spiked bed, knowing no patient eddy, and white-wreathed his dark, shiny rocks in spume and spray.

II

A far cry it was from bright June at Fort Chippewayan to dim October on Great Slave Lake.

Two long, laborious months Rea and Jones threaded the crooked shores of the great inland sea, to halt at the extreme northern end, where a plunging outlet formed the source of a river. Here they found a stone chimney and fireplace standing among the darkened, decayed ruins of a cabin.

"We mustn't lose no time," said Rea. "I feel the winter in the wind. An' see how dark the days are gettin' on us."

"I'm for hunting musk-oxen," replied Jones.

"Man, we're racin' the northern night; we're in the land of the midnight sun. Soon we'll be shut in for seven months. A cabin we want, an' wood, an' meat."

A forest of stunted spruce trees edged on the lake, and soon its dreary solitudes ran to the strokes of axes. The trees were small and uniform in size. Black stumps protruded, here and there, from the ground showing work of the steel in time gone by. Jones observed that the living trees were no larger in diameter than the stumps, and questioned Rea in regard to the difference in age.

"Cut twenty-five, mebbe fifty years ago," said the trapper.

"But the living trees are no bigger."

"Trees an' things don't grow fast in the northland."

They erected a fifteen-foot cabin round the stone chimney, roofed it with poles and branches of spruce, and a layer of sand. In digging near the fireplace Jones unearthed a rusty file and the head of a whisky keg, upon which was a sunken word in unintelligible letters.

"We've found the place," said Rea. "Franklin built a cabin here in 1819. An' in 1833 Captain Back wintered here when he was in search of the vessel *Fury*. It was those explorin' parties that cut the trees. I seen Indian sign out there, made last winter, I reckon; but Indians never cut down no trees."

The hunters completed the cabin, piled cords of firewood outside, stowed away the kegs of dried fish and fruits, the sacks of flour, boxes of crackers, canned meats and vegetables, sugar, salt, coffee, tobacco—all of the cargo; then took the boat apart and carried it up the bank, which labor took them less than a week.

Jones found sleeping in the cabin, despite the fire, uncomfortably cold, because of the wide chinks between the logs. It was hardly better than sleeping under the swaying spruces. When he essayed to stop up the cracks—a task by no means easy, considering the lack of material— Rea laughed his short easy, "Ho! Ho!" and stopped him with the word, "Wait." Every morning the green ice extended farther out into the lake; the sun paled dim and dimmer; the nights grew colder. On October 8th the thermometer registered several degrees below zero; it fell a little more next night and continued to fall.

"Ho! Ho!" cried Rea. "She's struck the toboggan, an' presently she'll commence to slide. Come on, Buff, we've work to do.

He caught up a bucket, made for their hole in the ice, rebroke a six inch layer, the freeze of a few hours, and filling his bucket, returned to the cabin. Jones had no inkling of the trapper's intention, and wonderingly he soused his bucket full of water and followed.

By the time he had reached the cabin, a matter of some thirty or forty paces, the water no longer splashed from his pail, for a thin film of ice prevented. Rea stood fifteen feet from the cabin, his back to the wind, and threw the water. Some of it froze in the air, most of it froze on the logs. The simple plan of the trapper to incase the cabin with ice was easily divined. All day the men worked, ceasing only when the cabin resembled a glistening mound. It had not a sharp corner nor a crevice. Inside it was warm and snug, and as light as when the chinks were open.

A slight moderation of the weather brought the snow. Such snow. A blinding white flutter of great flakes, as large as feathers. All day they rustled softly; all night they swirled, sweeping, seeping, brushing against the cabin. "Ho Ho!" roared Rea. "'Tis good; let her snow, an' the reindeer will migrate. We'll have fresh meat." The sun shone again but not brightly. A nipping wind cut down out of the frigid north and crusted the snow. The third night following the storm, when the hunters lay snug under their blankets, a commotion outside aroused them.

"Indians," said Rea, "come north for reindeer."

Half the night, shouting and yelling, barking dogs, hauling of sleds and cracking of dried-skin tepees murdered sleep for those in the cabin. In the morning the level plain and edge of the forest held as Indian village. Caribou hides, strung on forked poles, constituted tent-like habitations with no distinguishable doors. Fires smoked in the holes in the snow. Not till late in the day did any life manifest itself round the tepees, and then a group of children, poorly clad in ragged pieces of blankets and skins, gaped at Jones. He saw their pinched, brown faces, staring, hungry eyes, naked legs and throats, and noted particularly their dwarfish size. When he spoke they fled precipitously a little way, then turned. He called again, and all ran except one small lad. Jones went into the cabin and came out with a handful of sugar in square lumps.

"Yellow Knife Indians," said Rea. "A starved tribe! We're in for it."

Jones made motions to the lad, but he remained still, as if transfixed, and his black eyes stared wonderingly.

"*Molar nasu* (white man good)," said Rea.

The lad came out of his trance and looked back at his companions, who edged nearer. Jones at the lump of sugar, then handed one to the little Indian. He took it gingerly, put it into his mouth and immediately jumped up and down.

"*Hoppieshampoolie, Hoppieshampoolie!*" he shouted to his brothers and sisters. They came on the run.

"Think he means sweet salt," interpreted Rea. "Of course these beggars never tasted sugar."

The band of youngsters trooped round Jones, and after tasting the white lumps, shrieked in such delight that the braves and squaws shuffled out of the tepees.

In all his days Jones had never seen such miserable Indians. Dirty blankets hid all their person, except straggling black, hair, hungry, wolfish eyes and moccasined feet. They crowded into the path before the cabin door and mumbled and stared and waited. No dignity, no brightness, no suggestions of friendliness marked this peculiar attitude.

"Starved!" exclaimed Rea. "They've come to the lake to invoke the Great Spirit to send the reindeer. Buff, whatever you do, don't feed them. If you do, we'll have them on our hands all winter. It's cruel, but, man, we're in the north!"

Notwithstanding the practical trapper's admonition

Jones could not resist the pleading of the children. He could not stand by and see them starve. After ascertaining there was absolutely nothing to eat in the tepees, he invited the little ones into the cabin, and made a great pot of soup, into which he dropped compressed biscuits. The savage children were like wildcats. Jones had to call in Rea to assist him in keeping the famished little aborigines from tearing each other to pieces. When finally they were all fed, they had to be driven out of the cabin.

"That's new to me". said Jones. "Poor little beggars!"

Rea doubtfully shook his shaggy head.

Next day Jones traded with the Yellow Knives. He had a goodly number of baubles, besides blankets, gloves and boxes of canned goods, which he had brought for such trading. He secured a dozen of the large-boned, white and black Indian dogs—huskies, Rea called them—two long sleds with harness and several pairs of snowshoes. This trade made Jones rub his hands in satisfaction, for during all the long journey north he had failed to barter for such cardinal necessities to the success of his venture.

"Better have doled out the grub to them in rations," grumbled Rea.

Twenty four hours, sufficed to show Jones the wisdom of the trapper's words, for in just that time the crazed, ignorant savages had glutted the generous store of food, which should have lasted them for weeks. The next day they were begging at the cabin door. Rea cursed and threatened them with his fists, but they returned again and again.

Days passed. All the time, in light and dark, the Indians filled the air with dismal chant and doleful incantations to the Great Spirit, and the tum! tum! tum! of tomtoms, a specific feature of their wild prayer for food.

But the white monotony of the rolling land and level lake remained unbroken. The reindeer did not come. The days became shorter, dimmer, darker. The mercury kept on the slide.

Forty degrees below zero did not trouble the Indians. They stamped till they dropped, and sang till their voices vanished, and beat the tomtoms everlastingly. Jones fed the children once each day, against the trapper's advice.

One day, while Rea was absent, a dozen braves succeeded in forcing an entrance, and clamored so fiercely, and threatened so desperately, that Jones was on the point of giving them food when the door opened to admit Rea.

With a glance he saw the situation. He dropped the bucket he carried, threw the door wide open and commenced action. Because of his great bulk he seemed slow, but every blow of his sledge-hammer fist knocked a brave against the wall, or through the door into the snow. When he could reach two savages at once, by way of diversion, he swung their heads together with a crack. They dropped like dead things. Then he handled them as if they were sacks of corn, pitching them out into the snow. In two minutes the cabin was clear. He banged the door and slipped the bar in place.

"Buff, I'm goin' to get mad at these thievin' redskins some day," he said gruffly. The expanse of his chest heaved slightly, like the slow swell of a calm ocean, but there was no other indication of unusual exertion.

Jones laughed, and again gave thanks for the comradeship of this strange man.

Shortly afterward, he went out for wood, and as usual scanned the expanse of the lake. The sun shone mistier and wanner, and frost feathers floated in the air. Sky and sun and plain and lake—all were gray. Jones fancied he saw a distant moving mass of darker shade than the gray background. He called the trapper.

"Caribou," said Rea instantly. "The vanguard of the migration. Hear the Indians! Hear their cry: 'Aton! Aton! Aton! they mean reindeer. The idiots have scared the herd with their infernal racket, an' no meat will they get. The caribou will keep to the ice, an' man or Indian can't stalk them there."

For a few moments his companion surveyed the lake and shore with a plainsman's eye, then dashed within to reappear with a Winchester in each hand. Through the crowd of bewailing, bemoaning Indians he sped, to the low, dying bank. The hard crust of snow upheld him. The gray cloud was a thousand yards out upon the lake and moving southeast. If the caribou did not swerve from this course they would pass close to a projecting point of land, half mile up the lake. So, keeping a wary eye upon them, the hunter ran swiftly. He had not hunted antelope and buffalo on the plains all his life without learning how to approach moving game. As long as the caribou were in action, they could not tell whether he moved or was motionless. In order to tell if an object was inanimate or not, they must stop to see, of which fact the keen hunter took advantage. Suddenly he saw the gray mass slow down and bunch up. He stopped running, to stand like a stump. When the reindeer moved again, he moved, and when they slackened again, he stopped and became motionless. As they kept to their course, he worked gradually closer and closer. Soon he distinguished gray, bobbing heads. When the leader showed signs of halting in his slow trot the hunter again became a statue. He saw they were easy to deceive; and, daringly confident of success, he encroached on the ice and closed up the gap till not more than two hundred yards separated him from the gray, bobbing, antlered mass.

Jones dropped on one knee. A moment only his eyes lingered admiringly on the wild and beautiful spectacle; then he swept one of the rifle to a level. Old habit made the little beaded sight cover first the stately leader. Bang. The gray monarch leaped straight forward, forehoofs up, antlered head back, to fall dead with a crash. Then for a few moments the Winchester spat a deadly stream of fire, and when emptied was thrown down for the other gun, which in the steady, sure hands of the hunter, belched death to the caribou.

The herd rushed on, leaving the white surface of the lake

gray with a struggling, kicking, bellowing heap. When Jones reached the caribou he saw several trying to rise on crippled legs. With his knife he killed these, not without some hazard to himself. Most of the fallen ones were already dead, and the others soon lay still. Beautiful gray creatures they were, almost white, with wide reaching, symmetrical horns.

A medley of yells arose from the shore, and Rea appeared running with two sleds, with the whole tribe of Yellow Knives pouring out of the forest behind him.

"Buff, you're jest what old Jim said you was." thundered Rea, as he surveyed the gray pile. "Here's winter meat, an' I'd not given a biscuit for all the meat I thought you'd get."

"Thirty shots in less than thirty seconds," said Jones, "an' I'll bet every ball I sent touched hair. How many reindeer?"

"Twenty! twenty! Buff, or I've forgot how to count. I guess mebbe you can't handle them shootin' arns. Ho! here comes the howlin' redskins."

Rea whipped out a bowie knife and began disemboweling the reindeer. He had not proceeded far in his task when the crazed savages were around him. Every one carried a basket or receptacle, which he swung aloft, and they sang, prayed, rejoiced on their knees. Jones turned away from the sickening scenes that convinced him these savages were little better than cannibals. Rea cursed them, and tumbled them over, and threatened them with the big bowie. An altercation ensued, heated on his side, frenzied on theirs. Thinking some treachery might befall his comrade, Jones ran into the thick of the group.

"Share with them, Rea, share with them."

Whereupon the giant hauled out ten smoking carcasses. Bursting into a babel of savage glee and tumbling over one another, the Indians pulled the caribou to the shore.

"Thievin' fools!" growled Rea, wiping the sweat from his brow. "Said they'd prevailed on the Great Spirit to send the reindeer. Why, they'd never smelled warm meat but for you.

Now, Buff, they'll gorge every hair, hide an' hoof of their share in less than a week. Thet's the last we do for the damned cannibals. Didn't you see them eatin' of the raw innards? faugh! I'm calculatin' we'll see no more reindeer. It's late for the migration. The big herd has driven southward. But we're lucky, thanks to your prairie trainin'. Come on now with the sleds, or we'll have a pack of wolves to fight."

By loading the reindeers on each sled, the hunters were not long in transporting them to the cabin. "Buff, there ain't much doubt about them keepin' nice and cool," said Rea. "They'll freeze, an' we can skin them when we want."

That night the starved wolf dogs gorged themselves till they could not rise from the snow. Likewise the Yellow Knives feasted. How long the reindeer might have served the wasteful tribe, Rea and Jones never found out. The next day two Indians arrived with dog trains, and their advent was hailed with another feast, and a pow-wow that lasted into the night.

"Guess we're goin' to get rid of our blasted hungry neighbors," said Rea, coming in next morning with the water pail, "an' I'll be durned Buff, if I don't believe them crazy heathen have been told about you. Them Indians was messengers. Grab your gun, an' let's walk over and see."

The Yellow Knives were breaking camp, and the hunters were at once conscious of the difference in their bearing. Rea addressed several braves, but got no reply. He laid his broad hand on the old wrinkled chief, who repulsed him, and turned his back. With a growl, the trapper turned the Indian round, and spoke as many words of the language as he knew. He got a cold response, which ended in the ragged old chief starting up, stretching a long, dark arm northward and with eyes fixed in fanatical subjection, shouting: *"Naza! Naza! Naza!"*

"Heathen!" Rea shook his gun in the faces of the messengers. It'll go bad with you to come Nazain' any longer on our trail. Come, Buff, clear out before I get mad."

When they were once more in the cabin, Rea told Jones that the messengers had been sent to warn the Yellow Knives not to aid the white hunters in any way. That night the dogs were kept inside, and the men took turns in watching. Morning showed a broad trail southward. And with the going of the Yellow Knives the mercury dropped to fifty, and the long, twilight winter night fell.

So with this agreeable riddance and plenty of meat and fuel to cheer them, the hunters sat down in their snug cabin to wait many months for daylight.

Those few intervals when the wind did not blow were the only times Rea and Jones got out of doors. To the plainsman, new to the north, the dim gray world about him was of exceeding interest. Out of the twilight shone a wan, round, lusterless ring that Rea said was the sun. The silence and desolation were heart-numbing.

"Where are the wolves?" asked Jones of Rea.

"Wolves can't live on snow. They're farther south after caribou, or farther north after musk-ox."

In those few still intervals Jones remained out as long as he dared, with the mercury sinking to sixty degrees. He turned from the wonder of the unreal, remote sun, to the marvel in the north—Aurora borealis—ever present, ever changing, ever-beautiful! and he gazed in rapt attention.

"Polar lights," said Rea, as if he were speaking of biscuits. "You'll freeze. It's gettin' cold."

Cold it became, to the matter of seventy degrees. Frost covered the walls of the cabin and the roof, except just over the fire. The reindeer were harder

In those few still intervals Jones remained out as long as he dared, with the mercury sinking to sixty degrees. He turned from the wonder of the unreal, remote sun, to the marvel in the north—Aurora borealis—ever present, ever changing, ever-beautiful! and he gazed in rapt attention.

"Polar lights," said Rea, as if he were speaking of biscuits. "You'll freeze. It's gettin' cold."

Cold it became, to the matter of seventy degrees. Frost

covered the walls of the cabin and the roof, except just over the fire. The reindeer were harder than iron. A knife or an ax or a steel-trap burned as if it had been heated in fire, and stuck to the hand. The hunters experienced trouble in breathing; the air hurt their lungs.

The months dragged. Rea grew more silent day by day, and as he sat before the fire his wide shoulders sagged lower and lower. Jones, unaccustomed to the waiting, the restraint, the barrier of the north, worked on guns, sleds, harness, till he felt he would go mad. Then to save his mind he constructed a windmill of caribou hides and pondered over it trying to invent, to put into practical use an idea he had once conceived.

Hour after hour he lay under his blankets unable to sleep, and listened to the north wind. Sometimes Rea mumbled in his slumbers; once his giant form started up, and he muttered a woman's name. Shadows from the fire flickered on the walls, visionary, spectral shadows, cold and gray, fitting the north. At such times he longed with all the power of his soul to be among those scenes far southward, which he called home. For days Rea never spoke a word, only gazed into the fire, ate and slept. Jones, drifting far from his real self, feared the strange mood of the trapper and sought to break it, but without avail. More and more he reproached himself, and singularly on the one fact that, as he did not smoke himself, he had brought only a small store of tobacco. Rea, inordinate and inveterate smoker, had puffed away all the weed in clouds of white, then had relapsed into gloom.

III

At last the marvel in the north dimmed, the obscure gray shade lifted, the hope in the south brightened, and the mercury climbed—reluctantly, with a tyrant's hate to relinquish power.

Spring weather at twenty-five below zero! On April 12th a small band of Indians made their appearance. Of the Dog were they, an offcast of the Great Slaves, according to Rea, and as motley, staring and starved as the Yellow Knives. But they were friendly, which presupposed ignorance of the white hunters, and Rea persuaded the strongest brave to accompany them as guide northward after musk-oxen.

On April 16th, having given the Indians several caribou carcasses, and assuring them that the cabin was protected by white spirits, Rea and Jones, each with sled and train of dogs, started out after their guide, who was similarly equipped, over the glistening snow toward the north. They made sixty miles the first day, and pitched their Indian tepee on the shores of Artillery Lake. Traveling northeast, they covered its white waste of one hundred miles in two days. Then a day due north, over rolling, monotonously snowy plain, devoid of rock, tree or shrub, brought them into a country of the strangest, queerest little spruce trees, very slender, and none of them over fifteen feet in height. A primeval forest of saplings.

"*Ditchen Nechila!*" said the guide.

"Land of sticks Little," said Rea.

An occasional reindeer was seen and numerous foxes and hares trotted off into the woods, envincing more curiosity than fear. All were silver white, even the reindeer, at a distance, taking the hue of the north. Once a beautiful creature, unblemished as the snow it trod, ran up a ridge and stood watching the hunters. It resembled a monster dog, only it was inexpressibly more wild looking.

"Ho! Ho! there you are!" cried Rea, reaching for his Winchester. "Polar wolf! Them's the white devils we'll have hell with."

As if the wolf understood, he lifted his white, sharp head and uttered a bark or howl that was like nothing so much as a haunting, unearthly mourn. The animal then merged into the white, as if he were really a spirit of the world whence his cry seemed to come.

In this ancient forest of youthful appearing trees, the hunters cut firewood to the full carrying capacity of the sleds. For five days the Indian guide drove his dogs over the smooth crust, and on the sixth day, about noon, halting in a hollow he pointed to tracks in the snow and called out, "*Ageter! Ageter! Ageter!*"

The hunters saw sharply defined hoof-marks, not unlike the tracks of reindeer, except that they were longer. The tepee was set up on the spot and the dogs unharnessed.

The Indian led the way with the dogs, and Rea and

Jones followed, slipping over the hard crust without sinking in and traveling swiftly. Soon the guide, pointing, again let out the cry: "Ageter!" at the same moment loosing the dogs.

Some few hundred yards down the hollow, a number of large black animals, not unlike the shaggy, humpy buffalo, lumbered over the snow. Jones echoed Rea's yell, and broke into a run, easily distancing the puffing giant.

The musk-oxen squared round to the dogs, and were soon surrounded by the yelping pack. Jones came up to find six old bulls uttering grunts of rage and shaking ram-like horns at their tormentors. Notwithstanding that for Jones this was the culmination of years of desire, the crowning moment, the climax and fruition of long harbored dreams, he halted before the tame and helpless beasts, with joy not unmixed with pain.

"It will be murder!" he exclaimed. "It's like shooting down sheep."

Rea came crashing up behind him and yelled: "Get busy. We need fresh meat, an' I want the skins."

The bulls succumbed to well-directed shots, and the Indians and Rea hurried back to camp with the dogs to fetch the sleds, while Jones examined with warm interest the animals he had wanted to see all his life. He found the largest bull approached within a third of the size of a buffalo. He was of a brownish black color and very like a large, wooly ram. His head was broad, with sharp, small ears; the horns had wide and flattened bases and lay flat on the head, to run down back of the eyes, then curve forward to a sharp point. Like the bison, the musk-ox had short, heavy limbs, covered with very long hair, and small, hard hoofs with hairy tufts inside the curve of bone, which probably served as pads or checks to hold the hoof firm on ice. His legs seemed out of proportion to his body.

Two musk-oxen were loaded on a sled and hauled to camp in one trip. Skinning them was but short work for such expert hands. All the choice cuts of meat were saved.

No time was lost in broiling a steak, which they found sweet and juicy, with a flavor of musk that was disagreeable.

"Now, Rea, for the calves," exclaimed Jones, "and then we're homeward bound."

"I hate to tell this redskin," replied Rea. "He'll be like the others. But it ain't likely he'd desert us here. He's far from his base, with nothin' but thet old musket." Rea then commanded the attention of the brave, and began to mangle the Great Slave and Yellow Knife languages. Of this mixture Jones knew but a few words. *"Ageter nechila,"* which Rea kept repeating, he knew, however, meant "musk-oxen little."

The guide stared, suddenly appeared to get Rea's meaning, then vigorously shook his head and gazed at Jones in fear and horror. Following this came an action as singular and inexplicable. Slowly rising, he faced the north, lifted his hand, and remained statuesque in his immobility. Then he began deliberately packing his blankets and traps on his sled, which had not been unhitched from the train of dogs.

"Jackoway ditchen hula," he said, and pointed south.

"Jackoway ditchen hula," echoed Rea. "The damned Indian says 'wife sticks none.' He's goin' to quit us. What do you think of thet? His wife's out of wood. Jackoway out of wood, an' here we are two days from the Arctic Ocean! Jones, the damned heathen don't go back!"

The trapper coolly cocked his rifle. The savage, who plainly saw and understood the action, never flinched. He turned his breast to Rea, and there was nothing in his demeanor to suggest his relation to a craven tribe.

"Good heavens, Rea, don't kill him!" exclaimed Jones, knocking up the leveled rifle.

"Why not, I'd like to know?" demanded Rea, as if he were considering the fate of a threatening beast. "I reckon it'd be a bad thing for us to let him go."

"Let him go," said Jones. "We are here on the ground. We

have dogs and meat. We'll get our calves and reach the lake as soon as he does, and we might get there before."

"Mebbee we will," growled Rea.

No vacillation attended the Indian's mode. From a friendly guide, he had suddenly been transformed into a dark, sullen savage. He refused the musk-ox meat offered by Jones, and he pointed south and looked at the white hunters as if he asked them to go with him. Both men shook their heads in answer. The savage struck his breast a resounding blow and with his index finger pointed at the white of the north, he shouted dramatically: *"Naza! Naza! Naza!"*

He then leaped upon his sled, lashed his dogs into a run, and without looking back disappeared over a ridge.

The musk-ox hunters sat long silent. Finally Rea shook his shaggy locks and roared. "Ho! Ho! Jackoway out of wood! Jackoway out of wood!"

On the day following the desertion, Jones found tracks to the north of the camp, making a broad trail in which were numerous little imprints that sent him flying back to get Rea and the dogs. Musk-oxen in great numbers had passed in the night, and Jones and Rea had not trailed the herd a mile before they had it in sight. When the dogs burst into full cry, the musk-oxen climbed a high knoll and squared about to give battle.

"'Calves! Calves! Calves!" cried Jones.

"Hold back! Hold back! Thet's a big herd, an' they'll show fight."

As good fortune would have it, the herd split up into several sections, and one part, hard pressed by the dogs, ran down the knoll, to be cornered under the lee of a bank. The hunters, seeing this small number, hurried upon them to find three cows and five badly frightened little calves backed against the bank of snow, with small red eyes fastened on the barking, snapping dogs.

To a man of Jones's experience and skill, the capturing of the calves was a ridiculously easy piece of work. The cows tossed their heads, watched the dogs, and forgot their young. The first cast of the lasso settled over the neck of a little fellow. Jones hauled him out over the slippery snow and laughed as he bound the hairy legs. In less time than he had taken to capture one buffalo calf, with half the effort, he had all the little musk-oxen bound fast. Then he signaled his feat by pealing out an Indian yell of victory.

"Buff, we've got em," cried Rea; "an now for the hell of it—gettin' 'em home. I'll fetch the sleds. You might as well down the best cow for me. I can use another skin."

Of all Jones's prizes of captured wild beasts—which numbered nearly every species common to western North America—he took greatest pride in the little musk-oxen. In truth, so great had been his passion to capture some of these rare and inaccessible mammals, that he considered the day's work the fulfillment of his life's purpose. He was happy. Never had he been so delighted as when, the very evening of their captivity, the musk-oxen, envincing no particular fear of him began to dig with sharp hoofs into the snow for moss. And they found moss, and ate it, which solved Jones's greatest problem. He had hardly dared to think how to feed them, and here they were picking sustenance out of the frozen snow.

"Rea, will you look at that! Rea, will you look at that!" he kept repeating. "See, they're hunting feed."

And the giant, with his rare smile, watched him play with the calves. They were about two and a half feet high, and resembled long haired sheep. The ears and horns were undiscernible, and their color considerably lighter than that of the matured beasts.

"No sense of fear of man," said the life-student of animals. "But they shrink from the dogs."

In packing for the journey south, the captives were strapped on the sleds. This circumstance necessitated a sacrifice of meat and wood, which brought grave, doubtful shakes of Rea's great head.

Days of hastening over the icy snow, with short hours

for sleep and rest, passed before the hunters awoke to the consciousness that they were lost. The meat they had packed had gone to feed themselves and the dogs. Only a few sticks of wood were left.

"Better kill a calf, an' cook meat while we've got a little wood left," suggested Rea.

"Kill one of my calves? I'd starve first!" cried Jones.

The hungry giant said no more.

They headed southwest. All about them glared the grim monotony of the arctics. No rock or bush or tree made a welcome mark upon the hoary plain Wonderland of frost, white marble desert, infinitude of gleaming silences.

Snow began to fall, making the dogs flounder, obliterating the sun by which they traveled. They camped to wait for clearing weather. Biscuits soaked in tea made their meal. At dawn Jones crawled out of the tepee. The snow had ceased. But where were the dogs? He yelled in alarm. Then the little mounds of white, scattered here and there, became animated, heaved, rocked and rose to fall to pieces, exposing the dogs. Blankets of snow had been their covering.

Rea had ceased his "Jackoway out of wood," for a reiterated question: "Where are the wolves?"

"Lost," replied Jones in hollow humor.

Near the close of that day, in which they had resumed travel, from the crest of a ridge they descried a long, low, undulating dark line. It proved to be the forest of "little sticks," where, with grateful assurance of fire and of soon finding their old trail, they made camp.

"We've four biscuits left, an' enough tea for one drink each," said Rea. "I calculate we're two hundred miles from Great Slave Lake. Where are the wolves?"

At that moment the night wind wafted through the forest a long, haunting mourn. The calves shifted uneasily; the dogs raised sharp noses to sniff the air, and Rea, settling back against a tree, cried out: "Ho! Ho!" Again the savage sound, a keen wailing note with the hunger of the northland in it, broke the cold silence. "You'll see a pack of real wolves in a minute," said Rea. Soon a swift pattering of feet down a forest slope brought him to his feet with a curse to reach a brawny hand for his rifle. White streaks crossed the black of the tree trunks; then indistinct forms, the color of snow, swept up, spread out and streaked to and fro. Jones thought the great, gaunt, pure white beasts the spectral wolves of Rea's fancy, for they were silent, and silent wolves must belong to dreams only.

"Ho! Ho!" yelled Rea. "There's green-fire eyes for you, Buff. Hell itself ain't nothin' to these white devils. Get the calves in the tepee, an' stand ready to loose the dogs, for we've got to fight."

Raising his rifle he opened fire upon the white foe. A struggling, rustling sound followed the shots. But whether it was the threshing of wolves dying in agony, or the fighting of the fortunate ones over those shot, could not be ascertained in the confusion.

Following the example Jones also fired rapidly on the other side of the tepee. The same inarticulate, silently rustling wrestle succeeded this volley.

"Wait!" cried Rea. "Be sparin' of cartridges."

The dogs strained at their chains and bravely bayed the wolves. The hunters heaped logs and brush on the fire, which, blazing up, sent a bright light far into the woods. On the outer edge of that circle moved the white, restless, gliding forms.

"They're more afraid of fire than of us," said Jones.

So it proved. When the fire burned and crackled they kept well in the background. The hunters had a long respite from serious anxiety, during which time they collected all the available wood at hand. But at midnight, when this had been mostly consumed, the wolves grew bold again.

"Have you any shots left for the 45-90, besides what's in the magazine?" asked Rea.

"Yes, a good handful."

"Well, get busy."

With careful aim Jones emptied the magazine into the gray, gliding, groping mass. The same rustling, shuffling, almost silent strife ensued.

"Rea, there's something uncanny about those brutes. A silent pack of wolves."

"Ho! Ho!" rolled the giant's answer through the woods.

For the present the attack appeared to have been effectually checked. The hunters, sparingly adding a little of their fast diminishing pile of fuel to the fire, decided to lie down for much needed rest, but not for sleep. How long they lay there, cramped by the calves, listening for stealthy steps, neither could tell; it might have been moments and it might have been hours. All at once came a rapid rush of pattering feet, succeeded by a chorus of angry barks, then a terrible commingling of savage snarls, growls, snaps and yelps.

"Out!" yelled Rea. "They're on the dogs!"

Jones pushed his cocked rifle ahead of him and straightened up outside the tepee. A wolf, large as a panther and white as the gleaming snow, sprang at him. Even as he discharged his rifle, right against the breast of the beast, he saw its dripping jaws, its wicked green eyes, like spurts of fire and felt its hot breath. It fell at his feet and writhed in the death struggle. Slender bodies of black and white, whirling and tussling together, sent out fiendish uproar. Rea threw a blazing stick of wood among them, which sizzled as it met the furry coats, and brandishing another he ran into the thick of the fight. Unable to stand the proximity of fire, the wolves bolted and loped off into the woods.

"What a huge brute!" exclaimed Jones, dragging the one he had shot into the light. It was a superb animal, thin, supple, strong, with a coat of frosty fur, very long and fine. Rea began at once to skin it, remarking that he hoped to find other pelts in the morning.

Though the wolves remained in the vicinity of camp, none ventured near. The dogs moaned and whined; their restlessness increased as the dawn approached, and when the gray light came, Jones found that some of them had been badly lacerated by the fangs of the wolves. Rea hunted for dead wolves and found not so much as a piece of white fur.

Soon the hunters were speeding southward. Other than a disposition to fight among themselves, the dogs showed no evil effects of the attack. They were lashed to their best speed, for Rea said the white rangers of the north would never quit their trail. All day the men listened for the wild, lonesome, haunting mourn, but it came not.

A wonderful halo of white and gold, that Rea called a sundog, hung in the sky all afternoon, and dazzlingly bright over the dazzling world of snow, circled and glowed a mocking sun, brother of the desert mirage, beautiful illusion, smiling cold out of the polar blue.

The first pale evening star twinkled in the east when the hunters made camp on the shore of Artillery Lake. At dusk the clear, silent air opened to the sound of a long, haunting mourn.

"Ho! Ho!" called Rea. His hoarse, deep voice rang defiance to the foe.

While he built a fire before the tepee, Jones strode up and down, suddenly to whip out his knife and make for the tame little musk-oxen, now digging in the snow. Then he wheeled abruptly and held out the blade to Rea.

"What for?" demanded the giant.

"We've got to eat," said Jones. "And I can't kill one of them. I can't, so you do it."

"Kill one of our calves?" snorted Rea. "Not till hell freezes over! I ain't commenced to get hungry. Besides, the wolves are going to eat us, calves and all."

Nothing more was said. They ate their last biscuit. Jones packed the calves away in the tepee, and turned to the dogs. All day they had worried him; something was amiss with them, and even as he went among them a fierce fight broke out. Jones saw it was unusual, for the attacked dogs showed craven fear, and the attacking ones a howling, savage intensity that surprised him. Then one of the vicious brutes rolled his eyes, frothed at the mouth, shuddered and leaped in his harness, vented a hoarse howl and fell back shaking and retching.

"My God! Rea!" cried Jones in horror. "Come here! Look! That dog is dying of rabies! Hydrophobia! The white wolves have hydrophobia!"

"If you ain't right!" exclaimed Rea. "I seen a dog die of thet onct, an' he acted like this. An' thet one ain't all. Look, Buff! look at them green eyes! Didn't I say the white wolves was hell? We'll have to kill every dog we've got."

Jones shot the dog, and soon afterward three more that manifested signs of the disease. It was an awful situation. To kill all the dogs meant simply to sacrifice his life and Rea's; it meant abandoning hope of ever reaching the cabin. Then to risk being bitten by one of the poisoned, maddened brutes, to risk the most horrible of agonizing deaths that was even worse.

"Rea, we've one chance," cried Jones, with pale face. "Can you hold the dogs, one by one, while I muzzle them?"

"Ho! Ho!" replied the giant. Placing his bowie knife between his teeth, with gloved hands he seized and dragged one of the dogs to the campfire. The animal whined and protested, but showed no ill spirit. Jones muzzled his jaws tightly with strong cords. Another and another were tied up, then one which tried to snap at Jones was nearly crushed by the giant's grip. The last, a surly brute, broke out into mad ravings the moment he felt the touch of Jones's hands, and writhing, frothing, he snapped Jones's sleeve. Rea jerked him loose and held him in the air with one arm, while with the other he swung the bowie. They hauled the dead dogs out on the snow, and returning to the fire sat down to await the cry they expected.

Presently, as darkness fastened down tight, it came—the same cry, wild, haunting, mourning. But for hours it was not repeated.

"Better rest some," said Rea; "I'll call you if they come."

Jones dropped to sleep as he touched his blankets. Morning dawned for him, to find the great, dark, shadowy figure of the giant nodding over the fire.

"How's this? Why didn't you call me?" demanded Jones.

"The wolves only fought a little over the dead dogs."

On the instant Jones saw a wolf skulking up the bank. Throwing up his rifle, which he had carried out of the tepee, he took a snap shot at the beast. It ran off on three legs, to go out of sight over the bank. Jones scrambled up the steep, slippery place, and upon arriving at the ridge, which took several moments of hard work, he looked everywhere for the wolf. In a moment he saw the animal, standing still some hundred or more paces down a hollow. With the quick report of Jones's second shot, the wolf fell and rolled over. The hunter ran to the spot to find the wolf was dead. Taking hold of a front paw, he dragged the animal over the snow to camp. Rea began to skin the animal, when suddenly he exclaimed:

"This fellow's hind foot is gone."

"That's strange. I saw it hanging by the skin as the wolf ran up the bank. I'll look for it."

By the bloody trail on the snow he returned to the place where the wolf had fallen, and thence back to the spot where its leg had been broken by the bullet. He discovered no sign of the foot.

"Didn't find it, did you?" asked Rea.

"No, and it appears odd to me. The snow is so hard the foot could not have sunk."

"Well, the wolf ate his foot, that's what," returned Rea. "Look at them teeth marks!"

"Is it possible?" Jones stared at the leg Rea held up.

"Yes it is. These wolves are crazy at times. You've seen thet. An' the smell of blood, an' nothin' else, mind you, in my opinion, made him eat his own foot. We'll cut him open."

Impossible as the thing seemed to Jones—and he could

not but believe further evidence of his own eyes—it was even stranger to drive a train of mad dogs. Yet that was what Rea and he did, and lashed them, beat them to cover many miles in the long day's journey. Rabies had broken out in several dogs so alarmingly that Jones had to kill them at the end of the run. And hardly had the sound of the shots died, when faint and far away, but clear as a bell, bayed on the wind the same haunting mourn of a trailing wolf.

"Ho! Ho! where are the wolves?" cried Rea.

A waiting, watching, sleepless night followed. Again the hunters faced the south. Hour after hour, riding, running, walking, they urged the poor, jaded, poisoned dogs. At dark they reached the head of Artillery Lake. Rea placed the tepee between two huge stones. Then the hungry hunters, tired, grim, silent, desperate, awaited the familiar cry.

It came on the cold wind, the same haunting mourn, dreadful in its significance.

Absence of fire inspirited the wary wolves. Out of the pale gloom gaunt white forms emerged, agile and stealthy, slipping on velvet padded feet, closer, closer, closer. The dogs wailed in terror.

"Into the tepee!" yelled Rea.

Jones plunged in after his comrade. The despairing howls of the dogs, drowned in more savage, frightful sounds, knelled one tragedy and foreboded a more terrible one. Jones looked out to see a white mass, like leaping waves of a rapid.

"Pump lead into them," cried Rea.

Rappidly Jones emptied his rifle into the white fray. The mass split; gaunt wolves leaped high to fall back dead; others wriggled and limped away; others dragged their hind quarters; others darted at the tepee.

"No more cartridges!" yelled Jones.

The giant grabbed the ax, and barred the door of the tepee. Crash! the heavy iron cleaved the skull of the first brute. Crash! it lamed the second. Then Rea stood in the narrow passage between the rocks, waiting with uplifted ax. A shaggy, white demon, snapping his jaws, sprang like a dog. A sodden, thudding blow met him and he slunk away without a cry. Another rabid beast launched his white body at the giant. Like a flash the ax descended. In agony the wolf fell, to spin round and round, running on his hind legs, while his head and shoulders and forelegs remain in the snow. His back was broken.

Jones crouched in the opening of the tepee, knife in hand. He doubted his senses. This was a nightmare. He saw two wolves leap at once. He heard the crash of the ax; he saw one wolf go down and the other slip under the swinging weapon to grasp the giant's hip. Jones heard the rend of cloth, and then he pounced like a cat, to drive his knife into the body of the beast. Another nimble foe lunged at Rea, to sprawl broken and limp from the iron. It was silent fight. The giant shut the way to his comrade and the calves; he made no outcry; he needed but one blow for every beast; magnificent, he wielded death and faced it—silent. He brought the white wild dogs of the north down with lightning blows, and when no more sprang to the attack, down on the frigid silence he rolled his cry: "Ho! Ho!"

"Rea! Rea! how is it with you?" called Jones, climbing out.

"A torn coat—no more, my lad!"

Three of the poor dogs were dead; the fourth and last gasped at the hunters and died.

The wintry night became a thing of half conscious past, a dream to the hunters, manifesting its reality only by the stark, stiff bodies of wolves, white in the gray morning.

"If we can eat, we'll make the cabin," said Rea. "But the dogs an' wolves are poison."

"Shall I kill a calf?" asked Jones.

"Ho! Ho! when hell freezes over—if we must!"

Jones found one 45-90 cartridge in all the outfit, and with

that in the chamber of his rifle, once more struck south. Spruce trees began to show on the barrens and caribou trails roused hope in the hearts of the hunters.

"Look! in the spruces," whispered Jones, dropping the rope of his sled. Among the black trees gray objects moved.

"Caribou!" said Rea. "Hurry! Shoot! Don't miss!"

But Jones waited. He knew the value of the last bullet. He had a hunter's patience. When the caribou came out in an open space, Jones whistled. It was then the rifle grew set and fixed; it was then the red fire belched forth.

At four hundred yards, the bullet took some fraction of time to strike. What a long time that was! Then both hunters heard the spiteful spat of the lead. The caribou fell, jumped up, ran down the slope, and fell again to rise no more.

An hour of rest, with fire and meat, changed the world to the hunters; still glistening, it yet had lost its bitter cold, its deathlike clutch.

"What's this?" cried Jones.

Moccasin tracks of different sizes, all toeing north, arrested the hunters.

"Pointed north! Wonder what thet means?" Rea plodded on, doubtfully shaking his head.

Night again, clear, cold, silver, starlit, silent night! The hunters rested, listening ever for the haunting mourn. Day again, white, passion less, monotonous, silent day! The hunters traveled on—on—, ever listening for the haunting mourn.

Another dusk found them within thirty miles of their cabin. Only one more day now.

Rea talked of his furs, of the splendid white furs he could not bring. Jones talked of his little musk-oxen calves and joyfully watched them dig for moss in the snow.

Vigilance relaxed that night. Outworn nature rebelled, and both hunters slept.

Rea awoke first, and kicking off the blankets, went out. His terrible roar of rage made Jones fly to his side.

Under the very shadow of the tepee, where the little musk-oxen had been tethered, they lay stretched out pathetically on crimson snow—stiff, stone-cold, dead. Moccasin tracks told the story of the tragedy.

Jones leaned against his comrade.

The giant raised his huge fist.

"Jackoway out of wood! Jackoway out of wood!"

Then he choked.

The north wind, blowing through the thin, dark weird spruce trees, mounted and seemed to to sigh, *"Naza! Naza! Naza!"*

THE HOGAN OF OF NAS TA BEGA

John Shefford was a haunted man! He had hit the trail to forget he'd ever been a preacher—and to track down a legend that was as important to him as life itself!

Three desperate people had fled Mormon persecution, only to be imprisoned in a lost canyon. Among them was the beathtakingly beautiful Fay Larkin, whom Shefford had vowed would be his wife.

John Shefford was a tenderfoot and didn't even pack a gun, but he found an Indian friend, Nas Ta Bega, a former Navajo Chief who had heard his story, and for reasons that Shefford could not fathom himself, had vowed to help him. As Shefford was to find out, without the Indian his mission would have been doomed to failure.

I

Shefford halted his tired horse and gazed with slowly realizing eyes.

A league-long slope of sage rolled and billowed down to Red Lake, a dry red basin, denuded and glistening, a hollow in the desert, a lonely and desolate door to the vast, wild, and broken upland beyond.

All day Shefford had plodded onward with the clear horizon-line a thing unattainable; and for days before that he had ridden the wild bare flats and climbed the rocky desert benches. The great colored reaches and steps had led endlessly onward and upward through dim and deceiving distance.

A hundred miles of desert travel, with its mistakes and lessons and intimations, had not prepared him for what he now saw. He beheld what seemed a world that knew only vastness. Wonder and awe fixed his gaze, and thought remained aloof. Then that dark and unknown northland flung a menace at him. An irresistible call had drawn him to this seamed and peaked border of Arizona, this broken, battlemented wilderness of Utah upland; and at first sight they frowned upon him, as if to warn him not to search for what lay hidden beyond the ranges. But Shefford thrilled with both fear and exultation. That was the country which had been described to him. Far across the red valley, far beyond the ragged line of black mesa and yellow range, lay the wild canyon with its haunting secret.

Red Lake must be his Rubicon. Either he must enter the unknown to seek, to strive, to find, or turn back and fail and never know and be always haunted. A friend's strange story had prompted his singular journey; a beautiful rainbow with its mystery and promise had decided him. Once in his life he had answered a wild call to the kingdom of adventure within him, and once in his life he had been happy. But here in the horizon-wide face of that up-flung and cloven desert he grew cold; he faltered even while he felt more fatally drawn.

As if impelled Shefford started his horse down the sandy trail, but he checked his former far-reaching gaze. It was the month of April, and the waning sun lost heat and brightness. Long shadows crept down the slope ahead of him and the scant sage deepened its gray. He watched the lizards shoot like brown streaks across the sand, leaving their slender tracks. He heard the rustle of pack-rats as they darted into their brushy homes. The whir of a low-sailing hawk startled his horse.

Like ocean waves the slope rose and fell, its hollows choked with sand, its ridge tops showing scantier growth of sage and grass and weed. The last ridge was a sand-dune, beautifully ribbed and scalloped and lined by the wind, and from its knife-sharp crest a thin wavering sheet of sand blew, almost like smoke. Shefford wondered why the sand looked red at a distance, for here it seemed almost white. It rippled everywhere, clean and glistening, always leading down.

Suddenly Shefford became aware of a house looming out of the bareness of the slope. It dominated that long white incline. Grim, lonely, forbidding, how strangely it harmonized with the surroundings! The structure was octagon-shaped, built of uncut stone, and resembled a fort. There was no door on the sides exposed to Shefford's gaze, but small apertures two-thirds the way up probably served as windows and portholes. The roof appeared to be made of poles covered with red earth.

Like a huge cold rock on a wide plain this house stood there on the windy slope. It was an outpost of the trader Presbrey, of whom Shefford had heard at Flagstaff and Tuba. No living thing appeared in the limit of Shefford's vision. He gazed shudderingly at the unwelcoming habitation, at the dark eyelike windows, at the sweep of barren slope merging into the vast red valley, at the bold, bleak bluffs. Could any one live here? The nature of that sinister valley forbade a home there, and the spirit of the place hovered in the silence and space. Shefford thought irresistibly of how his enemies would have consigned him to just such a hell. He thought bitterly and mockingly of the narrow congregation that had proved him a failure in the ministry, that had repudiated his ideas of religion and immortality and God, that had driven him, at the age of twenty-four, from the calling forced upon him by his people. As a boy he had yearned to make himself an artist. His family had made him a clergyman; fate had made him a failure. A failure only so far in his life, something urged him to add—for in the lonely days and silent nights of the desert he had experienced a strange birth of hope. Adventure had called him, but it was a vague and spiritual hope, a dream of promise, a nameless attainment that fortified his wilder impulse.

As he rode around a corner of the stone house his horse snorted and stopped. A lean, shaggy pony jumped at sight of him, almost displacing a red long-haired blanket that covered an Indian saddle. Quick thuds of hoofs in sand drew Shefford's attention to a corral made of peeled poles, and here he saw another pony.

Shefford heard subdued voices. He dismounted and walked to an open door. In the dark interior he dimly descried a high counter, a stairway, a pile of bags of flour, blankets, and silver-ornamented objects, but the persons he had heard were not in that part of the house. Around another corner of the octagon-shaped wall he found another open door, and through it saw goat-skins and a mound of dirty sheep-wool, black and brown and white. It was light in this part of the building. When he crossed the threshhold he was astounded to see a man struggling with a girl—an Indian girl. She was straining back from him, panting, and uttering low guttural sounds. The man's face was corded and dark with passion. This scene affected Shefford strangely. Primitive emotions were new to him.

Before Shefford could speak the girl broke loose and turned to flee. She was an Indian and this place was the uncivilized desert, but Shefford knew terror when he saw it. Like a dog the man rushed after her. It was instinct that made Shefford strike, and his blow laid the man flat. He lay stunned a moment, then raised himself to a sitting posture, his hand to his face, and the gaze he fixed upon Shefford seemed to combine astonishment and rage.

"I hope you're not Presbrey," said Shefford, slowly. He felt awkward, not sure of himself.

The man appeared about to burst into speech, but repressed it. There was blood on his mouth and his hand. Hastily he scrambled to his feet. Shefford saw this man's amaze and rage change to shame. He was tall and rather stout; he had a smooth tanned face, soft of outline, with a weak chin. His eyes were dark. The look of him and his corduroys and his soft shoes gave Shefford an impression that he was not a man who worked hard. By contrast with the few other worn and rugged desert men Shefford had met this stranger stood out strikingly. He stooped to pick up a soft felt hat, and, jamming it on his head, he hurried out. Shefford followed him and watched him from the door. He went directly to the corral, mounted the pony, and rode out, to turn down the slope toward the south. When he reached the level of the basin, where evidently the sand was hard, he put the pony to a lope and gradually drew away.

"Well!" ejaculated Shefford. He did not know what to make of this adventure. Presently he became aware that the Indian girl was sitting on a roll of blankets near the wall. With curious interest Shefford studied her apperance. She had long, raven-black hair, tangled and dishevelled, and she wore a soiled white band of cord above her brow. The color of her face struck him; it was dark, but not red nor bronzed; it almost had a tinge of gold. Her profile was clear-cut, bold, almost stern. Long black eyelashes hid her eyes. She wore a tight-fitting waist garment of material resembling velveteen. It was ripped along her side, exposing a skin still more richly gold than that of her face. A string of silver ornaments and turquoise-and-white beads encircled her neck, and it moved gently up and down with the heaving of her full bosom. Her skirt was some gaudy print goods, torn and stained and dusty. She had little feet, encased in brown moccasins, fitting like gloves and buttoning over the ankles with silver coins.

"Who was that man? Did he hurt you?" inquired Shefford, turning to gaze down the valley where a moving black object showed on the bare sand.

"No savvy," replied the Indian girl.

"Where's the trader Presbrey?" asked Shefford.

She pointed straight down into the red valley.

"Toh," she said.

In the centre of the basin lay a small pool of water shining brightly in the sunset glow. Small objects moved around it, so small that Shefford thought he saw several dogs led by a child. But it was the distance that deceived him. There was a man down there watering his horses. That reminded Shefford of the duty owing to his own tired and thirsty beast. Whereupon he untied his pack, took off the saddle, and was about ready to start down when the Indian girl grasped the bridle from his hand.

"Me go," she said.

He saw her eyes then, and they made her look different. They were as black as her hair. He was puzzled to decide whether or not he thought her handsome.

"Thanks, but I'll go," he replied, and, taking the bridle again, he started down the slope. At every step he sank into the deep, soft sand. Down a little way he came upon a pile of tin cans; they were everywhere, buried, half buried, and lying loose; and these gave evidence of how the trader lived. Presently Shefford discovered that the Indian girl was following him with her own pony. Looking upward at her against the light, he thought her slender, lithe, picturesque. At a distance he liked her.

He plodded on, at length glad to get out of the drifts of sand to the hard level of the valley. This, too, was sand, but dried and baked hard, and red in colour. At some season of the year this immense flat must be covered with water. How wide it was, and empty! Shefford experienced again a feeling that had been novel to him—and it was that he was loose, free, unanchored, ready to veer with the wind. From the foot of the slope the water-hole had appeared to be a few hundred rods out in the valley. But the small size of the figures made Shefford doubt; and he had to travel many times a few hundred rods before those figures began to grow. Then Shefford made out that they were approaching him.

Thereafter they rapidly increased to normal proportions of man and beast. When Shefford met them he saw a powerful, heavily built young man leading two ponies.

"You're Mr. Presbrey, the trader?" inquired Shefford.

"Yes, I'm Presbrey, without the Mister," he replied.

"My name's Shefford. I'm knocking about on the desert. Rode from beyond Tuba to-day."

"Glad to see you," said Presbrey. He offered his hand. He was a stalwart man, clad in gray shirt, overalls, and boots. A shock of tumbled light hair covered his massive head; he was tanned, but not darkly, and there was red in his cheeks; under his shaggy eyebrows were deep, keen eyes; his lips were hard and set, as if occasion for smiles or words were rare, and his big strong jaw seemed locked.

"Wish more travellers came knocking around Red Lake," he added. "Reckon here's the jumping-off place."

"It's pretty—lonesome," said Shefford, hesitating as if at a loss for words.

Then the Indian girl came up. Presbrey addressed her in

her own language, which Shefford did not understand. She seemed shy and would not answer; she stood with downcast face and eyes. Presbrey spoke again at which she pointed down the valley, and then moved on with her pony toward the water-hole.

Presbrey's keen eyes fixed on the receding black dot far down that oval expanse.

"The fellow left—rather abruptly," said Shefford constrainedly. "Who was he?"

"His name's Willetts. He's a missionary. He rode in today with this Navajo girl. He was taking her to Blue Canyon, where he lives and teaches the Indians. I've met him only a few times. You see, not many white men ride in here. He's the first white man I've seen in six months, and you're the second. Both the same day! ... Red Lake's getting popular! It's queer, though, his leaving. He expected to stay all night. There's no other place to stay. Blue Canon is fifty miles away."

"I'm sorry to say—no, I'm not sorry, either—but I must tell you I was the cause of Mr. Willetts leaving," replied Shefford.

"How so?" inquired the other.

Then Shefford related the incident following his arrival.

"Perhaps my action was hasty," he concluded, apologetically. "I didn't think. Indeed, I'm surprised at myself."

Presbrey made no comment and his face was as hard to read as one of the distant bluffs.

"But what did the man mean?" asked Shefford, conscious of a little heat. "I'm a stranger out here. I'm ignorant of Indians—how they're controlled. Still I'm no fool ... If Willets didn't mean evil, at least he was brutal."

"He was teaching her religion," replied Presbrey.

Next morning the Indian girl was gone and the tracks of her pony led north. Shefford's first thought was to wonder if he would overtake her on the trail; and this surprised him with the proof of how unconsciously his resolve to go on had formed.

Presbrey made no further attempt to turn Shefford back. But he insisted on replenishing the pack, and that Shefford take weapons. Finally Shefford was persuaded to accept a revolver. The trader bade him goodbye and stood in the door while Shefford led his horse down the slope toward the waterhole. Perhaps the trader believed he was watching the departure of a man who would never return. He was still standing at the door of the post when Shefford halted at the pool.

Upon the level floor of the valley lay thin patches of snow which had fallen during the night. The air was biting cold, yet stimulated Shefford while it stung him. His horse drank rather slowly and disgustedly. Then Shefford mounted and reluctantly turned his back upon the trading-post.

As he rode away from the pool he saw a large flock of sheep approaching. They were very closely, even densely, packed, in a solid slow-moving mass, and coming with a precision almost like a march. This fact surprised Shefford, for there was not an Indian in sight. Presently he saw that a dog was leading the flock, and a little later he discovered another dog in the rear of the sheep. They were splendid, long-haired dogs, of a wild-looking shepherd breed. He halted his horse to watch the procession pass by. The flock covered fully an acre of ground and the sheep were black, white, and brown. They passed him, making a little pattering roar on the hard-caked sand. The dogs were taking the sheep in to water.

Shefford went on and was drawing close to the other side of the basin, where the flat red level was broken by rising dunes and ridges, when he spied a bunch of ponies. A shrill whistle told him that they had seen him. They stopped, threw up their heads, and watched him. Shefford certainly returned the attention. There was no Indian with them. Presently, with a snort, the leader, which appeared to be a stallion, trotted behind the others, seemed to be driving them, and went clear round the band to get in the lead again. He was taking them in to water, the same as the dogs had taken the sheep.

These incidents were new and pleasing to Shefford. How ignorant he had been of life in the wilderness. Once more he received subtle intimations of what he might learn out in the open; and it was with a less weighted heart that he faced the gateway between the huge yellow bluffs on his left and the slow rise of ground to the black mesa on his right. He looked back in time to see the trading-post, bleak and lonely on the bare slope, pass out of sight behind the bluffs. Shefford felt no fear—he really had little experience of physical fear—but it was certain that he gritted his teeth and welcomed whatever was to come to him. He had lived a narrow, insulated life with his mind on spiritual things; his family and his congregation and his friends—except that one new friend whose story had enthralled him—were people of quiet religious habit. The man deep down in him had never had a chance. He breathed hard as he tried to imagine the world opening to him, and almost dared to be glad for the doubt that had set him adrift.

The tracks of the Indian girl's pony were plain in the sand. Also there were other tracks, not so plain, and these Shefford decided had been made by Willetts and the girl the day before. He climbed a ridge, half soft sand and half hard, and saw right before him, rising in striking form, two great yellow buttes, like elephant legs. He rode between them, amazed at their height. Then before him stretched a slowly ascending valley, walled on one side by the black mesa and on the other by low bluffs. For miles a dark-green growth of greasewood covered the valley, and Shefford could see where the green thinned and failed, to give place to sand. He trotted his horse and made good time on this stretch.

The day contrasted greatly with any he had yet experienced. Gray clouds obscured the walls of rock a few miles to the west, and Shefford saw squalls of snow like huge veins dropping down and spreading out. The wind cut with the keenness of a knife. Soon he was chilled to the bone. A squall swooped and roared down upon him, and the wind that bore the driving white pellets of snow, almost like hail, was so freezing bitter cold that the former wind seemed warm in comparison. The squall passed as swiftly as it had come, and it left Shefford so benumbed he could not hold the bridle. He tumbled off his horse and walked. By and by the sun came out and soon warmed him and melted the thin layer of snow on the sand. He was still on the trail of the Indian girl, but hers were now the only tracks he could see.

All morning he gradually climbed, with limited view, until at last he mounted to a point where the country lay open to his sight on all sides except where the endless black mesa ranged on into the north. A rugged yellow peak dominated the landscape to the fore, but it was far away. Red and ragged country extended westward to a huge flat-topped wall of gray rock. Lowering swift clouds swept across the sky, like drooping mantles, and they darkened the sun. Shefford built a little fire out of dead greasewood sticks, and with his blanket round his shoulders he hung over the blaze, scorching his clothes and hands. He had been cold before in his life, but he had never before appreciated fire. This desert blast pierced him. The squall enveloped him, thicker and colder and windier than any other, but, being better fortified, he did not suffer so much. It howled away, hiding the mesa and leaving a white desert behind. Shefford walked on, leading his horse, until the exercise and the sun had once more warmed him.

This last squall had rendered the Indian girl's trail difficult to follow. The snow did not quickly melt, and, besides, sheep tracks and the tracks of horses gave him trouble, until at last he was compelled to admit that he could not follow her any longer. A faint path or trail led north, however, and, following that, he soon forgot the girl. Every surmounted ridge held a surprise for him. The desert seemed never to change in the vast whole that encompassed him, yet near him it was always changing. From Red Lake he had seen a peaked, walled, and canyoned country, as rough as a stormy sea; but when he rode into that country the sharp and broken features held to the distance.

He was glad to get out of the sand. Long narrow flats,

gray with grass and dotted with patches of greasewood, and lined by low bare ridges of yellow rock, stretched away from him, leading toward the yellow peak that seemed never to be gained upon.

Shefford had pictures in his mind, pictures of stone walls and wild valleys and domed buttes, all of which had been painted in colourful and vivid words by his friend Venters. He believed he would recognize the distinctive and remarkable landmarks Venters had portrayed, and he was certain that he had not yet come upon one of them. This was his second lonely day of travel and he had grown more and more susceptible to the influence of the horizon and the different prominent points. He attributed a gradual change in his feelings to the loneliness and the increasing wildness. Between Tuba and Flagstaff he had met Indians and an occasional prospector and teamster. Here he was alone, and though he felt some strange gladness, he could not help but see the difference.

He rode on during the gray, lowering, chilly day, and toward evening the clouds broke in the west, and a setting sun shone through the rift, burnishing the desert to red and gold. Shefford's instinctive but deadened love of the beautiful in nature stirred into life, and the moment of its rebirth was a melancholy and sweet one. Too late for the artist's work, but not too late for his soul!

For a place to make camp he halted near a low area of rock that lay like an island in a sea of grass. There was an abundance of dead greasewood for a camp-fire, and, after searching over the rock, he found little pools of melted snow in the depressions. He took off the saddle and pack, watered his horse, and, hobbling him as well as his inexperience permitted, he turned him loose on the grass.

Then while he built a fire and prepared a meal the night came down upon him. In the lee of the rock he was well sheltered from the wind, but the air was bitter cold. He gathered all the dead greasewood in the vicinity, replenished the fire, and rolled in his blanket, back to the blaze. The loneliness and the coyotes did not bother him this night. He was too tired and cold. He went to sleep at once and did not awaken until the fire died out. Then he rebuilt it and went to sleep again. Every half-hour all night long he repeated this, and was glad indeed when the dawn broke.

The day began with misfortune. His horse was gone; it had been stolen, or had worked out of sight, or had broken the hobbles and made off. From a high stone ridge Shefford searched the grassy flats and slopes, all to no purpose. Then he tried to track the horse, but this was equally futile. He had expected disasters, and the first one did not daunt him. He tied most of his pack in the blanket, threw the canteen across his shoulder, and set forth, sure at least of one thing—that he was a very much better traveller on foot than on horseback.

Walking did not afford him the leisure to study the surrounding country. However, from time to time, when he surmounted a bench he scanned the different landmarks that had grown familiar. It took hours of steady walking to reach and pass the yellow peak that had been a kind of goal. He saw many sheep trails and horse tracks in the vicinity of this mountain, and once he was sure he espied an Indian watching him from a bold ridge-top.

The day was bright and warm, with air so clear it magnified objects he knew to be far away. The ascent was gradual; there were many narrow flats connected by steps; and the grass grew thicker and longer. At noon Shefford halted under the first cedar-tree, a lonely, dwarfed shrub that seemed to have had a hard life. From this point the rise of ground was more perceptible, and straggling cedars led the eye on to a purple slope that merged into green of pinon and pine. Could that purple be the sage Venters had so feelingly described, or was it merely the purple of deceiving distance? Whatever it might be, it gave Shefford a thrill and made him think of the strange, shy, and lovely woman Venters had won out here in this purple-sage country.

He calculated that he had ridden thirty miles the day before and had already travelled ten miles today, and therefore could hope to be in the pass before night. Shefford resumed his journey with too much energy and enthusiasm to think of being tired. And he discovered presently that the straggling cedars and the slope beyond were much closer than he had judged them to be. He reached the sage to find it gray instead of purple. Yet it was always purple a little way ahead, and if he half shut his eyes it was purple near at hand. He was surprised to find that he could not breathe freely, or it seemed so, and soon made the discovery that the sweet, pungent, penetrating fragrance of sage and cedar had this strange effect upon him. This was an exceedingly dry and odorous forest, where every open space between the clumps of cedars was choked with luxuriant sage. The pinons were higher up on the mesa, and the pines still higher. Shefford appeared to lose himself. There were no trails. The black mesa on the right and the wall of stone on the left could not be seen, but he pushed on with what was either singular confidence or rash impulse. And he did not know whether that slope was long or short.

Once at the summit he saw with surprise that it broke abruptly and the descent was very steep and short on that side. Through the trees he once more saw the black mesa, rising to the dignity of a mountain; and he had glimpses of another flat, narrow valley, this time with a red wall running parallel with the mesa. He could not help but hurry down to get an unobstructed view. His eagerness was rewarded by a splendid scene, yet to his regret he could not force himself to believe it had any relation to the pictured scenes in his mind. The valley was half a mile wide, perhaps several miles long, and extended in a curve between the cedar-sloped mesa and a looming wall of red stone. There was not a bird or a beast in sight. He found a well-defined trail, but it had not been recently used. He passed a low structure made of peeled logs and mud, with a dark opening like a door. It did not take him many minutes to learn that the valley was longer than he had calculated. He walked swiftly and steadily, in spite of the fact that the pack had become burdensome. What lay beyond the jutting corner of the mesa had increasing fascination for him and acted as a spur. At last he turned the corner, only to be disappointed at sight of another cedar slope. He had a glimpse of a single black shaft of rock rising far in the distance, and it disappeared as his striding forward made the crest of the slope rise toward the sky.

Again his view became restricted, and he lost the sense of a slow and gradual uplift of rock and an increase in the scale of proportion. Halfway up this ascent he was compelled to rest, and again the sun was slanting low when he entered the cedar forest. Soon he was descending, and he suddenly came into the open to face a scene that made his heart beat thick and fast.

He saw lofty crags and cathedral spires, and a wonderful canyon winding between huge beetling red walls. He heard the murmur of flowing water. The trail led down to the canyon floor, which appeared to be level and green and cut by deep washes in red earth. Could this canyon be the mouth of Deception Pass? It bore no resemblance to any place Shefford had heard described, yet somehow he felt rather than saw that it was the portal to the wild fastness he had travelled so far to enter.

Not till he had descended the trail and had dropped his pack did he realize how weary and footsore he was. Then he rested. But his eyes roved to and fro, and his mind was active. What a wild and lonesome spot! The low murmur of shallow water came up to him from a deep, narrow cleft. Shadows were already making the canon seem full of blue haze. He saw a bare slope of stone out of which cedar-trees were growing. And as he looked about him he became aware of a singular and very perceptible change in the lights and shades. The sun was setting, the crags were gold-tipped, the shadows crept upward, the sky seemed to darken swiftly. Then the gold changed to red, slowly dulled, and the grays and purples stood out. Shefford was entranced with the beautiful changing effects, and watched till the walls turned black and the sky grew steely and a faint star peeped out. Then he set about the necessary camp tasks.

Dead cedars right at hand assured him a comfortable night with steady fire, and when he had satisfied his hunger he arranged an easy seat before the blazing logs, and gave his mind over to thought of his weird, lonely environment.

The murmur of running water mingled in harmonious accompaniment with the moan of the wind in the cedars—wild, sweet sounds that were balm to his wounded spirit! They seemed a part of the silence, rather than a break in it or a hindrance to the feeling of it. But suddenly that silence did break to the rattle of a rock. Shefford listened, thinking some wild animal was prowling around. He felt no alarm. Presently he heard the sound again and again. Then he recognized the crack of unshod hoofs upon rock. A horse was coming down the trail. Shefford rather resented the interruption, though he still had no alarm. He believed he was perfectly safe. As a matter of fact, he had never in his life been anything but safe and padded around with wool, hence, never having experienced peril, he did not know what fear was.

Presently he saw a horse and rider come into dark prominence on the ridge just above his camp. They were silhouetted against the starry sky. The horseman stopped and he and his steed made a magnificent black statue, somehow wild and strange, in Shefford's sight. Then he came on, vanished in the darkness under the ridge, presently to emerge into the circle of camp-fire light.

He rode to within twenty feet of Shefford and the fire. The horse was dark, wild-looking, and seemed ready to run. The rider appeared to be an Indian, and yet had something about him suggesting the cowboy. At once Shefford remembered what Presbrey had said about half-breeds. A little shock, inexplicable to Shefford, rippled over him.

He greeted his visitor but received no answer. Shefford saw a dark, squat figure bending forward in the saddle. The man was tense. All about him was dark except the glint of a rifle across the saddle. The face under the sombrero was only a shadow. Shefford kicked the fire-logs and a brighter blaze lightened the scene. Then he saw this stranger a little more clearly, and made out an unusually large head, broad, dark face, a sinister tight-shut mouth, and gleaming black eyes.

Those eyes were unmistakably hostile. They roved searchingly over Shefford's pack and then over his person. Shefford felt for the gun that Presbrey had given him. But it was gone. He had left it back where he had lost his horse, and had not thought of it since. Then a strange, slow-coming cold agitation possessed Shefford. Something gripped his throat.

Suddenly Shefford was stricken at a menacing movement on the part of the horseman. He had drawn a gun. Shefford saw it shine darkly in the firelight. The Indian meant to murder him. Shefford saw the grim, dark face in a kind of horrible amazement. He felt the meaning of that drawn weapon as he had never felt anything before in his life. And he collapsed back into his seat with an icy, sickening terror. In a second he was dripping wet with cold sweat. Lightning-swift thoughts flashed through his mind. It had been one of his platitudes that he was not afraid of death. Yet here he was a shaking, helpless coward. What had he learned about either life or death? Would this dark savage plunge him into the unknown? It was then that Shefford realized his hollow philosophy and the bittersweetness of life. He had a brain and a soul, and between them he might have worked out his salvation. But what were they to this ruthless night-wanderer, this raw and horrible wildness of the desert?

Incapable of voluntary movement, with tongue cleaving to the roof of his mouth, Shefford watched the horseman and the half-poised gun. It was not yet levelled. Then it dawned upon Shefford that the stranger's head was turned a little, his ear to the wind. He was listening. His horse was listening. Suddenly he straightened up, wheeled his horse, and trotted away into the darkness. But he did not climb the ridge down which he had come.

Shefford heard the click of hoofs upon the stony trail. Other horses and riders were descending into the canyon. They had been the cause of his deliverance, and in the relaxation of feeling he almost fainted. Then he sat there, slowly recovering, slowly ceasing to tremble, divining that this situation was somehow to change his attitude toward life.

Three horses, two with riders, moved in dark shapes across the skyline above the ridge, disappeared as had

Shefford's first visitor, and then rode into the light. Shefford saw two Indians—a man and a woman; then with surprise recognized the latter to be the Indian girl he had met at Red Lake. He was still more surprised to recognize in the third horse the one he had lost at the last camp. Shefford rose, a little shaky on his legs, to thank these Indians for a double service. The man slipped from his saddle and his moccasined feet thudded lightly. He was tall, lithe, erect, a singularly graceful figure, and as he advanced Shefford saw a dark face and sharp, dark eyes. The Indian was bareheaded, with his hair bound in a band. He resembled the girl, but appered to have a finer face.

"How do?" he said, in a voice low and distinct. He extended his hand, and Shefford felt a grip of steel. He returned the greeting. Then the Indian gave Shefford the bridle of the horse, and made signs that appeared to indicate the horse had broken his hobbles and strayed. Shefford thanked him. Thereupon the Indian unsaddled and led the horses away, evidently to water them. The girl remained behind. Shefford addressed her, but she was shy and did not respond. He then set about cooking a meal for his visitors, and was busily engaged at this when the Indian returned without the horses. Presently Shefford resumed his seat by the fire and watched the two eat what he had prepared. They certainly were hungry and soon had the pans and cups empty. Then the girl drew back a little into the shadow, while the man sat with his legs crossed and his feet tucked under him.

His dark face was smooth, yet it seemed to have lines under the surface. Shefford was impressed. He had never seen an Indian who interested him as this one. Looked at superficially, he appeared young, wild, silent, locked in his primeval apathy, just a healthy savage. But looked at more attentively, he appeared matured, even old, a strange, sad, brooding figure, with a burden on his shoulders. Shefford found himself growing curious.

"What place?" asked Shefford, waving his hand toward the dark opening between the black cliffs.

"Sagi," replied the Indian.

That did not mean anything to Shefford, and he asked if the Sagi was the pass, but the Indian shook his head.

"Wife?" asked Shefford, pointing to the girl.

The Indian shook his head again. *"Bi-la,"* he said.

"What you mean?" asked Shefford. "What *bi-la?*"

"Sister," replied the Indian. He spoke the word reluctantly, as if the white man's language did not please him, but the clearness and correct pronunciation surprised Shefford.

"What name—what call her?" he went on.

"Glen Naspa."

"What your name?" inquired Shefford, indicating the Indian.

"Nas Ta Bega," answered the Indian.

"Navajo?"

The Indian bowed with what seemed pride and stately dignity.

"My name John Shefford. Come far 'way back toward rising sun. Come stay here long."

Nas Ta Bega's dark eyes were fixed steadily upon Shefford. He reflected that he could not remember having felt so penetrating a gaze. But neither the Indian's eyes nor face gave any clue to his thoughts.

"Navajo no savvy Jesus Christ," said the Indian, and his voice rolled out low and deep.

Shefford felt both amaze and pain. The Indian had taken him for a missionary.

"No!... Me no missionary," cried Shefford, and he flung up a passionately repudiating hand.

A singular flash shot from the Indian's dark eyes. It struck Shefford even at this stinging moment when the past came back.

"Trade—buy wool—blanket?" queried Nas Ta Bega.

"No," replied Shefford. "Me want ride—walk far." He waved his hand to indicate a wide sweep of territory. "Me sick."

Nas Ta Bega laid a significant finger upon his lungs.

"No," replied Shefford. "Me strong. Sick here." And with motions of his hands he tried to show that his was a trouble of the heart.

Shefford received instant impression of this Indian's intelligent comprehension, but he could not tell just what had given him the feeling. Nas Ta Bega rose then and walked away into the shadow. Shefford heard him working around the dead cedar-tree, where he had probably gone to get fire-wood. Then Shefford heard a splintering crash, which was followed by a crunching, bumping sound. Presently he was astounded to see the Indian enter the lighted circle dragging the whole cedar-tree, trunk first. Shefford would have doubted the ability of two men to drag that tree, and here came Nas Ta Bega, managing it easily. He laid the trunk on the fire, and then proceeded to break off small branches, to place them advantageously where the red coals kindled them into a blaze.

The Indian's next move was to place his saddle, which he evidently meant to use for a pillow. Then he spread a goat-skin on the ground, lay down upon it, with his back to the fire, and, pulling a long-haired saddle-blanket over his shoulders, he relaxed and became motionless. His sister, Glen Naspa, did likewise, except that she stayed farther away from the fire, and she had a larger blanket, which covered her well. It appeared to Shefford that they went to sleep at once.

Shefford felt as tired as he had ever been, but he did not think he could soon drop into slumber, and in fact he did not want to.

There was something in the companionship of these Indians that he had not experienced before. He still had a strange and weak feeling—the aftermath of that fear which had sickened him with its horrible icy grip. Nas Ta Bega's arrival had frightened away that dark and silent prowler of the night; and Shefford was convinced the Indian had saved his life. The measure of his gratitude was a source of wonder to him. Had he cared so much for life? Yes—he had, when face to face with death. That was something to know. It helped him. And he gathered from his strange feelings that the romantic quest which had brought him into the wilderness might turn out to be an antidote for the morbid bitterness of heart.

With new sensations had come new thoughts. Right

then it was very pleasant to sit in the warmth and light of the roaring cedar fire. There was a deep-seated ache of fatigue in his bones. What joy it was to rest! He had felt the dry scorch of desert thirst and the pang of hunger. How wonderful to learn the real meaning of water and food! He had just finished the longest, hardest day's work of his life! Had that anything to do with a something almost like peace which seemed to hover near in the shadows, trying to come to him? He had befriended an Indian girl, and now her brother had paid back the service. Both the giving and receiving were somehow sweet to Shefford. They opened up hitherto vague channels of thought. For years he had imagined he was serving people, when he had never lifted a hand. A blow given in the defence of an Indian girl had somehow operated to make a change in John Shefford's existence. It had liberated a spirit in him. Moreover, it had worked its influence outside his mind. The Indian girl and her brother had followed his trail to return his horse, perhaps to guide him safely, but, unknowingly perhaps, they had done infinitely more than that for him. As Shefford's eye wandered over the dark, still figures of the sleepers he had a strange, dreamy premonition, or perhaps only a fancy, that there was to be more come of this fortunate meeting.

For the rest, it was good to be there in the speaking silence, to feel the heat on his outstretched palms and the cold wind on his cheek, to see the black wall lifting its bold outline and the crags reaching for the white stars.

The stamping of horses awoke Shefford. He saw a towering crag, rosy in the morning light, like a huge red spear splitting the clear blue of the sky. He got up, feeling cramped and sore, yet with unfamiliar exhilaration. The whipping air made him stretch his hands to the fire. An aroma of coffee and broiled meat mingled with the fragrance of wood smoke. Glen Naspa was on her knees broiling a rabbit on a stick over the red coals. Nas Ta Bega was saddling the ponies. The canyon appeared to be full of purple shadows under one side of dark cliffs and golden streaks of mist on the other where the sun struck high up on the walls.

"Good morning," said Shefford.

Glen Naspa shyly replied in Navajo.

"How," was Nas Ta Bega's greeting.

In daylight the Indian lost some of the dark sombreness of face that had impressed Shefford. He had a noble head, in poise like that of an eagle; a bold, clean-cut profile, and stern, close-shut lips. His eyes were the most striking and attractive feature about him. They were coal-black and piercing and the intent look out of them seemed to come from a keen and inquisitive mind.

Shefford ate breakfast with the Indians, and then helped with the few preparations for departure. Before they mounted, Nas Ta Bega pointed to horse tracks in the dust. They were those that had been made by Shefford's threatening visitor of the night before. Shefford explained by word and sign, and succeeded at least in showing that he had been in danger. Nas Ta Bega followed the tracks a little way and presently returned.

"Shadd," he said, with an ominous shake of his head. Shefford did not understand whether he meant the name of his visitor or something else, but the menace connected with the word was clear enough.

Glen Naspa mounted her pony, and it was a graceful action that pleased Shefford. He climbed a little stiffly into his own saddle. Then Nas Ta Bega got up and pointed northward.

"Kayenta?" he inquired.

Shefford nodded and then they were off, with Glen Naspa in the lead. They did not climb the trail which they had descended, but took one leading to the right along the base of the slope. Shefford saw down into the red wash that bisected the canyon floor. It was a sheer wall of red clay or loam, a hundred feet high, and at the bottom ran a swift, shallow stream of reddish water. Then for a time a high growth of greasewood hid the surroundings from Shefford's sight. Presently the trail led out into the open, and

Shefford saw that he was at the neck of a wonderful valley that gradually widened with great jagged red peaks on the left and the black mesa, now a mountain, running away to the right. He turned to find that the opening of the Sagi could no longer be seen, and he was conscious of a strong desire to return and explore that canyon.

Soon Glen Naspa put her pony to a long, easy, swinging canter and her followers did likewise. As they got outward into the valley Shefford lost the sense of being overshadowed and crowded by the nearness of the huge walls and crags. The trail appeared level underfoot, but at a distance it was seen to climb. Shefford found where it disappeared over the foot of a slope that formed a graceful rising line up to the cedared flank of the mesa. The valley floor, widening away to the north, remained level and green. Beyond rose the jagged range of red peaks, all strangely cut and slanting. These distant, deceiving features of the country held Shefford's gaze until the Indian drew his attention to things near at hand. Then Shefford saw flocks of sheep dotting the gray-green valley, and bands of beautiful long-maned, long-tailed ponies.

For several miles the scene did not change except that Shefford imagined he came to see where the upland plain ended or at least broke its level. He was right, for presently the Indian pointed, and Shefford went on to halt upon the edge of a steep slope leading down into a valley vast in its barren gray reaches.

"Kayenta," said Nas Ta Bega.

Shefford at first saw nothing except the monotonous gray valley reaching far to the strange, grotesque monuments of yellow cliff. Then, close under the foot of the slope, he espied two squat stone houses with red roofs, and a corral with a pool of water shining in the sun.

The trail leading down was steep and sandy, but it was not long. Shefford's sweeping eyes appeared to take in everything at once—the crude stone structures with their earthen roofs, the piles of dirty wool, the Indians lolling around, the tents, and wagons, and horses, little lazy burrows and dogs, and scattered everywhere, saddles, blankets, guns, and packs.

Then a white man came out of the door. He waved a hand and shouted. Dust and wool and flour were thick upon him. He was muscular and weatherbeaten, and appeared young in activity rather than face. A gun swung at his hip and a row of brass-tipped cartridges showed in his belt. Shefford looked into a face that he thought he had seen before, until he realized the similarity was only the bronze and hard line and rugged cast common to desert men. The gray searching eyes went right through him.

"Glad to see you. Get down and come in. Just heard from an Indian that you were coming. I'm the trader Withers," he said to Shefford. His voice was welcoming and the grip of his hand made Shefford's ache.

Shefford told his name and said he was as glad as he was lucky to arrive at Kayenta.

"Hello! Nas Ta Bega!" exclaimed Withers. His tone expressed a surprise his face did not show. "Did this Indian bring you in?"

Withers shook hands with the Navajo while Shefford briefly related what he owed to him. Then Withers looked at Nas Ta Bega and spoke to him in the Indian tongue.

"Shadd," said Nas Ta Bega.

Withers let out a dry little laugh and his strong hand tugged at his mustache.

"Who's Shadd?" asked Shefford.

"He's a half-breed Ute—bad Indian; outlaw, murderer. He's in with a gang of outlaws who hide in the San Juan country... Reckon you're lucky. How'd you come to be there in the Sagi alone?"

"I travelled from Red Lake. Presbrey, the trader there, advised against it, but I came anyway."

"Well." Withers' gray glance was kind, if it did express the foolhardiness of Shefford's act. "Come into the house.... Never mind the horse. My wife will sure be glad to see you."

Withers led Shefford by the first stone house, which

evidently was the trading-store, into the second. The room Shefford entered was large, with logs smouldering in a huge open fireplace, blankets covering every foot of floor space, Indian baskets and silver ornaments everywhere, and strange Indian designs painted upon the whitewashed walls. Withers called his wife and made her acquainted with Shefford. She was a slight, comely little woman, with keen, earnest, dark eyes. She seemed to be serious and quiet, but she made Shefford feel at home immediately. He refused, however, to accept the room offered him, saying that he meant to sleep out under the open sky. Withers laughed at this and said he understood. Shefford, remembering Presbrey's hunger for news of the outside world, told this trader and his wife all he could think of, and he was listened to with that close attention a traveller always gained in the remote places.

"Sure am glad you rode in," said Withers, for the fourth time. "Now you make yourself at home. Stay here—come over to the store—do what you like. I've got to work. Tonight we'll talk."

Shefford went out with his host. The store was as interesting as Presbrey's, though much smaller and more primitive. It was full of everything, and smelled strongly of sheep and goats. There was a narrow aisle between sacks of flour and blankets on one side and a high counter on the other. Behind this counter Withers stood to wait upon the buying Indians. They sold blankets and skins and bags of wool, and in exchange took silver money. Then they lingered and with slow, staid reluctance bought one thing and then another—flour, sugar, canned goods, coffee, tobacco, ammunition. The counter was never without two or three Indians leaning on their dark, silver-braceleted arms. But as they were slow to sell and buy and go, so were others slow to come in. Their voices were soft and low and it seemed to Shefford they were whispering. He liked to hear them and to look at the banded heads, the long, twisted rolls of black hair tied with white cords, the still dark faces and watchful eyes, the silver ear-rings, the slender, shapely brown hands, the lean and sinewy shapes, the corduroys with a belt and gun, and the small, close-fitting buckskin moccasins buttoned with coins. These Indians all appeared young, and under the quiet, slow demeanor there was fierce blood and fire.

By and by two women came in, evidently squaw and daughter. The former was a huge, stout Indian with a face that was certainly pleasant if not jolly. She had the corners of a blanket tied under her chin and in the folds behind on her broad back was a naked Indian baby, round and black of head, brown-skinned, with eyes as bright as beads. When the youngster caught sight of Shefford he made a startled dive into the sack of the blanket. Manifestly, however, curiosity got the better of fear, for presently Shefford caught a pair of wondering dark eyes peeping at him.

"They're good spenders, but slow," said Withers. "The Navajos are careful and cautious. That's why they're rich. This squaw, Yan As Pa, has flocks of sheep and more mustangs than she knows about."

"Mustangs. So that's what you call the ponies?" replied Shefford.

"Yep. They're mustangs, and mostly wild as jackrabbits."

Shefford strolled outside and made the acquaintance of Wither's helper, a Mormon named Whisner. He was a stockily built man past maturity, and his sun-blistered face and watery eyes told of the open desert. He was engaged in weighing sacks of wool brought in by the Indians. Near by stood a framework of poles from which an immense bag was suspended. From the top of this bag protruded the head and shoulders of an Indian, who appeared to be stamping and packing wool with his feet. He grinned at the curious Shefford. But Shefford was more interested in the Mormon. So far as he knew, Whisner was the first man of that creed he had ever met, and he could scarcely hide his eagerness. Venters' stories had been of a long-past generation of Mormons; fanatical, ruthless, and unchangeable. Shefford did not expect to meet Mormons of this kind. But any man of that religion would have interested him. Besides this, Whisner seemed to bring him closer to that wild secret canyon he had come West to find. Shefford was somewhat amazed and discomfited to have his polite and friendly overtures repulsed. Whisner might have been an Indian. He was cold, incommunicative, aloof, and there was something about him that made the sensitive Shefford feel his presence was resented.

Presently Shefford strolled on to the corral, which was full of shaggy mustangs. They snorted and kicked at him. He had a half-formed wish that he would never be called upon to ride one of those wild brutes, and then he found himself thinking that he would ride one of them, and after a while any of them. Shefford did not understand himself, but he fought his natural instinctive reluctance to meet obstacles, peril, suffering.

He traced the white-bordered little stream that made the pool in the corral, and when he came to where it oozed out of the sand under the bluff he decided that was not the spring which had made Kayenta famous. Presently down below the trading-post he saw a trough from which burros were drinking. Here he found the spring, a deep well of eddying water walled in by stones, and the overflow made a shallow stream meandering away between its borders of alkali, like a crust of salt. Shefford tasted the water. It bit, but it was good.

Shefford had no trouble in making friends with the lazy sleepy-eyed burros. They let him pull their long ears and rub their noses, but the mustangs standing around were unapproachable. They had wild eyes; they raised long ears and looked vicious. He let them alone.

Evidently this trading-post was a great deal busier than Red Lake. Shefford counted a dozen Indians lounging outside, and there were others riding away. Big wagons told how the bags of wool were transported out of the wilds and how supplies were brought in. A wide, hard-packed road led off to the east, and another, not so clearly defined, wound away to the north. And Indian trails streaked off in all directions.

Shefford discovered, however, when he had walked off a

mile or so across the valley to lose sight of the post, that the feeling of wildness and loneliness returned to him. It was a wonderful country. It held something for him besides the possible rescue of an imprisoned girl from a wild canyon.

That night after supper, when Withers and Shefford sat alone before the blazing logs in the huge fireplace, the trader laid his hand on Shefford's and said, with directness and force:

"I've lived my life in the desert. I've met many men and have been a friend to most.... You're no prospector or trader or missionary?"

"No," replied Shefford.

"You've had trouble?"

"Yes."

"Have you come in here to hide? Don't be afraid to tell me. I won't give you away."

"I didn't come to hide."

"Then no one is after you? You've done no wrong?"

"Perhaps I wronged myself, but no one else," replied Shefford, steadily.

"I reckoned so. Well, tell me, or keep your secret—it's all one to me."

Shefford felt a desire to unburden himself. This man was strong, persuasive, kindly. He drew Shefford.

"You're welcome in Kayenta," went on Withers. "Stay as long as you like. I take no pay from a white man. If you want work I have it aplenty."

"Thank you. That is good. I need to work. We'll talk of it later.... But just yet I can't tell you why I came to Kayenta, what I want to do, how long I shall stay. My thoughts put in words would seem so like dreams. Maybe they are dreams. Perhaps I'm only chasing a phantom—perhaps I'm only hunting the treasure at the foot of the rainbow."

"Well, this is the country for rainbows," laughed Withers. "In summer from June to August when it storms we have rainbows that'll make you think you're in another world. The Navajos have rainbow mountains, rainbow canyons, rainbow bridges of stone, rainbow trails. It sure is rainbow country."

That deep and mystic chord in Shefford thrilled. Here it was again—something tangible at the bottom of his dream.

Withers did not wait for Shefford to say any more, and almost as if he read his visitor's mind he began to talk about the wild country he called home.

He had lived at Kayenta for several years—hard and profitless years by reason of marauding outlaws. He could not have lived there at all but for the protection of the Indians. His father-in-law had been friendly with the Navajos and Piutes for many years, and his wife had been brought up among them. She was held in peculiar reverence and affection by both tribes in that part of the country. Probably she knew more of the Indians' habits, religion, and life than any white person in the West. Both tribes were friendly and peaceable, but there were bad Indians, half-breeds, and outlaws that made the trading-post a venture Withers had long considered precarious, and he wanted to move and intended to some day. His nearest white neighbors in New Mexico and Colorado were a hundred miles distant and at some seasons the roads were impassable. To the north, however, twenty miles or so, was situated a Mormon village named Stonebridge. It lay across the Utah line. Withers did some business with this village, but scarcely enough to warrant the risks he had to run. During the last year he had lost several pack-trains, one of which he had never heard of after it left Stonebridge.

"Stonebridge!" exclaimed Shefford, and he trembled. He had heard that name. In his memory it had a place beside the name of another village Shefford longed to speak of to this trader.

"Yes—Stonebridge," replied Withers. "Ever heard the name?"

"I think so. Are there other villages in—in that part of the country?"

"A few, but not close. Glaze is now only a water-hole. Bluff and Monticello are far north across the San

Juan.... There used to be another village—but that wouldn't interest you."

"Maybe it would," replied Shefford, quietly.

But his hint was not taken by the trader. Withers suddenly showed a semblance to the aloofness Shefford had observed in Whisner.

"Withers, pardon an impertinence—I am deeply serious.... Are you a Mormon?"

"Indeed I'm not," replied the trader, instantly.

"Are you for the Mormons or against them?"

"Neither. I get along with them. I know them. I believe they are a misunderstood people."

"That's for them."

"No. I'm only fair-minded."

Shefford paused, trying to curb his thrilling impulse, but it was too strong.

"You said there used to be another village.... Was the name of it—Cottonwoods?"

Withers gave a start and faced round to stare at Shefford in blank astonishment.

"Say, did you give me a straight story about yourself?" he queried, sharply.

"So far as I went," replied Shefford.

"You're no spy on the lookout for sealed wives?"

"Absolutely not. I don't even know what you mean by sealed wives."

"Well, it's damn strange that you'd know the name Cottonwoods.... Yes, that's the name of the village I meant—the one that used to be. It's gone now, all except a few stone walls."

"What became of it?"

"Torn down by Mormons years ago. They destroyed it and moved away. I've heard Indians talk about a grand spring that was there once. It's gone, too. Its name was—let me see—"

"Amber Spring," interrupted Shefford.

"By George, you're right!" rejoined the trader, again amazed. "Shefford, this beats me. I haven't heard that name for ten years. I can't help seeing what a tenderfoot—

171

stranger—you are to the desert. Yet, here you are—speaking of what you should know nothing of.... And there's more behind this."

Shefford rose, unable to conceal his agitation.

"Did you ever hear of a rider named Venters?"

"Rider? You mean a cowboy? Venters. No, I never heard that name."

"Did you ever hear of a gunman named Lassiter?" queried Shefford, with increasing emotion.

"No."

"Did you ever hear of a Mormon woman named—Jane Withersteen?"

"No."

Shefford drew his breath sharply. He had followed a gleam—he had caught a fleeting glimpse of it.

"Did you ever hear of a child—a girl—a woman—called Fay Larkin?"

Withers rose slowly with a paling face.

"If you're a spy it'll go hard with you—though I'm no Mormon," he said, grimly.

Shefford lifted a shaking hand.

"I *was* a clergyman. Now I'm nothing—a wanderer—least of all a spy."

Withers leaned closer to see into the other man's eyes; he looked long and then appeared satisfied.

"I've heard the name Fay Larkin," he said, slowly. "I reckon that's all I'll say till you tell your story."

Shefford stood with his back to the fire and he turned the palms of his hands to catch the warmth. He felt cold. Withers had affected him strangely. What was the meaning of the trader's sombre gravity? Why was the very mention of Mormons attended by something austere and secret?

"My name is John Shefford. I am twenty-four," began Shefford. "My family—"

Here a knock on the door interrupted Shefford.

"Come in," called Withers.

The door opened and like a shadow Nas Ta Bega slipped in. He said something in Navajo to the trader.

"How," he said to Shefford, and extended his hand. He was stately, but there was no mistaking his friendliness. Then he sat down before the fire, doubled his legs under him after the Indian fashion, and with dark eyes on the blazing logs seemed to lose himself in meditation.

"He likes the fire," explained Withers. "Whenever he comes to Kayenta he always visits me like this.... Don't mind him. Go on with your story."

"My family were plain people, well-to-do, and very religious," went on Shefford. "When I was a boy we moved from the country to a town called Beaumont, Illinois. There was a college in Beaumont and eventually I was sent to it to study for the ministry. I wanted to be— But never mind that.... By the time I was twenty-two I was ready for my career as a clergyman. I preached for a year around at different places and then got a church in my home town of Beaumont. I became exceedingly good friends of a man named Venters, who had recently come to Beaumont. He was a singular man. His wife was a strange, beautiful woman, very reserved, and she had wonderful dark eyes. They had money and were devoted to each other, and perfectly happy. They owned the finest horses ever seen in Illinois, and their particular enjoyment seemed to be riding. They were always taking long rides. It was something worth going far for to see Mrs. Venters on a horse.

"It was through my own love of horses that I became friendly with Venters. He and his wife attended my church, and as I got to see more of them, gradually we grew intimate. And it was not until I did get intimate with them that I realized that both seemed to be haunted by the past. They were sometimes sad even in their happiness. They drifted off into dreams. They lived back in another world. They seemed to be listening. Indeed, they were a singularly interesting couple, and I grew genuinely fond of them. By and by they had a little girl whom they named Jane. The coming of the baby made a change in my friends. They were happier, and I observed that the haunting shadow did not so often return.

"Venters had spoken of a journey west that he and his wife meant to take some time. But after the baby came he never mentioned his wife in connection with the trip. I gathered that he felt compelled to go to clear up a mystery or to find something—I did not make out just what. But eventually, and it was about a year ago, he told me his story—the strangest, wildest, and most tragic I ever heard.

"I can't tell it all now. It is enough to say that fifteen years before he had been a rider for a rich Mormon woman named Jane Withersteen, of this village Cottonwoods. She had adopted a beautiful Gentile child named Fay Larkin. Her interest in Gentiles earned the displeasure of her churchmen, and as she was proud there came a breach. Venters and a gunman named Lassiter became involved in her quarrel. Finally Venters took to the canyons. Here in the wilds he found the strange girl he eventually married. For a long time they lived in a wonderful hidden valley, the entrance to which was guarded by a huge balancing rock. Venters got away with the girl. But Lassiter and Jane Withersteen and the child Fay Larkin were driven into the canyon. They escaped to the valley where Venters had lived. Lassiter rolled the balancing rock, and, crashing down the narrow trail, it loosened the weathered walls and closed the narrow outlet forever."

Shefford ended his narrative out of breath, pale and dripping with sweat. Withers sat leaning forward with an expression of intense interest. Nas Ta Bega's easy, graceful pose had succeeded to one of strained rigidity. He seemed a statue of bronze. Could a few intelligible words, Shefford wondered, have created that strange, listening posture?

"Venters got out of Utah, of course, as you know," went on Shefford. "He got out, knowing—as I feel I would have known—that Jane, Lassiter, and little Fay Larkin were shut up, walled up in Surprise Valley. For years Venters considered it would not have been safe for him to venture to rescue them. He had no fears for their lives. They could live in Surprise Valley. But Venters always intended to come back with Bess and find the valley and his friends. No wonder he and Bess were haunted. However, when his wife had the baby that made a difference. It meant he had to go alone. And he was thinking seriously of starting when I— when there were developments that made it desirable for me to leave Beaumont. Venters' story haunted me as he had been haunted. I dreamed of that wild valley—of little Fay Larkin grown to womanhood—such a woman as Bess Venters was. And the longing to come was great.... And, Withers—here I am."

The trader reached out and gave Shefford the grip of a man in whom emotion was powerful, but deep and difficult to express.

"Listen to this.... I wish I could help you. Life is a queer deal.... Shefford, I've got to trust you. Over here in the wild canyon country there's a village of Mormons' sealed wives. It's in Arizona, perhaps twenty miles from here, and near the Utah line. When the United States government began to persecute, or prosecute, the Mormons for polygamy, the Mormons over in Stonebridge took their sealed wives and moved them out of Utah, just across the line. They built houses, established a village there. I'm the only Gentile who knows about it. And I pack supplies every few weeks in to these women. There are perhaps fifty women, mostly young—second or third or fourth wives of Mormons— sealed wives. And I want you to understand that sealed means *sealed* in all that religion or loyalty can get out of the word. There are also some old women and old men in the village, but they hardly count. And there's a flock of the finest children you ever saw in your life.

"The idea of the Mormons must have been to escape prosecution. The law of the government is one wife for each man—no more. All over Utah polygamists have been arrested. The Mormons are deeply concerned. I believe they are a good, law-abiding people. But this law is a direct blow at their religion. In my opinion they can't obey both. And therefore they have not altogether given up plural wives. Perhaps they will some day. I have no proof, but I believe the Mormons of Stonebridge pay secret night visits to their sealed wives across the line in the lonely, hidden village.

"Now once over in Stonebridge I overheard some Mormons talking about a girl who was named Fay Larkin. I never forgot the name. Later I heard the name in this sealed-wife village. But, as I told you, I never heard of Lassiter or Jane Withersteen. Still, if Mormons had found them I would never have heard of it. And Deception Pass—that might be the Sagi.... I'm not surprised at your rainbow-chasing adventure. It's a great story.... This Fay Larkin I've heard of *might* be your Fay Larkin—I almost believe so. Shefford, I'll help you find out."

"Yes, yes—I must know," replied Shefford. "Oh, I hope, I pray we can find her! But—I'd rather she was dead—if she's not still hidden in the valley."

"Naturally. You've dreamed yourself into rescuing this lost Fay Larkin.... But, Shefford, you're old enough to know life doesn't work out as you want it to. One way or another I fear you're in for a bitter disappointment."

"Withers, take me to the village."

"Shefford, you're liable to get in bad out here," said the trader, gravely.

"I couldn't be any more ruined than I am now," replied Shefford, passionately.

"But there's risk in this—risk such as you never had," persisted Withers.

"I'll risk anything."

"Reckon this's a funny deal for a sheep-trader to have on his hands," continued Withers. "Shefford, I like you. I've a mind to see you through this. It's a damn strange story.... I'll tell you what—I will help you. I'll give you a job packing supplies into the village. I meant to turn that over to a Mormon cowboy—Joe Lake. The job shall be yours, and I'll go with you first trip. Here's my hand on it.... Now, Shefford, I'm more curious about you than I was before you told your story. What ruined you? As we're to be partners, you can tell me now. I'll keep your secret. Maybe I can do you good."

Shefford wanted to confess, yet it was hard. Perhaps, had he not been so agitated, he would not have answered to impulse. But this trader was a man—a man of the desert—he would understand.

"I told you I was a clergyman," said Shefford in low voice. "I didn't want to be one, but they made me one. I did my best. I failed.... I had doubts of religion—of the Bible—of God, as my church believed in them. As I grew older thought and study convinced me of the narrowness of religion as my congregation lived it. I preached what I believed. I alienated them. They put me out, took my calling from me, disgraced me, ruined me."

"So that's all!" exclaimed Withers, slowly. "You didn't believe in the God of the Bible.... Well, I've been in the desert long enough to know there *is* a God, but probably not the one your church worships.... Shefford, go to the Navajo for a faith!"

Shefford had forgotten the presence of Nas Ta Bega, and perhaps Withers had likewise. At this juncture the Indian rose to his full height, and he folded his arms to stand with the sombre pride of a chieftain while his dark, inscrutable eyes were riveted upon Shefford. At that moment he seemed magnificent. How infinitely more he seemed than just a common Indian who had chanced to befriend a white man! The difference was obscure to Shefford. But he felt that it was there in the Navajo's mind. Nas Ta Bega's strange look was not to be interpreted. Presently he turned and passed from the room.

"By George!" cried Withers, suddenly, and he pounded his knee with his fist. "I'd forgotten."

"What?" ejaculated Shefford.

"Why, that Indian understood every word we said. He knows English. He's educated. Well, if this doesn't beat me.... Let me tell you about Nas Ta Bega."

Withers appeared to be recalling something half forgotten.

"Years ago, in fifty-seven, I think, Kit Carson with his soldiers chased the Navajo tribes and rounded them up to be put on reservations. But he failed to catch all the members of one tribe. They escaped up into wild canyons like the Sagi. The descendants of these fugitives live there now and are the finest Indians on earth—the finest because they're unspoiled by the white man. Well, as I got the story, years after Carson's round-up one of his soldiers guided some interested travellers in there. When they left they took an Indian boy with them to educate. From what I know of Navajos I'm inclined to think the boy was taken against his parents' wish. Anyway, he was taken. That boy was Nas Ta Bega. The story goes that he was educated somewhere. Years afterward, and perhaps not long before I came in here, he returned to his people. There have been missionaries and other interested fools who have given Indians a white man's education. In all the instances I know of, these educated Indians returned to their tribes, repudiating the white man's knowledge, habits, life, and religion. I have heard that Nas Ta Bega came back, laid down the white man's clothes along with the education, and never again showed that he had known either.

"You have just seen how strangely he acted. It's almost certain he heard our conversation. Well, it doesn't matter. He won't tell. He can hardly be made to use an English word. Besides, he's a noble red man, if there ever was one. He has been a friend in need to me. If you stay long out here you'll learn something from the Indians. Nas Ta Bega has befriended you, too, it seems. I thought he showed unusal

"Perhaps that was because I saved his sister—well, to be charitable, from the rather rude advances of a white man," said Shefford, and he proceeded to tell of the incident that occurred at Red Lake.

"Willets!" exclaimed Withers, with much the same expression that Presbrey had used. "I never met him. But I know about him. He's—well, the Indians don't like him much. Most of the missionaries are good men—good for the Indians, in a way, but sometimes one drifts out here who is bad. A bad missionary teaching religion to savages! Queer, isn't it! The queerest part is the white people's blindness— the blindness of those who send the missionaries. Well, I dare say Willetts isn't very good. When Presbrey said that was Willett's way of teaching religion he meant just what he said. If Willetts drifts over here he'll be risking much.... This you told me explains Nas Ta Bega's friendliness toward you, and also sending his sister Glen Naspa to live with relatives up in the pass. She had been living near Red Lake."

"Do you mean Nas Ta Bega wants to keep his sister far removed from Willetts?" inquired Shefford.

"I mean that," replied Withers, "and I hope he's not too late."

Later Shefford went outdoors to walk and think. There was no moon, but the stars made light enough to cast his shadow on the ground. The dark, illimitable expanse of blue sky seemed to be glittering with numberless points of fire. The air was cold and still. A dreaming silence lay over the land. Shefford saw and felt all these things, and their effect was continuous and remained with him and helped calm him. He was conscious of a burden removed from his mind. Confession of his secret had been like tearing a thorn from his flesh, but, once done, it afforded him relief and a singular realization that out here it did not matter much. In a crowd of men all looking at him and judging him by their standards he had been made to suffer. Here, if he were judged at all, it would be by what he could do, how he sustained himself and helped others.

He walked far across the valley toward the low bluffs, but they did not seem to get any closer. And, finally, he stopped beside a stone and looked around at the strange horizon and up at the heavens. He did not feel utterly aloof from them, nor alone in a waste, nor a useless atom amid incomprehensible forces. Something like a loosened mantle fell from about him, dropping down at his feet; and all at once he was conscious of freedom. He did not understand in the least why abasement left him, but it was so. He had come a long way, in bitterness, in despair, believing himself to be what men had called him. The desert and the stars and the wind, the silence of the night, the loneliness of this vast country where there was room for a thousand cities—these somehow vaguely, yet surely, bade him lift his head. They withheld their secret, but they made a promise. The thing which he had been feeling every day and every night was a strange enveloping comfort. And it was at this moment that Shefford, divining whence his help was to come, embraced all that wild and speaking nature around and above and surrendered himself utterly.

"I am young. I am free. I have my life to live," he said. "I'll be a man. I'll take what comes. Let me learn here!"

When he had spoken out, settled once and for ever his attitude toward his future, he seemed to be born again, wonderfully alive to the influences around him, ready to trust what yet remained a mystery.

Then his thoughts reverted to Fay Larkin. Could this girl be known to the Mormons? It was possible. Fay Larkin was an unusual name. Deep into Shefford's heart had sunk the story Venters had told. Shefford found that he had unconsciously created a like romance—he had been loving a wild and strange and lonely girl, like beautiful Bess Venters. It was a shock to learn the truth, but, as it had been only a dream, it could hardly be vital.

Shefford retraced his steps toward the post. Half-way back he espied a tall, dark figure moving toward him, and presently the shape and the step seemed familiar. Then he recognized Nas Ta Bega. Soon they were face to face. Shefford felt that the Indian had been trailing him over the sand, and that this was to be a significant meeting. Remembering Withers' revelation about the Navajo, Shefford scarcely knew how to approach him now. There was no difference to be made out in Nas Ta Bega's dark face and inscrutable eyes, yet there was a difference to be felt in his presence. But the Indian did not speak, and turned to walk by Shefford's side. Shefford could not long be silent.

"Nas Ta Bega, were you looking for me?" he asked.

"You had no gun," replied the Indian.

But for his very low voice, his slow speaking of the words, Shefford would have thought him a white man. For Shefford there was indeed instinct in this meeting, and he turned to face the Navajo.

"Withers told me you had been educated, that you came back to the desert, that you never showed your training .... Nas Ta Bega, did you understand all I told Withers?"

"Yes," replied the Indian.

"You won't betray me?"

"I am a Navajo."

"Nas Ta Bega, you trail me—you say I had no gun." Shefford wanted to ask this Indian if he cared to be the white man's friend, but the question was not easy to put, and, besides, seemed unnecessary. "I am alone and strange in this wild country. I must learn."

"Nas Ta Bega will show you the trails and the waterholes and how to hide from Shadd."

"For money—for silver you will do this?" inquired Shefford.

Shefford felt that the Indian's silence was a rebuke. He remembered Withers' singular praise of this red man. He realized he must change his idea of Indians.

"Nas Ta Bega, I know nothing. I feel like a child in the wilderness. When I speak it is out of the mouths of those who have taught me. I must find a new voice and a new life.... You heard my story to Withers. I am an outcast from my own people. If you will be my friend—be so."

The Indian clasped Shefford's hand and held it in a response that was more beautiful for its silence. So they stood for a moment in the starlight.

"Nas Ta Bega, what did Withers mean when he said go to the Navajo for a faith?" asked Shefford.

"He meant the desert is my mother.... Will you go with Nas Ta Bega into the canyons and the mountains?"

"Indeed I will."

They unclasped hands and turned toward the trading-post.

"Nas Ta Bega, have you spoken my tongue to any other white man since you returned to your home?" asked Shefford.

"No."

"Why do you—why are you different for me?"

The Indian maintained silence.

"Is it because of—of Glen Naspa?" inquired Shefford.

Nas Ta Bega stalked on, still silent, but Shefford divined that, although his service to Glen Naspa would never be forgotten, still it was not wholly responsible for the Indian's subtle sympathy.

"Bi Nai! The Navajo will call his white friend Bi Nai—brother," said Nas Ta Bega, and he spoke haltingly, not as if words were hard to find, but strange to speak. "I was stolen from my mother's hogan and taken to California. They kept me ten years in a mission at San Bernardino and four years in a school. They said my color and my hair were all that was left of the Indian in me. But they could not see my heart. They took fourteen years of my life. They wanted to make me a missionary among my own people. But the white man's ways and his life and his God are not the Indian's. They never can be."

How strangely productive of thought for Shefford to hear the Indian talk! What fatality in this meeting and friendship! Upon Nas Ta Bega had been forced education, training, religion and that had made him something more and something less than an Indian. It was something assimilated from the white man which made the Indian unhappy and alien in his own home—something meant to be good for him and his kind that had ruined him. For Shefford felt the passion and the tragedy of this Navajo.

"Bi Nai, the Indian is dying!" Nas Ta Bega's low voice was deep and wonderful with its intensity of feeling. "The white man robbed the Indian of lands and homes, drove him into the deserts, made him a gaunt and sleepless spiller of blood.... The blood is all spilled now, for the Indian is broken. But the white man sells him rum and seduces his daughters.... He will not leave the Indian in peace with his own God!... Bi Nai, the Indian is dying!"

The home of Nas Ta Bega lay far up the cedared slope, with the craggy yellow cliffs and the black canyons and the pine-fringed top of Navajo Mountain behind, and to the fore the vast, rolling descent of cedar groves and sage flats and sandy washes. No dim, dark range made bold outline along the horizon; the stretch of gray and purple and green extended to the blue line of the sky.

Down the length of one sage level Shefford saw a long lane where the brush and grass had been beaten flat. This, the Navajo said, was a track where the young braves had raced their mustangs and had striven for supremacy before the eyes of maidens and the old people of the tribe.

"Nas Ta Bega, did you ever race here?" asked Shefford.

"I am a chief by birth. But I was stolen from my home, and now I cannot ride well enough to race the braves of my tribe," the Indian replied bitterly.

In another place Nas Ta Bega halted his horse and called Shefford's attention to a big yellow rock lying along the trail. And then he spoke in Navajo to the Mormon cowboy, Joe Lake.

"I've heard of this stone—Isende Aha," said Joe, after Nas Ta Bega had spoken. "Get down, and let's see."

Shefford dismounted, but the Indian kept his seat in the saddle.

Joe placed a big hand on the stone and tried to move it. According to Shefford's eye measurement the stone was nearly oval, perhaps three feet high, by a little over two in width. Joe threw off his sombrero, took a deep breath, and, bending over, clasped the stone in his arms. He was an exceedingly heavy and powerful man, and it was plain to Shefford that he meant to lift the stone if that were possible. Joe's broad shoulders strained, flattened; his arms bulged, his joints cracked, his neck corded, and his face turned black. By gigantic effort he lifted the stone and moved it about six inches. Then as he released his hold he fell, and when he sat up his face was wet with sweat.

"Try it," he said to Shefford, with his lazy smile. "See if you can heave it."

Shefford was strong, and there had been a time when he took pride in his strength. Something in Joe's supreme effort and in the gloom of the Indian's eyes made Shefford curious about the stone. He bent over and grasped it as Joe had done. He braced himself and lifted with all his power, until a red blur obscured his sight and shooting stars seemed to explode in his head. But he could not even stir the stone.

"Shefford, maybe you'll be able to heft it some day," observed Joe. Then he pointed to the stone and addressed Nas Ta Bega.

The Indian shook his head and spoke for a moment.

"This is the Isende Aha of the Navajos," explained Joe. "The young braves are always trying to carry this stone. As soon as one of them can carry it he is a man. He who carries it farthest is the biggest man. And just so soon as any Indian can no longer lift it he is old. Nas Ta Bega says the stone has been carried two miles in his lifetime. His own father carried it the length of six steps."

"Well! It's plain to me that I am not a man," said Shefford, "or else I am old."

Joe Lake drawled his lazy laugh and, mounting, rode up the trail. But Shefford lingered beside the Indian.

"Bi Nai," said Nas Ta Bega, "I am a chief of my tribe, but I have never been a man. I never lifted that stone. See what the pale-face education has done for the Indian!"

The Navajo's bitterness made Shefford thoughtful. Could greater injury be done to man than this—to rob him of his heritage of strength?

Joe drove the bobbing pack-train of burros into the cedars where the smoke of the hogans curled upward, and soon the whistling of mustangs, the barking of dogs, the bleating of sheep, told of his reception. And presently Shefford was in the midst of an animated scene. Great, woolly, fierce dogs, like wolves, ran out to meet the visitors. Sheep and goats were everywhere, and little lambs scarcely able to walk, with others frisky and frolicsome. There were pure-white lambs, and some that appeared to be painted, and some so beautiful with their fleecy white all except black faces or ears or tails or feet. They ran right under Nack-yal's legs and bumped against Shefford, and kept bleating their thin-piped welcome. Under the cedars surrounding the several hogans were mustangs that took Shefford's eye. He saw an iron-gray with white mane and tail sweeping to the ground; and a fiery black, wilder than any other beast he had ever seen; and a pinto as wonderfully painted as the little lambs; and, most striking of all, a pure, cream-coloured mustang with grace and fine lines and beautiful mane and tail, and, strange to see, eyes as blue as azure. This albino mustang came right up to Shefford, an action in singular contrast with that of the others, and showed a tame and friendly spirit toward him and Nack-yal. Indeed, Shefford had reason to feel ashamed of Nack-yal's temper or jealousy.

The first Indians to put in an appearance were a flock of children, half naked, with tangled manes of raven-black hair and skin like gold bronze. They appeared bold and shy by turns. Then a little, sinewy man, old and beaten and gray, came out of the principal hogan. He wore a blanket round his bent shoulders. His name was Hosteen Doetin, and it meant gentle man. His fine, old, wrinkled face lighted with a smile of kindly interest. His squaw followed him, and she was as venerable as he. Shefford caught a glimpse of the shy, dark Glen Naspa, Nas Ta Bega's sister, but she did not come out. Other Indians appeared, coming from adjacent hogans.

Nas Ta Bega turned the mustangs loose among those Shefford had noticed, and presently there rose a snorting, whistling, kicking, plunging melee. A cloud of dust hid them, and then a thudding of swift hoofs told of a run through the cedars. Joe Lake began picking over stacks of goatskins, and bags of wool that were piled against the hogan.

"Reckon we'll have one grand job packing out this load," he growled. "It's not so heavy, but awkward to pack."

It developed, presently, from talk with the old Navajo, that this pile was only a half of the load to be packed to Kayenta, and the other half was round the corner of the mountain in the camp of the Piutes. Hosteen Doetin said he would send to the camp and have the Piutes bring their share over. The suggestion suited Joe, who wanted to save his burros as much as possible. Accordingly, a messenger was dispatched to the Piute camp. And Shefford, with time on his hands and poignant memory to combat, decided to recall his keen interest in the Navajo, and learn, if possible, what the Indian's life was like. What would a day of his natural life be?

In the gray of dawn, when the hush of the desert night still lay deep over the land, the Navajo stirred in his blanket and began to chant to the morning light. It began very soft and low, a strange, broken murmur, like the music of a brook, and as it swelled that weird and mournful tone was slowly lost in one of hope and joy. The Indian's soul was coming out of night, blackness, the sleep that resembled death, into the day, the light that was life.

Then he stood in the door of his hogan, his blanket around him, and faced the east.

Night was lifting out of the clefts and ravines; the rolling cedar ridges and the sage flats were softly gray, with thin veils like smoke mysteriously rising and vanishing; the colorless rocks were changing. A long, horizon-wide gleam of light, rosiest in the centre, lay low down in the east and momentarily brightened. One by one the stars in the deep-blue sky paled and went out and the blue dome changed and lightened. Night had vanished on invisible wings and silence broke to the music of a mocking-bird. The rose in the east deepened. A wisp of cloud turned gold. Dim distant mountains showed dark against the red, and low down in a notch a rim of fire appeared. Over the soft ridges and valleys crept a wondrous transfiguration. It was as if every blade of grass, every leaf of sage, every twig of cedar, the flowers, the trees, the rocks came to life at sight of the sun. The red disk rose, and a golden fire burned over the glowing face of that lonely waste.

The Navajo, dark, stately, inscrutable, faced the sun—his god. This was his Great Spirit. The desert was his mother, but the sun was his life. To the keeper of the winds and rains, to the master of light, to the maker of fire, to the giver of life the Navajo sent up his prayer:

*Of all the good things of the Earth let me always
   have plenty.*

*Of all the beautiful things of the Earth let me
  always have plenty.
Peacefully let my horses go and peacefully let my
  sheep go.
God of the Heavens, give me many sheep and
  horses.
God of the Heavens, help me to talk straight.
Goddess of the Earth, my Mother, let me walk
  straight.
Now all is well, now all is well, now all is well, now
  all is well.*

Hope and faith were his.

A chief would be born to save the vanishing tribe of Navajos. A bride would rise from a wind—kiss of the lilies in the moonlight.

He drank from the clear, cold spring bubbling from under mossy rocks. He went into the cedars, and the tracks in the trails told him of the visitors of night. His mustangs whistled to him from the ridge-tops, standing clear with heads up and manes flying, and then trooped down through the sage. The shepherd dogs, guardians of the flocks, barked him a welcome, and the sheep bleated and the lambs pattered round him.

In the hogan by the warm, red fire his women baked his bread and cooked his meat. And he satisfied his hunger. Then he took choice meat to the hogan of a sick relative, and joined in the song and the dance and the prayer that drove away the evil spirit of illness. Down in the valley, in a sandy, sunny place, was his corn field, and here he turned in the water from the ditch, and worked awhile, and went his contented way.

He loved his people, his women, and his children. To his son he said: "Be bold and brave. Grow like a pine. Work and ride and play that you may be strong. Talk straight. Love your brother. Give half to your friend. Honour your mother that you may honour your wife. Pray and listen to your gods."

Then with his gun and his mustang he climbed the slope of the mountain. He loved the solitude, but he was never alone. There were voices on the wind and steps on his trail. The lofty pine, the lichened rock, the tiny bluebell, the seared crag—all whispered their secrets. For him their spirits spoke. In the morning light Old Stone Face, the mountain, was a red god calling him to the chase. He was a brother of the eagle, at home on the heights where the winds swept and the earth lay revealed below.

In the golden afternoon, with the warm sun on his back and the blue canyons at his feet, he knew the joy of doing nothing. He did not need rest, for he was never tired. The sage-sweet breath of the open was thick in his nostrils, the silence that had so many whisperings was all about him, the loneliness of the wild was his. His falcon eye saw mustang and sheep, the puff of dust down on the cedar level, the Indian riding on a distant ridge, the gray walls, and the blue clefts. Here was home, still free, still wild, still untainted. He saw the eyes of his ancestors. He felt them around him. They had gone into the elements from which their voices came on the wind. They were the watchers on his trails.

At sunset he faced the west, and this was his prayer:
Great Spirit, God of my Fathers,
Keep my horses in the night.
Keep my sheep in the night.
Keep my family in the night.
Let me wake to the day.
Let me be worthy of the light.
Now all is well, now all is well,
Now all is well, now all is well.

And he watched the sun go down and the gold sink from the peaks and the red die out of the west and the gray shadows creep out of the canyons to meet the twilight and the slow, silent, mysterious approach of night with its gift of stars.

Night fell. The white stars blinked. The wind sighed in the cedars. The sheep bleated. The shepherd dogs bayed the mourning coyotes. And the Indian lay down in his blankets with his dark face tranquil in the starlight. All was well in his lonely world. Phantoms hovered, illness lingered, injury and pain and death were there, the shadow of a strange white hand flitted across the face of the moon—but now all was well—the Navajo had prayed to the god of his Fathers. Now all was well!

And this, thought Shefford in revolt, was what the white man had killed in the Indian tribes; was reaching out now to kill in this wild remnant of the Navajos. The padre, the trapper, the trader, the prospector, and the missionary—so the white man had come, some of him good, no doubt, but more of him evil; and the young brave learned a thirst that could never be quenched at the cold, sweet spring of his forefathers, and the young maiden burned with a fever in her blood, and lost the sweet, strange, wild fancies of her tribe.

Joe Lake came to Shefford and said, "Withers told me you had a mix-up with a missionary at Red Lake."

"Yes, I regret to say," replied Shefford.

"About Glen Naspa?"

"Yes, Nas Ta Bega's sister."

"Withers just mentioned it. Who was the missionary?"

"Willetts, so Presbrey, the trader, said."

"What'd he look like?"

Shefford recalled the smooth, brown face, the dark eyes, the weak chin, the mild expression, and the soft, lax figure of the missionary.

"Can't tell by what you said," went on Joe. "But I'll bet a peso to a horse-hair that's the fellow who's been here. Old Hosteen Doetin just told me. First visits he ever had from the priest with the long gown. That's what he called the missionary. These old fellows will never forget what's come down from father to son about the Spanish padres. Well, anyway, Willetts has been here twice after Glen Naspa.

The old chap is impressed, but he doesn't want to let the girl go. I'm inclined to think Glen Naspa would as lief go as stay. She may be a Navajo, but she's a girl. She won't talk much."

"Where's Nas Ta Bega?" asked Shefford.

"He rode off somewhere yesterday. Perhaps to the Piute camp. These Indians are slow. They may take a week to pack that load over here. But if Nas Ta Bega or some one doesn't come with a message today I'll ride over there myself."

"Joe, what do you think about this missionary?" queried Shefford, bluntly.

"Reckon there's not much to think, unless you see him or find out something. I heard of Willetts before Withers spoke of him. He's friendly with Mormons. I understand he's worked for Mormon interests, someway or other. That's on the quiet. Savvy? This matter of him coming after Glen Naspa, reckon that's all right. The missionaries all go after the young people. What'd be the use to try to convert the old Indians? No, the missionary's work is to educate the Indian, and, of course, the younger he is the better."

"You approve of the missionary?"

"Shefford, if you understood a Mormon you wouldn't ask that. Did you ever read or hear of Jacob Hamblin?... Well, he was a Mormon missionary among the Navajos. The Navajos were as fierce as Apaches till Hamblin worked among them. He made them friendly to the white man."

"That doesn't prove he made converts of them," replied Shefford, still bluntly.

"No. For the matter of that, Hamblin let religion alone. He made presents, then traded with them, then taught them useful knowledge. Mormon or not, Shefford, I'll admit this: A good man, strong with his body, and learned in ways with his hands, with some knowledge of medicine, can better the condition of these Indians. But just as soon as he begins to preach his religion, then his influence wanes. That's natural. These heathen have their ideals, their gods."

"Which the white man should leave them!" replied Shefford, feelingly.

"That's a matter of opinion. But don't let's argue... Willets is after Glen Naspa. And if I know Indian girls he'll persuade her to go to his school."

"Persuade her?" Then Shefford broke off and related the incident that had occurred at Red Lake.

"Reckon any means justifies the end," replied Joe, imperturbably. "Let him talk love to her or rope her or beat her, so long as he makes a Christian of her."

Shefford felt a hot flush and had difficulty in controlling himself. From this single point of view the Mormon was impossible to reason with.

"That, too, is a matter of opinion. We won't discuss it," continued Shefford. "But—if old Hosteen Doetin objects to the girl leaving, and if Nas Ta Bega does the same, won't that end the matter?"

"Reckon not. The end of the matter is Glen Naspa. If she wants to go she'll go."

Shefford thought best to drop the discussion. For the first time he had occasion to be repelled by something in this kind and genial Mormon, and he wanted to forget it. Just as he had never talked about men to the sealed wives in the hidden valley, so he could not talk of women to Joe Lake.

Nas Ta Bega did not return that day, but next morning a messenger came calling Lake to the Piute camp. Shefford spent the morning high on the slope, learning more with every hour in the silence and loneliness, that he was stronger of soul than he had dared to hope, and that the added pain which had come to him could be borne.

Upon his return toward camp, in the cedar grove, he caught sight of Glen Naspa with a white man. They did not see him. When Shefford recognized Willetts an embarrassment as well as an instinct made him halt and step into a bushy, low-branched cedar. It was not his intention to spy on him. He merely wanted to avoid a meeting. But the missionary's hand on the girl's arm, and her uplifted head, her pretty face, strange, intent, troubled, struck Shefford with an unusual and irresistible curiosity. Willetts was talking earnestly; Glen Naspa was listening intently. Shefford watched long enough to see that the girl loved the missionary, and that he reciprocated or was pretending. His manner scarcely savoured of pretence, Shefford concluded, as he slipped away under the trees.

He did not go at once into camp. He felt troubled, and wished that he had not encountered the two. His duty in the matter, of course, was to tell Nas Ta Bega what he had seen. Upon reflection Shefford decided to give the missionary the benefit of a doubt; and if he really cared for the Indian girl, and admitted or betrayed it, to think all the better of him for the fact. Glen Naspa was certainly pretty enough, and probably lovable enough, to please any lonely man in this desert. The pain and the yearning in Shefford's heart made him lenient. He had to fight himself—not to forget, for that was impossible—but to keep rational and sane when a white flower-like face haunted him and a voice called.

The cracking of hard hoofs on stones caused him to turn toward camp, and as he emerged from the cedar grove he saw three Indian horsemen ride into the cleared space before the hogans. They were superbly mounted and well armed, and impressed him as being different from the Navajos. Perhaps they were Piutes. They dismounted and led the mustangs down to the pool below the spring. Shefford saw another mustang, standing bridle down and carrying a pack behind the saddle. Some squaws with children hanging behind their skirts were standing at the door of Hosteen Doetin's hogan. Shefford glanced in to see Glen Naspa, pale, quiet, almost sullen. Willetts stood with his hands spread. The old Navajo's seamed face worked convulsively as he tried to lift his bent form to some semblance of dignity, and his voice rolled out, sonorously: "Me no savvy Jesus Christ! Me hungry!... Me no eat Jesus Christ!"

Shefford drew back as if he had received a blow. That had been Hosteen Doetin's reply to the importunities of the missionary. The old Navajo could work no longer. His sons were gone. His squaw was worn out. He had no one save Glen Naspa to help him. She was young, strong. He was hungry. What was the white man's religion to him?

With long, swift stride Shefford entered the hogan,

Willetts, seeing him, did not look so mild as Shefford had him pictured in memory, nor did he appear surprised. Shefford touched Hosteen Doetin's shoulder and said, "Tell me."

The aged Navajo lifted a shaking hand.

"Me no savvy Jesus Christ! Me hungry... Me no eat Jesus Christ!"

Shefford then made signs that indicated the missionary's intention to take the girl away.

"Him come—big talk—Jesus—all Jesus.... Me no want Glen Naspa go," replied the Indian.

Shefford turned to the missionary.

"Willetts, is he a relative of the girl?"

"There's some blood tie, I don't know what. But it's not close," replied Willetts.

"Then don't you think you'd better wait till Nas Ta Bega returns? He's her brother."

"What for?" demanded Willetts. "That Indian may be gone a week. She's willing to go."

Shefford looked at the girl.

"Glen Naspa, do you want to go?"

She was shy, ashamed, and silent, but manifestly willing to accompany the missionary. Shefford pondered a moment. How he hoped Nas Ta Bega would come back! It was thought of the Indian that made Shefford stubborn. What his stand ought to be was hard to define, unless he answered to impulse; and here in the wilds he had become imbued with the idea that his impulses and instincts were no longer false.

"Willetts, what do you want with the girl?" queried Shefford, coolly, and at the question he seemed to find himself. He peered deliberately and searchingly into the other's face. The missionary's gaze shifted and a tinge of red crept up from under his collar.

"Absurd thing to ask a missionary!" he burst out, impatiently.

"Do you care for Glen Naspa?"

"I care as God's disciple—who cares to save the soul of heathen," he replied, with the lofty tone of prayer.

"Has Glen Naspa no—no other interest in you—except to be taught religion?"

The missionary's face flamed, and his violent tremor showed that under his exterior there was a different man.

"What right have you to question me?" he demanded. "You're an adventurer—an outcast. I've my duty here. I'm a missionary with church and state and government behind me."

"Yes, I'm an outcast," replied Shefford, bitterly. "And you may be all you say. But we're alone now out here on the desert. And this girl's brother is absent. You haven't answered me yet.... Is there anything between you and Glen Naspa except religion?"

"No, you insulting beggar!"

Shefford had forced the reply that he had expected and which damned the missionary beyond any consideration.

"Willets, you are a liar?" said Shefford, steadily.

"And what are you?" cried Willetts, in shrill fury. "I've heard all about you. Heretic! Atheist! Driven from your church! Hated and scorned for your blasphemy!"

Then he gave way to ungovernable rage, and cursed Shefford as a religious fanatic might have cursed the most debased of sinners. Shefford heard with the blood beating, strangling the pulse in his ears. Somehow this missionary had learned his secret. And the terms of disgrace were coals of fire upon Shefford's head. Strangely, however, he did not bow to them, as had been his humble act in the past, when his calumniators had arraigned and flayed him. Passion burned in him now, and hate, for the first time in his life, made a tiger of him. And these raw emotions, new to him, were difficult to control.

"You can't take the girl," he replied, when the other had ceased. "Not without her brother's consent."

"I will take her!"

Shefford threw him out of the hogan and strode after him. Willetts had stumbled. When he straightened up he was white and shaken. He groped for the bridle of his horse while keeping his eyes upon Shefford, and when he found it he whirled quickly, mounted, and rode off. Shefford saw him halt a moment under the cedars to speak with the three strange Indians, and then he galloped away. It came to Shefford then that he had been unconscious of the last strained moment of that encounter. He seemed all cold, tight, locked, and was amazed to find his hand on his gun. Verily the wild environment had liberated strange instincts and impulses, which he had answered. That he had no regrets proved how he had changed.

Shefford heard the old woman scolding. Peering into the hogan, he saw Glen Naspa flounce sullenly down, for all the world like any other thwarted girl. Hosteen Doetin came out and pointed down the slope at the departing missionary.

"Heap talk Jesus—all talk—all Jesus!" he exclaimed, contemptuously. Then he gave Shefford a hard rap on the chest. "Small talk—heap man!"

The matter appeared to be adjusted for the present. But Shefford felt that he had made a bitter enemy, and perhaps a powerful one.

He prepared and ate his supper alone that evening, for Joe Lake and Nas Ta Bega did not put in an appearance. He observed that the three strange Indians, whom he took for Piutes, kept to themselves, and, so far as he knew, had no intercourse with any one at the camp. This would not have seemed unusual, considering the taciturn habit of Indians, had he not remembered seeing Willetts speak to the trio. What had he to do with them? Shefford was considering the situation with vague doubts when, to his relief, the three strangers rode off into the twilight. Then he went to bed.

He was awakened by violence. It was the gray hour before dawn. Dark forms knelt over him. A cloth pressed down hard over his mouth. Strong hands bound it while other strong hands held him. He could not cry out. He could not struggle. A heavy weight, evidently a man, held down his feet. Then he was rolled over, securely bound, and carried, to be thrown like a sack over the back of a horse.

All this happened so swiftly as to be bewildering. He was too astounded to be frightened. As he hung head downward he saw the legs of a horse and a dim trails. A stirrup swung to and fro, hitting him in the face. He began to feel exceedingly uncomfortable, with a rush of blood to his head, and cramps in his arms and legs. This kept on and grew worse for what seemed a long time. Then the horse was stopped and a rude hand tumbled him to the ground. Again he was rolled over on his face. Strong fingers plucked at his clothes, and he believed he was being searched. His captors were as silent as if they had been dumb. He felt when they took his pocketbook and his knife and all that he had. Then they cut, tore, and stripped off all his clothing. He was lifted, carried a few steps, and dropped upon what seemed a soft, low mound, and left lying there still tied and naked. Shefford heard the rustle of sage and the dull thud of hoofs as his assailants went away.

His first sensation was one of immeasurable relief. He had not been murdered. Robbery was nothing. And though roughly handled, he had not been hurt. He associated the assault with the three strange visitors of the preceding day. Still, he had no proof of that. Not the slightest clue remained to help him ascertain who had attacked him.

It might have been a short while or a long one, his mind was so filled with growing conjectures, but a time came when he felt cold. As he lay face down, only his back felt cold at first. He was grateful that he had not been thrown upon the rocks. The ground under him appeared soft, spongy, and gave somewhat as he breathed. He had really sunk down a little in this pile of soft earth. The day was not far off, as he could tell by the brightening of the gray. He began to suffer with the cold, and then slowly he seemed to freeze and grow numb. In an effort to roll over upon his back he discovered that his position, or his being bound, or the numbness of his muscles was responsible for the fact that he could not move. Here was a predicament. It began to look serious. What would a few hours of the powerful sun do to his uncovered skin? Somebody would trail and find him; still, he might not be found soon.

He saw the sky lighten, turn rose and then gold. The sun shone upon him, but some time elapsed before he felt its warmth. All of a sudden a pain, like a sting, shot through his shoulder. He could not see what caused it; probably a bee. Then he felt another upon his leg, and about simultaneously with it a tiny, fiery stab in his side. A sickening sensation pervaded his body, slowly moving, as if poison had entered the blood of his veins. Then a puncture, as from a hot wire, entered the skin of his breast. Unmistakably it was a bite. By dint of great efforts he twisted his head to see a big red ant on his breast. Then he heard a faint sound, so exceedingly faint that he could not tell what it was like. But presently his strained ears detected a low, swift, rustling, creeping sound, like the slipping rattle of an infinite number of tiny bits of moving gravel. Then it was a sound like the seeping of wind-blown sand. Several hot bites occurred at once. And then with his head twisted he saw a red stream of ants pour out of the mound and spill over his quivering flesh.

In an instant he realized his position. He had been dropped intentionally upon an ant-heap, which had sunk with his weight, wedging him between the crusts. At the mercy of those terrible desert ants! A frantic effort to roll out proved futile, as did another and another. His violent muscular contractions infuriated the ants, and in an instant he was writhing in pain so horrible and so unendurable that he nearly fainted. But he was too strong to faint suddenly. A bath of vitriol, a stripping of his skin and red embers of fire thrown upon raw flesh, could not have equalled this. There was fury in the bites and poison in the fangs of these ants. Was this an Indian's brutal trick or was it the missionary's revenge? Shefford realized that it would kill him soon. He sweat what seemed blood, although perhaps the blood came from the bites. A strange, hollow, buzzing roar filled his ears, and it must have been the pouring of the angry ants from their mound.

Then followed a time that was hell—worse than fire, for fire would have given merciful death—agony under which his physical being began spasmodically to jerk and retch— and his eyeballs turned and his breast caved in.

A cry rang through the roar in his ears. "Bi Nai! Bi Nai!"

His fading sight seemed to shade round the dark face of Nas Ta Bega.

Then powerful hands dragged him from the mound, through the grass and sage, rolled him over and over, and brushed his burning skin with strong, swift motions.

That hard experience was but the beginning of many cruel trials for John Shefford.

He never knew who his assailants were, nor their motive other than robbery, and they had gotten little, for they had not found the large sum of money sewed in the lining of his coat. Joe Lake declared it was Shadd's work, and the Mormon showed the stern nature that lay hidden under his habitual mild manner. Nas Ta Bega shook his head and would not tell what he thought. But a somber fire burned in his eyes.

The three started with a heavily laden pack-train and went down the mountain slope into West Canyon. The second day they were shot at from the rim walls. Lake was wounded, hindering the swift flight necessary to escape deeper into the canyon. Here they hid for days, while the Mormon recovered and the Indian took stealthy trips to try to locate the enemy. Lack of water and grass for the burros drove them on. They climbed out of a side canyon, losing several burros on a rough trail, and had proceeded to within half a day's journey of Red Lake when they were attacked while making camp in a cedar grove. Shefford sustained a painful injury to his leg, but, fortunately, the bullet went through without breaking a bone. With that burning pain there came to Shefford the meaning of fight, and his rifle grew hot in his hands. Night alone saved the trio from certain fatality. Under the cover of darkness the Indian helped Shefford to escape. Joe Lake looked out for himself. The pack-train was lost, and the mustangs, except Nack-yal.

Shefford learned what it meant to lie out at night, listening for pursuit, cold to his marrow, sick with dread, and enduring frightful pain from a ragged bullet hole. Next day the Indian led him down into the red basin, where the sun shone hot and the sand reflected the heat. They had no water. A wind arose and the valley became a place of flying sand. Through a heavy, stifling pall Nas Ta Bega somehow got Shefford to the trading-post at Red Lake. Presbrey attended to Shefford's injury and made him comfortable. Next day Joe Lake limped in, surly and somber, with the news that Shadd and eight or ten of his outlaw gang had gotten away with the pack-train.

In short time Shefford was able to ride, and with his companions went over the pass to Kayenta. Withers already knew of his loss, and all he said was that he hoped to meet Shadd some day.

Shefford showed a reluctance to go again to the hidden village in the silent canyon with the rounded walls. The trader appeared surprised, but did not press the point. And Shefford meant sooner or later to tell him, yet never quite reached the point. The early summer brought more work for the little post, and Shefford toiled with the others. He liked the outdoor tasks, and at night was grateful that he was too tired to think. Then followed trips to Durango and Bluff and Monticello. He rode fifty miles a day for may days. He knew how a man fares who packs light and rides far and fast. When the Indian was with him he got along well, but Nas Ta Bega would not go near the towns. Thus many mishaps were Shefford's fortune.

Many and many a mile he trailed his mustang, for Nackyal never forgot the Sagi, and always headed for it when he broke his hobbles. Shefford accompanied an Indian teamster in to Durango with a wagon and four wild mustangs. Upon the return, with a heavy load of supplies, accident put Shefford in charge of the outfit. In despair he had to face the hardest task that could have been given him... to take care of a crippled Indian; catch, water, feed, harness and drive four wild mustangs that did not know him and tried to kill him at every turn, and to get that precious load of supplies home to Kayenta. That he accomplished it proved to him the possibilities of a man, for both endurance and patience. From that time he never gave up in front of any duty.

He rode to Durango and back in record time. Upon one occasion he was lost in a canyon for days, with no food and little water. Upon another he went through a sand-storm in the open desert, facing it in forty miles and keeping to the trail. When he rode in to Kayenta that night the trader, in grim praise, said there was no worse to endure. At Monticello, Shefford stood off a band of desperadoes, and this time Shefford experienced a strange, sickening shock in the wounding of a man. Later he had other fights, but in none of them did he know whether or not he had shed blood.

The heat of midsummer came, when the blistering sun shone, and a hot blast blew across the sand, and the furious storms made floods in the washes. Day and night Shefford was always in the open, and any one who had ever known him in the past would have failed to recognize him now.

In the early fall, with Nas Ta Bega as companion, he set out to the south of Kayenta upon long-neglected business of the trader. They visited Red Lake, Blue Canyon, Keams Canyon, Oribi, the Moki villages, Tuba, Moencopie, and Moen Ave. This trip took many weeks and gave Shefford all the opportunity he wanted to study the Indians, and the conditions near to the border of civilization. He learned the truth about the Indians and the missionaries.

Upon the return trip he rode over the trail he had followed alone to Red Lake and thence on to the Sagi, and it seemed that years had passed since he first entered this wild region which had come to be home, years that had molded him in the stern and fiery crucible of the desert. But he knew he must plunge on and on until he fulfilled his mission—to find Fay Larkin and make her his wife.

ZANE GREY CLASSICS

THE LAST RANGER BT50651 95¢
(Original title: Betty Zane)

A lusty frontier novel. Only Zane Grey could have created such flesh-and-blood characters as fiery Betty Zane; Wetzel, the Indian fighter, McColloch, the brawling empire builder.

**THE SPIRIT OF
THE BORDER** BT50652 95¢

An action-packed Western epic by American's most beloved writer. The story of how a handful of hard-living riflemen stood between the hate-crazed Indians and the greatest massacre in the history of the West.

**ZANE GREY'S GREATEST
ANIMAL STORIES** BT50771 $1.25
Edited by Loren Grey

A superb collection of stories by the greatest Western writer who ever lived. A legendary hunter and sportsman, Zane Grey wrote about men and animals with an intensity that has never been surpassed, not even by Hemingway. A sure seller by a writer whose books sell millions of copies every year.

**ZANE GREY'S
SAVAGE KINGDOM** BT50778 $1.25
Edited by Loren Grey

Man against Nature is the theme, and more often than not, Zane Grey is on the side of the animals.

**ZANE GREY'S GREATEST
WESTERN STORIES** BT50799 $1.25
Edited by Loren Grey

Hell for leather tales by the champion Western writer of all time.

FARGO
Western Adventure Series

by John Benteen

Fargo is a hard-bitten soldier-of-fortune who names his own price. Only a liar or a fool would call him a nice guy, but when he takes a job, he finishes it—no matter how many dead bodies he has to step over.

FARGO   BT50861 $1.25

No matter how dirty the job, Fargo will do it if the price is right. Fargo lives with a gun in his fist. Guns and killing are all he knows. While he lasts, Fargo plans to grab the world by the throat and take what he wants. If the world doesn't like that, it can try to stop him—if it can.

HELL ON WHEELS   BT50889 $1.25
John Benteen

He was a soldier of fortune, for sale to the highest bidder. He had grown up hard and he never looked back. He had joined Teddy Roosevelt's Rough Riders and found his true calling—combat. Fargo set out to get his man and he didn't worry about getting paid if he failed. If he failed, he'd be dead.

THE BORDER JUMPERS   BT50899 $1.25
John Benteen

Cattle rustlers were hitting the spreads of the biggest Texas ranchers. They were striking the most vulnerable, those along the Rio and running the cattle into Mexico. These rustlers were breaking the ranchers. Fargo had to break them.

LASSITER
Western Series

by Jack Slade

Lassiter would shoot his best friend for a new pair of boots. He can be as cold as a corpse in January, as tough as a chuck-wagon steak, and as cruel as a wounded Apache. He has the morals of a jackrabbit, the ethics of a landgrabber, and the conscience of a cold-blooded gunslick.

#18 RIMFIRE   BT50749 95¢

Want to commit suicide? The quickest way is to tangle with Lassiter, the dirtiest, meanest desperado to cross the Mesa. Lassiter is a new breed of Western hero for the new breed of Western reader.

#17 BLOOD RIVER   BT50734 95¢

Lassiter was a soldier of fortune with a gun for hire. He turned the Texas prairie into a river of blood— and then moved on. . . .

#16 RIDE INTO HELL   BT50681 95¢

Whip Brazeen was the richest and most vicious cattle baron in the Great Southwest. He brandished a whip that would slice away the flesh in hunks. Lassiter was the only dude around with guts enough to cross him —and for the $150,000 in diamonds at stake, he'd RIDE INTO HELL.

#15 HELL AT YUMA   BT50646 95¢

At times, Lassiter can be meaner than the worst black hat in the West—especially when he's doublecrossed. They tried to bake him to death in the desert, then drown him in the Colorado River, but Lassiter came back to collect his fee—in blood and money.

WESTERNS

BUSHWHACKED   BT50763   95¢
Jeff Jeffries

Fanning was bushwhacked and left to die on the desert. But even half-dead, Fanning had more guts than the hired killers who gunned him down and the cattle barons who ordered the job done.

THE PISTOLEROS   BT50762   95¢
E.E. Halleran

The notorious Ed Cragg and his band of Confederate raiders threatened to turn to the entire Southwest into Rebel territory. Only one man was big enough to stand up to Ed Cragg. And even hard-bitten Sam Kimbrell didn't know if he could stop them.

THE DAY
THE KILLERS CAME   BT50761   95¢
John S. Daniels

Deputy Sheriff Carl Sturtz just wanted to settle down after a lifetime of town-taming. But when Black Jack Connor rode into town, Platte City became a hellhole of murder and Sturtz knew that relaxation would have to wait.

STARBUCK'S BRAND   BT50748   95¢
Theodore V. Olsen

Battle-scarred and hungry for power, Starbuck came through the Civil War determined to carve for himself an empire from the wide-open Texas plains. First time in paperback from the author of *The Stalking Moon*, one of the greatest names in Westerns.

CHEYENNE VENGEANCE BT50841 $.95
Robert J. Steelman
John Beaver was just an infant when his people, the Cheyenne, were massacred. For the few survivors only the destruction of the officer who had organized the attack could avenge the tribe's honor. Years later, it was to John Beaver, whose light skin belied his real identity, that the burden of vengeance fell.

AMBUSH ON THE MESA BT50769 95¢
Gordon D. Shirreffs
They needed a regiment but the U.S. Army sent only one—veteran scout Hugh Kinzie. Red Sleeves was on the warpath, raiding, burning, killing women and children. Kinzie's job was to stop him. A tough-as-nails Western by one of the gutsiest writers in America. Several of Gordon D. Shirreffs' books have been made into big budget movies.

IRON HAND BT50770 95¢
Lee Floren
The South Texas white man and the brooding black made a strange pair. Iron Hand was what they called the black, because a deadly curved steel hook was where his right hand had been. The two partners didn't look for trouble, but it found them just the same. Then the killing started. A blistering action-Western by a proven winner.

COPPER CANYON BT50851 95¢
Edward N. Todd
Young Fergie Harrison and his uncle Tom ride into San Antonio intending to hire out as cowhands. Instead they meet Will Rawley, who offers to take them in on a chance to recover a lost shipment of silver in return for running guns to Mexico. For the youth the trip marks a coming of age in which the true value of the treasure suddenly becomes clear—almost at the cost of his life.

SHOTGUN LAW BT50871 $.95
Nelson Nye

They called him Tin Badge and tried to play him for a sucker—but one day they went too far. Girt Sasabe had just arrived in town when he was made sheriff of Broken Stirrup. He found himself in the middle of a savage range war—with both sides gunning for him.

KINKAID BT50872 $.95
Leslie Ernenwein

Lon Kinkaid was the fighting young marshal of Red Butte Junction. Even though he wore the lawbadge when he killed, Kinkaid felt disgusted with what he was becoming. In this town, even an honest marshal had to become a professional killer to survive.

TRACK THE MAN DOWN BT50873 $.95
Bob Haning

Framed into jail, Lomax spent five years thinking of nothing but revenge. Now he was out. Years in the man-killing sun had baked all softness out of him. He was out to find Ted Durham—once his closest friend—and set things right.

THE MARAUDERS BT50883 $.95
Lee Floren

Darr Gardner and his gunslicks rode into town at dawn, tough and ready to kill. "Kill every farmer you see! This time we're wiping them out for good!" It was a day of slaughter such as the town of Burnt Wagon had never seen—and would never see again.

DEPUTIES FROM HELL BT50902 95¢
Chuck Martin

Only hate kept Joel Landon alive. Hate for the sheriff who sentenced him to die in the desert.

RIFLES ON THE RIMROCK BT50903 95¢
Lee Floren

"Funeral" O'Neill was the town undertaker. When he started to check into the deaths of two harmless old codgers, somebody tried to turn him into one of his own customers.

TEXAS SPURS BT50880 $.95
J.L. Bouma

The tough cattle drive from Texas to Colorado was finally over. Mark Regan looked forward to peaceful living in the town of Pine City but when he reached the town his herd blasted and his best friend was murdered. He set out on a mission of vengeance.

DANGER TRAIL BT50881 $.95
J.L. Bouma

Webb McLane was a peaceful man. He owned a small ranch, surrounded by the vast spreads of powerful men. They didn't trouble him at first, but then there were a few threats and soon the talk turned to action. This is the explosive story of a peaceful man forced to violence.

THE HELL RAISERS BT50882 $.95
Lee Floren

When Jess Roberts and War Dog Smith heard an old friend was in trouble, they rode fast to back him up. They found themselves in the middle of a war between the farmers and the cattlemen. Before it was over, the range would be red with blood—with two bullets marked for Jess and War Dog.

THE FASTEST GUN BT50892 95¢
Chuck Martin

This is the savage story of two violent men who lived by the gunfighter's code—and were ready to die by it. They knew the showdown had to come. Both men wanted blood and nothing else mattered.

BUGLES IN THE NIGHT BT50893 95¢
Burt Arthur

Major Bonesteele smiled cynically when he handed the orders to his hated subordinate, Captain Zachary Swain. The Major knew the hills were swarming with blood-thirsty Indians and that twenty-one brave soldiers were being sent into an ambush—by their own commanding officer.

BELMONT TOWER BOOKS
P.O. Box 2050
NORWALK, CONN. 06852

Please send me the books listed below.

ORDER BY BOOK NUMBER ONLY.

Quantity	Book No.	Price
....	....	....
....	....	....
....	....	....
....	....	....
....	....	....
....	....	....

In the event we are out of stock of any of the books listed, please list alternate selections below.

....	....	....
....	....	....
....	....	....
....	....	....

I enclose $...............

Add 25¢ per book to help cover cost of postage and handling. Buy 4 or more books and we will pay the cost. Send cash, check or money order. No stamps. Allow 4 weeks for delivery.

NAME ....
(Please print)

ADDRESS ....

CITY .... STATE .... ZIP ....